Legend of Lost Basin

Legend of Lost Basin

a novel by

Bruce Hartman

Swallow Tail Press

Legend of Lost Basin

Published by Swallow Tail Press

Philadelphia, PA, USA

ISBN 978-0-9997564-7-8

Part I

1.

Nobody knew where Slater came from or even if that was his real name. Some say he drove his ramshackle herd up from Texas, others claim he rustled it from some Indians up north. If you'd seen those crook-horned cattle drifting through town after an early snow, stumbling like blind men, mere skeletons in cowhide, massive skulls and horns tipping them forward to bite at the frozen ground—if you'd even noticed them, or their threadbare drover shambling back of the herd with his string of castoff nags, the boy behind him in the dilapidated two-mule wagon, you'd have forgotten about them by the end of the day. Those were drought years when men sold off their stock and nobody cared if another few dozen cattle starved on the parched range.

The drover looked like he'd crawled out of a cleft in the earth. It was one of those bleary November days when an ice fog rises off the snow and a figure a dozen yards ahead can loom up like a ghost in the time it takes to draw a breath. He rode with his battered hat pulled down to the eyebrows, deerskin slicker wrapped over his shoulders, his dark silent eyes warning you not to ask any questions. He stopped in town to trade for supplies, not that he had much to trade with. A few furs, a wagonload of axe-hewn cordwood, some greasy old Spanish coins that might have been counterfeit. He needed a bucksaw, a whetstone, a sledge hammer, a keg of twenty-pound nails. Building a cabin and corral, he told the men in the general store, alongside a sand wash they knew had been dry for years. None of them mentioned that, nor did they ask what he expected his cattle to live on. He'd staked his claim out at Seven Mile Ridge and that's where he would stay. After he drove away they took bets on how long he would last on the bone-dry range.

"That fella's trouble," one of the men said, and the others nodded. "I'd like to put a torch to his cabin."

The storekeeper cocked a smile. "Can't you wait till he's done building it?"

The cattlemen paid Slater no mind as long as he kept his gaunted stock off their land. It wasn't their land, of course. It was open range, owned by the Indians or the government or God Almighty, but they'd made it their own and they weren't about to let some ragged cowpuncher out of nowhere crowd them off it. Everything that followed—the deadly rivalry, the raids, the killings—traced back to Slater's determination to stay in the basin. A prophet or doomsayer might have seen it all coming four months later when he drove his wagon back into town behind his span of sullen gray mules and hitched it in front of an empty stock pen across from the feed store. Another dreary afternoon, clouds swirling in a gunmetal sky, the mules restless and uneasy. His boy, nineteen or twenty years old, huddled in the back of the wagon. Did Slater know that stock pen was owned by Captain Devaney, the man folks called the cattle king? Who drove more stock out of that basin every year than any ten ranchers put together. Who had a reputation as a great man, a visionary and a vindictive S.O.B. you'd better not turn your back on.

The Captain stood on the plank sidewalk with his wife Jacinta and their two children, a nineteen-year-old son Luke and a daughter one year younger, having just climbed down from their own wagon on the way to the general store. He waited for Slater to finish hitching his mules with a rawhide rope before he spoke. Slater turned to face him, his black eyes poised, disquieting, not the eyes of a man inclined to deference. Slater's boy—they called him Rory—climbed out of the wagon and hauled himself up beside Slater. He was big and blond but not yet in the shape of a man. He looked at the Captain's daughter, lithe and dark and almost a woman, and kept his eyes on her until she stared back at him, both of them astonished to glimpse any such creature in that rough basin. Elena turned away, not out of bashfulness or embarrassment but to capture his attention and make it clear that yes, as he hoped, she liked him but she would at all times be in control of whether his eyes met hers and whether she paid him any mind, and then she tilted her head slightly, just enough to hold him taut without returning his gaze.

"Kindly move your wagon from in front of my stock pen, if you please," the Captain said in a mocking imitation of politeness. His voice was southern, polished as cold as a knife blade.

Slater stared back in wonderment, as if he'd never heard anybody talk that way before. The Captain's face—dark, craggy, whip-scarred on the lower lip—was new to him but seemed somehow familiar, especially that whip scar, whose tale he'd heard somewhere on those vast plains.

The Captain's expression tightened at that hint of recognition. "Maybe you don't understand English," he said.

"I know what your words mean," Slater said, holding his eyes on the whip scar. "I just don't understand what you mean by saying them. Them's two different things."

"You're smarter than you look. Let me translate for you. Get your wagon out of here, and yourself and your boy out of this basin."

"Now I understand," Slater said, and followed by the boy he turned his back and walked across the muddy street to the feed store.

That first disobedience—the Captain's wife, Jacinta, called it insolence—bore bitter fruit. Years later people talked about it as if it had changed the course of time or the alignment of the planets or brought death into the world. To the Captain it became the germ of an obsession. Slater's vacant face and his hooded, indomitable eyes—and his pausing over the fishhook-shaped whip scar on his lip—had struck an unaccustomed anxiety into the Captain's heart. His pride and his empire over men which that pride had made

possible would not suffer a slight or a challenge to go unpunished—
that was something Slater, even as a newcomer, ought to have
known. What strange presumption lurked in those eyes that made
him think it could be otherwise? Was it the whip scar that
emboldened him? Had it reminded him of a tale never to be repeated
in this basin?

That night, after Luke and Elena had gone to bed, Jacinta
brushed the back of her hand across the Captain's lower lip. "His
eyes lit on this," she said. "Came back to it a second time."

"Don't you think I know that?"

"Do you know him?"

"Never seen him before."

"It's just hearsay, then. He can't be sure."

"I told him to get out, but what good would that do? If he's got
a story to tell, he'll spread it around before he leaves."

In the weeks that followed, the Captain's mood was dark, wary,
short-tempered: he would curse and fly into a rage at the mention of
Slater's name. The cowhands talked about the insult, the defiance,
the Captain's rage. If you had said that within a year he'd give Slater
his daughter in marriage, you would have been horsewhipped and
laughed out of the territory.

2.

It was never about revenge or an insult to his pride. Right from the start, it was about domination and power. The Captain had the right to rule—it was as much a burden as a right—and he could not allow his authority to be undermined by defiance or slight, or by a stranger's familiarity with the ghosts of his past. And in a way nobody could have grasped until later, when, as it seemed, a shapeshifting spirit of destruction, relentless, indifferent to life, had taken over the basin, it was about shame, and fear, and fate.

Ten years earlier the Captain had driven a herd of longhorns up from New Mexico to claim his kingdom. He couldn't have approached it from the north or the west or even the south, so jealously was it guarded on those sides by badlands and winding canyons and battlements that no livestock could surmount. He had to ford the herd, after driving it north, across the river from the east. The nearest railroad—the only railroad—was a hundred parched miles to the north. And so he staked out his domain with natural boundaries thirty, forty miles apart, a desert island in a sea of thirst rimmed by mountains and labyrinthine fissures in the earth. A thin patina of high cold wilderness over a ledge of brittle rock, bone dry in summer, knee-deep in snow in the winter, rutted with ridges and sand washes and sinkholes, speckled with sagebrush and bunchgrass, saltbush and scraggly piñon pine. A natural basin with no outlet except to a shadowy underworld from which there was no return. A blank spot on the map, if there had been a map, that knew nothing of lawmen or avengers or bounty hunters or government spies. Exactly what the Captain was looking for.

The family lived in a two-story log house constructed of timber skidded over the snow from the mountains, with a high, wide front porch colonnaded by a dozen enormous hemlock boles. That house, less than a mile from the town (which the Captain had also built and largely owned), was the nerve center of his ranch, ringed with corrals and pens and outbuildings: sheds, barns, a bunkhouse for the men. In the springtime when the frost eased its grip on the land and the cold nights brightened into shimmering days, the snow pack trickled down off the headlands and for a few precious weeks the draws and washes in the basin bloomed with bluestem and fireweed and bitter root. If that water found an outlet to the sea it must have been deep underground, for the rivers that rimmed the basin on three sides were sealed off by the jagged remains of ancient peaks. The river to the east ran blood red in summer, wintered white and hard as a tombstone. Then one day—usually in the middle of April—the pressure of the snow melt converging under its marble crust made it explode with the crack of a rifle shot, as blocks and slabs of ice heaved in the air and swirled in a tumult of foam and black water. The Captain's son and daughter, Luke and Elena, often raced on their horses across the range lands their father claimed, hoping to be near the river when the ice broke up. When it happened—violently, without warning—they recoiled as if that rifle shot was meant for them. Scrambling to higher ground, they watched the water surge and jet upwards as the explosion worked its way upstream. In this way they learned that there is violence in all things, even in the unlocking of the spring. For a long time they remained innocent of the brutality that sustained their father's kingdom. It dawned on them, like the knowledge of good and evil itself, in tiny increments, each inconclusive in itself so that the whole could be denied. There was no sudden irruption like the ice breaking up that showed them the savagery beneath the surface of things.

Luke was a year older than Elena and he thought that made him smarter. He was tall and slender like his mother but without her natural grace, as ungainly as a strutting crow. The Captain, who craved an heir to rule his domain, no longer tried to hide his disappointment in Luke's weakness, his foolishness, his poor judgment—they gnawed at his heart and often (secretly, because Jacinta fiercely defended Luke from any criticism) made him ashamed to have such a son.

April brought a warm wind scouring down from the buttes and mesas, stirring the bunchgrass and bluestem and sage back to life under the melting snow. Then came the rain, the only real rain of the year. If the ground hadn't been frozen it might have done some good. Instead it flooded the washes and gulches and ran down into cracks and crevices along the stony rim that divided the basin from the world unknown to it.

One morning when the sun hung cold and bright in the sky, Luke and Elena came across a herd of mustangs in a swale behind the clay butte. Dappled mares with foals under them, chestnut colts and fillies kicking up their hoofs, black stallions with stars on their foreheads, their tails up, pawing the grass, unwilling to yield the ground to these two chimerical intruders. Prancing among them was a beautiful strawberry roan with a full white face and a long black mane, a yearling filly. The next morning Luke rode up to the clay butte by himself and snared the roan filly with his lasso and dragged her to the corral nearest the house. The yearling's bone-white face had the appearance of a skull. She stumbled along, her hind legs hobbled together, her neck galled by the rope, her eyes swollen where he'd slapped them with his quirt. Once inside the corral he yanked the rope off his saddle and lashed it to the stubbing post. "Caught this gal on the ridge where we were yesterday," he told Elena.

"Looks like you already about ruined her," Elena said.

"She'll live."

The mustang was wild and frantic to escape. Behind her mask of death, she blazed with life and spirit and freedom and defiance, like the wild horses in Elena's dreams. Elena wanted to take that freedom and defiance into herself to keep it away from Luke and his leaden stupidity. She reached across the rail to pat the roan filly but the horse reared and stumbled away, almost toppling as she fought the rope, wailing in fright. "You must be proud of yourself," Elena told Luke.

"I drug her down here, didn't I? I bet I can break her in about ten minutes."

The Captain had drifted down from the wide front porch, six or seven dogs boiling up around him. As he strode toward the corral, the filly skittered backwards and almost went down, showing the Captain her skull-like face. He frowned at Luke. "What in hell are you doing with that mustang?"

"I caught her up on the ridge," Luke said. "Fought off the rest of them and drug her down here." His dark eyes begged his father to be proud of him.

"Get them hobbles off her before she breaks a leg."

The boy slipped through the chute and tried to approach the horse, which lurched back and forth in a half-circle to keep him in her sight. He staggered behind her like a drunk.

"You get a saddle on that horse by a week from today or you're going to have to shoot her."

Elena felt the filly's desperation beat through her own heart. "Shoot her? Why can't we just let her go?"

"You can't mix the wild ones with the livestock. They'll come back and trick the other horses away. And those others—you'll be lucky to get a saddle on them after they see what it's like to be free."

She knew Luke would never be able to break the mustang. "But why do you have to shoot her?"

"In this business you do what needs to be done."

The Captain whistled to his dogs and gathered them back onto the porch.

Elena had lived her whole life—all eighteen years of it—on those unforgiving plains. Parched brittle ground under a malign sky, prickly pears up over her ankles, rattlesnakes thick as her leg. Thin grass in the high meadows and vanishing streambeds. Leathern men bent to the shape of their saddles, preening their beards with bear claws and suet, salving their solitary hearts with whiskey and tobacco. Bleak and barren headlands loomed in the distance like prison walls.

She had never known another girl her own age, or any other beauty or ugliness or passion but what made its home on those plains. Lean and lithe with straight black hair and fierce amber eyes from the Spanish blood on her mother's side, she could do the work of a ranch hand—riding and roping, cutting and branding cattle, tending the horses—far better than her brother. The Captain encouraged her to wear britches and boots and he boasted of her prowess just to shame Luke. Still she was just a girl, as innocent and hopeful as the day she was born. Inside her quivered a force she'd heard the name of but couldn't imagine and she knew that someday it would burst forth with the power and spirit of that mustang.

In the week after their father's ultimatum, she slipped out to the corral every morning ahead of Luke to tame the mustang with soft words and carrots she stole from the cookhouse. She named her Susannah, after the girl in the song.

Luke was furious when he found out. "Who said you could name her? I caught her and drug her down here."

"I named her first so that's her name."

All his efforts to tame the mustang went for naught. Elena's secret plan to rescue Susannah occupied her every waking minute and most of her dreams. She imagined herself standing on the mustang's bare back like the acrobat on a circus pony she'd seen in a picture book: a barefoot girl in a short flaring skirt waving one hand in the air, twirling a stick-and-string whip in the other as she galloped past the spectators, Slater's boy Rory gaping in astonishment as she raced by. She'd only seen Rory the once, that time in town when her father had ordered Slater out of the basin. She still had never spoken to Rory and couldn't imagine what she'd say to him if they chanced to meet. They were supposed to hate each other the way her father and Slater did, but she'd felt the pull of his eyes and let him feel the pull of hers, and part of her secret plan for Susannah was to watch for Rory every second as she galloped wantonly across the range.

The season was changing, the wind skittish and fickle. It would soothe you one minute and sting you the next. One sky followed another in a widening arc, each one warmer and windier than the last. On the seventh day the Captain came down to the corral with his dogs, fawning mixes of all breeds found on the plains, including wolves and coyotes. Luke had the mustang in the chute. He dropped into the saddle and the horse bolted and slammed him against the rail until he fell off, then reared and tried to trample him as he dodged away.

"Better get your rifle, son."

Luke vaulted the rail and stumbled toward his father, his eyes glistening, his cheeks on fire. "I don't want to shoot her."

"You will, though," the Captain said. "The world has no place for a coward."

"I can't. I won't. I ain't going to shoot her."

"Go get your rifle."

Luke cast a sullen eye on the mustang and marched toward the porch. Elena was beside herself. She threw the corral gate open and leaped astride the mustang, which reared and screamed and tried to throw her.

"Damn it! Get down off that horse!"

She heard the command and instinctively ignored it. Twisting her fingers into the long black mane, she pulled herself forward, head down along the mustang's neck, arms wrapped around it, and in that position, not standing up like the circus girl she'd envisioned but almost flat, hugging the mustang as if the two of them were the same animal, she bolted out of the corral and across the range.

3.

The old west was still new, the buffalo but lately gone, the Indians scoured off the plains like brush in a wildfire. Men slept on the ground among beasts with twisted horns seven and eight feet across which could grind them into the dust at the squeak of a saddle and nobody but the wolves and the ravens would have noticed or cared. They loved their horses more than anything except whisky and of course gold when they could scoop it out of a creek bed or off a faro table. Women were scarcer than hens' teeth, scarcer than hens, in fact, or any other female creature except cows in that embryonic Eden, where men yearned for helpmates to lure them to sin, of which they as yet knew nothing, living outside of time and without guile or regret in a state of perfect obedience to the instincts they were created with, knowing in their childish hearts only that without women they could not become men.

The sole exception to all this being the Captain, whose misfortune it was (so men said) to have found a wife. Jacinta Devaney née Gallegos was a proud woman, heiress to ten generations of pure-blooded Spanish landowners in northern New Mexico who had been dispossessed and impoverished after America seized the region from Old Mexico. Her hair was black, her eyes fierce, her complexion as white and cold as bone china. Her mother having died giving her birth, she'd been raised by a high-strung, superstitious aunt from Hidalgo who taught her to be haughty, melancholic, and fanatical. As she grew older she rebelled against the strictures that society imposed on a girl: by the time she was sixteen she was so ungovernable that she had to be kept under lock and key. The Captain paid her bankrupt father a hundred dollars in gold to let him have her, subduing her with the fairytale promise of a cattle kingdom to the north where she would reign as queen. She married him and followed a herd of belching longhorns from one forlorn domain to another, ranging across New Mexico, Colorado and Wyoming behind a span of windgalled mules for ten years before he finally found his kingdom in the sere emptiness of the basin. Throughout those years he was restless, relentless, tormented by demons he refused to name. He fought off Indians, rustlers, cavalry troops, stampeded herds of buffalo over cliffs, did whatever was needed to grow and protect his herd. Jacinta asked herself if a queen didn't deserve better than this. To be navigating a mile-wide track of mire with a husband who cared only for cattle and horses and dominion over men. To sleep in a wagon surrounded by stinking unshaven brutes who would barely grunt when she condescended to speak to them. To spend her days choking on dust and stench and if she chanced off the wagon to sink to her ankles in mud.

One night about a year into the marriage, not long after their first child Luke had been born, the Captain found her sobbing into a scrap of cloth left over from making a dress, which was the closest she had to a handkerchief. Her obsidian eyes seemed to peer out from some impenetrable region deep in the earth.

He tilted her head back and squinted down her throat as if she were a colicky foal. "What's ailing you?"

She explained to his astonishment that she hated this life and would not stand for it. That she would not stand for his drinking, his card playing, his stinking, his spitting, his impiety. That if they did not settle down and live in a proper house with a roof and a floor and keep the cattle and the cowhands away from it, she would take the baby and return to her family in Santa Fe.

"You ought to be happy," he told her, regretting the hundred dollars he'd paid her father to let him marry her. "You're the only white woman within a hundred miles who ain't a whore."

She whirled her arm around and smacked him, leaving a handprint burned into his cheek like a brand, which remained visible for three weeks. The origin of that mark was no mystery to the cowhands. They said Jacinta was a hard woman, as in hard case, hard times, hard luck, who had powers and proclivities, some said, that were not of this earth, or of heaven either. They said the Captain was a leader of men but had no power over women, which, they all agreed, nobody could.

A little over a year later their second child—a daughter—was born.

The boy named Rory wasn't Slater's son. Slater had been married once: his wife died giving birth and the child had not lived. He fled from Missouri in a rage when he learned that that child—a son—had not been his. Then on a cattle drive out of Texas to New Mexico he almost lost his mind in the mirage country between the Brazos and the Rio Concho. In the delirium of thirst he'd seen poison lakes rimmed with the bleached bones of prehistoric beasts, elk and buffalo driven to drown in their toxic waters. He'd seen men blinded by dust and riven by the compulsion of heat and wind, horses lamed and swallowed by wolves and rattlesnakes, cattle stampeded into quicksand, drowning each other in their fury of thirst. Like as not it was the heat and the mirages that drove him to the brink of madness, but he'd tell you it was the newborn calves, yanked away every morning from the cows that dropped them in the night because they couldn't survive on the trail, made to stand up together trapped in rope corrals to be clubbed to death amid the bawling of their dams. The mothers bellowed all day after they were yoked to steers and dragged to the next night's killing ground. Slater rode a hundred miles with that mournful roar echoing inside him, the way you might hum a tune without making a sound anyone else can hear, and it stayed in his brain, he liked to say, every day of his life.

When they reached the Concho there was a wagon train stopped ten days by the spring flood. One frustrated emigrant tried to take his wagon across and it rolled over and tumbled in the current. Slater shook off his madness—or succumbed to it, he could never say which—and spurred his horse into the river to rescue the little boy whose family had swirled to the bottom. The boy was eight years old and he called himself Rory. His face was stone cold when Slater comforted him for the loss of his parents. They weren't his real parents, he said, and that was the last time he mentioned them. He rode with Slater and took his name, hitching himself to a man of few words who had no education and no money and as little hope, and who would sometimes break down in tears for no reason the boy could discern or imagine. Those bad times passed and Slater gained a new strength from Rory as he taught him to face the rigors of the cattle drives, which was the only life he knew. Rory clung to Slater's saddle and rattled in his wagon from Mexico to Montana and back a dozen times, learned to ride and rope and cull the herd, brand calves, round up strays, swelter and shiver on the windswept plains the year around without it ever dawning on him that there could be any other way to live. By the time he arrived in the basin with Slater he was as big and almost as strong as a man without the hardness or wariness or guile a man needed to survive in that country. He had a big open smile that made you like him but in some men's eyes invited disrespect. There were men out there who never met your gaze and you'd be well advised not to meet theirs, men who saw friendliness or sincerity as unmanly weakness spoiling for a fight. And Rory could be cocky, like any young kid, sure of himself with no real reason to be. Too big for his britches sometimes, a jokester, but often stubborn, quick to take offense. What he is is innocent, Slater realized, surprised by the thought, but not so innocent that you could tell him that. How could Slater, who'd brought him up with kindness and generosity, teach him the heartlessness and guile and distrust he'd need in a tribe of lawless men? He couldn't let on like he thought Rory was innocent or anything like that. The boy would take it as an insult, a dare to be the opposite—and Slater shuddered to think what that might mean in the kind of world they had to live in.

"I reckon we might ought to be moving on," he told Rory one morning before sunrise as they fixed their breakfast on the cast-iron stove in the cabin. Biscuits with bacon grease gravy and one egg apiece, washed down with hot coffee that was blacker (Slater liked to say) than devil spit. It was a month after their confrontation with the Captain. That whip scar on the Captain's lower lip was all Slater could remember of his face. He'd heard tell of it before, he fancied, but he couldn't be sure. It might have been a different man he'd heard that tale about—a tale which, until then, he would have been glad to forget.

"Why do you want to leave?" Rory asked him.

"There's other places we could take our herd and do just as well."

Rory had stood beside Slater in town, embarrassed for Slater's sake at the Captain's taunting parody of respect in his order to move their wagon (but innocent of their taut exchange about the whip scar, which Slater still hadn't mentioned). What would he do if he'd been insulted like Slater was? he wondered. Would he want to walk away? "You afraid of the Captain?" he asked.

Afraid, Slater thought. That's part of his innocence. The notion that self-respect comes before survival in this hair-trigger world, that if a man lets himself be afraid of a killer he's less than a man. Slater had seen a dozen fools go down in the dust with that thought trembling on their lips.

"I hear the Captain didn't take kindly to my walking away from him," he said. "They say he's the type to carry a grudge."

"A grudge for what?" Rory laughed. "For not moving your wagon? How could you run away from that?"

Slater's temper flared—that was one of his tender spots, being laughed at—but he tamped it down before he made a fool of himself. From his own point of view Rory was right. A young man needs a dash of innocence and scorn even against death or he'd run away before he's had a chance to make a life for himself. Might as well skip ahead to being an old man as do that. Even then he'd be at the mercy of the killers who'd shoot him and leave him for dead as a gift to the crows and coyotes.

"I reckon you're in favor of staying," he said.

"At least long enough to hire a crew and bring our herd down from the high country. We at least ought to do that."

Rory drew a long sip of devil spit and shuffled out into the breaking dawn. In town, the day they were confronted by the Captain, he'd seen the girl, the Captain's daughter, and for that reason alone (which he kept secret from Slater, almost secret from himself) he wanted to stay in the basin, not only to avoid the disgrace of running away but because he wanted that girl, and he imagined, from the way she'd looked back at him and jerked her eyes away, the way you'd twitch your line to snag a trout, that she wanted him.

It wasn't much of a town and for a long time it didn't even have a name. First there was a trading post which later they called a general store. Then a saloon, set up under a tent, a feed mill, the Captain's stock pen—but still no name. The big dusty basin it sat in didn't have a name either, or it had as many names as there were men to name it. Sandwash Basin in spring and early summer, Dugout Basin in August, Consternation Basin in the fall. Same with the ridges and the mesas and the battlements you could see on the far horizon. People gave them names, but out of deference to the Captain none of those names stuck. It was up to him to affix the names and he was in no rush to do it. In his mind he owned the basin and everything in it and he must have thought that if it had a name that just anybody could use, folks might get the impression he didn't own it. He wouldn't name that basin any more than he'd name his front porch or the northwest corner of his corral. In the early days a surveyor showed up who wanted to put it on a map. "This basin don't care to be on any map," the Captain told him. The discussion grew heated. Threats were made, weapons drawn, until the surveyor fled north into the badland and was never seen again. When a search party came from Denver they found his bones and his field notes with a sketch of the basin where he'd written the name you'll find on maps to this day. Lost.

All her life Elena had dreamed of escaping from the basin. Canyons and cliffs on three sides, where if you tried to escape you'd likely fall to your death or drown in a waterfall. The badland to the north, where depending on the season you'd either go mad from thirst or sink waist-deep in mud. That was her world, the stage where her dreams would play out.

Until she galloped away on Susannah it had never crossed her mind to disobey her father. Now freedom beat in her heart as she clenched its unruly mane. She raced five or six miles to the high meadow back of the clay butte before the mustang stopped long enough to let her slide off. The herd idled nearby around a puddle that passed for a watering hole in that muddy season. They whinnied and lashed their tails as the yearling pranced toward them. Elena stood still, waiting for the wild horses to decide that she posed no threat. She crooned in her most soothing voice and held up her sack of carrots, swinging it from side to side until it caught their attention. Then she poured the carrots out on a flat rock and turned around to walk away. It took her all morning to hike back to the ranch, wishing she could walk out of the basin and never come back. A bitter morning it was, with a skirling wind and a few icy snowflakes that prickled her face. The sun struggled against that wind and lost its way in the ragged clouds. She kept an eye out for Rory, who sometimes rode the high meadows and mesas looking for strays. She imagined that if she called out to him he'd gallop forward and lift her up and carry her away, her arms wrapped around his waist. That long moment in town when she'd caught his glance was the entire history of their acquaintance, except in her dreams. At some unforeseeable time they'd meet again, but not today. Today the range was as empty as a cowboy's promises.

The family had just finished their midday dinner when she stamped inside in her boots and took her place at the long pine table. The table occupied what her mother called the dining room, one end of the open space which at the other end she called the parlor, the kitchen being in a separate cookhouse out back, tended by an old cowhand named Zeke. Elena dreaded what punishment her father would decree for her riding off on the mustang. She could take it, whatever it was.

She dished out some beef stew for herself and sat back down. Huddled beside her, Luke peeked at his sister with a resentful eye. He tried to think of a clever remark but nothing came to his unclever mind. The Captain, sullen and watchful as he'd been for the past few weeks, soaked up the last of his stew with a crust of bread, studying the crust and his daughter with equal detachment.

Jacinta broke the silence in her high, crooning voice. "You shouldn't have ridden off like that when your father told you to stop."

"He didn't tell me to stop," Elena said.

"He said get down off that horse." She must have been listening through the window.

"He was going to make Luke shoot Susannah."

"Susannah?" Jacinta seemed shocked, as if the name was a vital piece of information that had been withheld from her. "Is that the horse's name? Susannah?"

"No, it ain't," Luke said. "She was my horse and I didn't name her that. I didn't name her anything."

The Captain stretched out his legs and pushed his chair back, scraping the pinewood floor. All watched his movements, his impassive expression, waiting for him to render judgment. "It's about time you got married," he told Elena.

"Married?"

"I decided that as soon as I saw you ride off on that mustang."

She felt weak, clammy, out of breath. "That's impossible." She knew it was the wrong thing to say. "I don't know any men I would marry."

His face bent into a sly smile. "You only need one."

"I don't even know one. Anyway I'm not getting married."

"There's suitable men within three days' ride, with enough land and cattle to keep you. I'll arrange for you to meet one of them."

She turned to her mother, pleading with her eyes. "Don't I have anything to say about this? Don't my own feelings count for anything? Don't—"

He cut her off. "It's the same as shooting the mustang, like we talked about. You've got your feelings on the subject, I understand that. But if something's necessary, you've got to do it. There's no arguing about it."

He pulled on his boots and his jacket and stalked out without saying another word.

Elena was in tears. Her mother touched her hand as if in sympathy. "Everything he does," she told her daughter, "he does for us. He's looking to the future. Someday Luke will have this place and you'll need a place of your own."

Late that afternoon, as they did their chores in the barn, Elena and Luke talked about what had happened at dinner. Despite their disagreements they had always been close, each the sole ally of the other in the family regime. Between themselves they called their father the Captain with no hint of irony. They knew how hopeless it was to resist him, how determined their mother was in propping him up. He imposed an order within the family that gave their lives meaning and purpose, as the order he imposed within the basin brought the same benefit to the men. A benefit which justified sacrificing most of their freedom—though not all of it, as Elena, in her private thoughts, had begun to discern.

"Are you serious about not getting married?" Luke asked her as he tossed a forkful of hay into a stall. "What in hell else would you do?"

She picked up an empty bucket to carry out to the pump. "Work on the ranch like I always have."

"You ain't a man."

There was no answer to that. "I want to decide things for myself," she said.

Luke burst out laughing in that giggling way which made men say he was a fool. "You looking for some kind of freedom? Because if so, this ain't the right place to look."

"I've never been any place else and neither have you."

"There ain't any freedom in this basin. Oh, it looks free enough, but what does anybody do because they chose it? Even that mustang you call Susannah. She seems free but she's just doing what she's got to do. And you claim you own her. How free is that?"

Sometimes Luke wasn't such a fool after all.

"What about the Captain?" Elena asked him. "Nobody makes him do what he does."

"He makes himself do it. That ain't no different."

4.

The cattlemen in those days were hard-working, hard-drinking, certain of their salvation or indifferent to it. Without compunction or debate they drove out intruders, burned their camps, dressed their motley herds in blood. On moonlit summer nights they hung rustlers, drove away horses, stampeded sheep over cliffs by the thousands. Where his own interests were at stake, the Captain discouraged such tactics because he had the law on his side—the law of custom, which was the only law in that country. His kingdom was a patchwork of watering holes, draws, swales and wallows, any place a blade of grass might see daylight in a wet year. A man who encroached on that domain was either a rustler or a squatter as far as the Captain was concerned. He'd be given fair warning, a chance to move on, and if he refused, the law of custom would apply, which was the law of the rope.

A man named Hortter had run up against that law shortly before Slater arrived. He grazed his cattle on the Captain's land and helped himself to one of the maverick calves. He was warned to leave the basin, a warning he ignored. On a moonlit night he was escorted to a lonely crossroads, where he was tried and convicted by a jury of cowhands and hanged from a gatepost with a note pinned to his shirt labeling him a rustler and warning others not to follow in his path.

To the men it seemed that Slater was in a special category, unlike any man who'd ever set foot in the basin. He ran his cattle over land the Captain called his own (though in truth he had no more right to it than anyone else) and ignored the Captain's order to leave the basin—instead he built corrals, brought in more stock, hired a crew—and yet nothing had happened. And Slater didn't seem to be afraid. It was as if he had a power over the Captain that no other man had. Time was, and not so long ago, when the Captain would have meted out justice quickly and unsparingly, but now, some of the men said, he seemed indecisive, wary, shadowed by the hesitancy of timeworn authority. Nobody suggested cowardice, or that Slater, rather than being the object of justice, might be the bringer of it. His time would come, they agreed. They speculated on whether the Captain's wife (a dire, spectral figure to the men) was holding him back or pushing him forward.

The speculation came to a head in early May, at the time of the spring roundup. Men from all the outfits in and around the basin rode to the far corners of the range, driving cattle out of the thickets and timber bottoms—cows, bulls, yearlings, steers, heifers coming around to their first heat—most of them branded to one herd or another but commingled, so the outfits had to fight each other to claim their stock. It had been a long day on the range, clouds tumbling past on a chill north wind. As dusk drew on, Slater rode flushing cows out of a timber gulch along the yellow bluffs, with Rory trailing twenty yards behind. The Captain cantered up with his hard-bitten foreman Vickery and two weathered cowhands whose faces might have been chipped out of the cap rock. They set their narrow eyes on Slater, shotguns poised across their saddles. Half a dozen of the Captain's dogs cringed and cowered around them.

The Captain's foreman Vickery was an unsightly and unlikeable man, his teeth stained by tobacco, his face scarred by burns during the war. He had an odd nervous tic: at intervals he clicked like a blackbird, involuntarily, probably unconsciously. It happened when his facial expression changed, which was never a good sign. The men who worked with him ignored it. You didn't want to mention it or even let on like you heard it. One of the cowhands made the mistake of doing that and Vickery whipped him within an inch of his life.

Slater never carried a sidearm but kept a Winchester rifle in the scabbard hanging by his leg. He shot a sharp glance at Rory, to make sure the boy had no visions of going down in a blaze of glory. Rory's hands were on his reins, his eyes fixed on the Captain under a mask of defiance, though in fact he was terrified. Vickery pulled up his mount between Rory and the Captain and spit a mouthful of tobacco in the dirt.

The Captain addressed Slater with his usual punctilio, even offered him a cigar, which he refused. They exchanged observations about the weather, the drought, the dust in the air, before the Captain came to the point. "Roundup makes you realize this country can't support more than one big operation, doesn't it?" he said, staring past Slater toward the gulch where two of Slater's men shuffled into view prodding a cow and her calf. "A few small outfits, fine, but not more than one big one. That's why we've got certain customs everybody's got to observe. They aren't written down anywhere"— he glanced at Slater and shrugged—"even supposing a man could read."

He nudged his horse a step closer and lifted the brim of his hat so Slater could look into his eyes, which were as gray and empty as the range in front of them. "Here's the main thing you need to remember, Slater. All the cattle born in this basin belong to me. Even a calf dropped by the gaunted, tick-eaten vermin you drove in here, soon as it's weaned, belongs to me. That's the custom of the country and it ain't about to change because some swamp trash trespasser shows up and builds himself a corral. You lay a hand on any of my stock, that's rustling. We've got a rope for that."

Vickery shifted position and his horse jostled forward, snorted, tossed its head. Every little sound—a meadowlark flapping out of the brush, the creak of saddle leather, the clink of metal on metal— seized its moment and faded into the still wind. In the silence around those moments Slater could hear himself inhaling and exhaling,

Vickery clicking, the Captain puffing his cigar, his men chuffing along with their horses, and he thought: This is the sound of men breathing for the last time. This might not be the last time, but when the last time comes this is what it will sound like. Ordinary, unexpected, quickly lost in the wind. Later, when it really was the last time, he would hear that sound again.

The Captain held up his palm as if to fend off an objection. "Don't bother arguing," he said pleasantly. "I won't be out-talked by the likes of you. Just round up your stock and get the hell back to wherever you came from. You've got three days."

Slater bobbed his head slightly, as if to show that he was paying attention. He saw the Captain's whip-scarred lower lip with its white slash on the edge, and lingered on it longer than would have been polite even in that uncouth country. The Captain caught him staring and his gray eyes darkened—with anger, fear, shame: the moment passed too quickly to know what instinct they succumbed to. But Slater knew this: it was the strange familiarity of that scar, shaped like a fishhook, which the Captain could read on Slater's face, that triggered his clench of desperation. In that instant Slater knew that the Captain was the man he'd thought he was, and the Captain knew that he knew. The entire transaction took less than a second.

"This is hard country, Captain," Slater said, turning toward the speckled range. Broken sandstone under a thin veneer of dust, a patina of edible plants wilting in the stony soil, desperate cattle devouring the plants, and men, the damned fools dangling at the end of this chain of folly, offering to kill each other for the right to be there. "We all got our reasons for coming here, and when we leave we'll have our reasons for leaving. We could all die tomorrow, or today. Come a good stiff wind out of the north and nobody fifty miles away'd ever know we were here."

The Captain's livid eyes searched Slater's for some sign of acquiescence, some recognition that a line had been crossed. "Like

I say," Slater repeated—he didn't know what he hoped to gain, maybe an acknowledgement that they could both exist on that range without having to kill each other—"it's hard country."

The Captain stepped his white Arabian closer and spoke so his men couldn't hear him. They watched silently, slack-jawed and stupid, their mounts staring with a curiosity that was beyond them. "Not half so hard as I am, Slater," he said between clenched teeth. "I'd see this range strewn with corpses before I'd let you get the better of me."

The sounds came at Slater again in single file: the Captain's low, almost chanting voice, each word spat at him like a curse. Jangling tack, groaning cattle, men holding and releasing their breath. The wind bristling around them. He sat motionless, silent. Rory's horse lashed its tail at a bug and Vickery spun around.

Now the Captain's voice added mockery to its mix of timbres. "Not that I expect anything like that to happen," he said. "But there'd be a certain justice in it that almost makes me hope you'll force my hand. Hell, you'd be less than a man if you didn't."

"Don't mock me, Captain," Slater said.

The Captain rolled his eyes over the motionless herd of men and beasts that surrounded them. "Not one of these men is worth the dirt that'll be dug up to bury him. That includes you and that boy of yours."

For every man there are some indignities which, if he can't avoid them, he must strike back against in fury or relentless defiance. In Slater's case there were three: to be betrayed by those he trusted, to be laughed at, and to be taunted by evil. The last was the hardest. Slater was no innocent, and no saint. When he came upon evil, he could ride past it and not look back. But he would not be mocked by it, or scorned by any man for shrinking from it. At that roundup the Captain had taken his high-handedness a step too far. He had warned Slater off the land, threatened him, yet at the same time dared him to defy the warning—even said he'd be less than a man if he didn't. This was the evil that mocks its victims, the taunting evil Slater could not abide.

It left him throbbing with a defiance he knew could destroy him. The Captain and his foreman Vickery and the two cowhands turned their backs and faded into the gathering dusk, Slater squinting furiously after them. His horse whinnied, eager to follow them. He pulled him back.

"Now what?" Rory asked. "We going to pull out?" He was thinking about the girl. He wanted her and he was determined not to leave the basin without her.

Slater leaned sideways and spat on the ground. "It's a big country," he said. "Still plenty of open range for all of us."

"The Captain was daring you not to run away."

So are you, Slater wanted to say, but he let it go. "I know that," he said. "He won't be satisfied with seeing the back of me. He wants to see me hung."

They gathered the cattle they'd flushed out of the thickets and drove them to an open flat where they'd left a dozen cows and their calves in a makeshift rope corral. The ropes had been cut, the stock harried back into the gulch. It took an hour to flush the strays out of the gulch and bring them back to the herd. By then the dusk had thickened to darkness. The stock milled and bawled for water but they would not advance in a straight line. Some folded their legs and settled on the ground. There was no choice but to bed them down for the night.

The men collected brush and built a cookfire while Slater stood apart, mulling the aftertaste of insult and defiance. In the smoke of that fire he savored a story he'd heard long ago around a campfire along the Rio Concho. A Comanche raid on a cattle drive in west Texas. A cowhand left to be scalped while his foreman ran away. A whip-scar that made a white slash shaped like a fishhook at the edge of that foreman's lower lip. And now that old tale had sprung to life in front of them. He and the Captain could no longer pretend that they didn't know that tale and who the foreman was. Knowing what they knew, could they both exist on that range without killing each other?

Rory wanted to stay in the basin because of the girl but there was more to it than that. He didn't want to tuck tail and run. He didn't want to surrender. It was that innocence again: only a child would think he could beat the odds he faced on those plains. If you were Slater and you could read Rory's mind, you'd have forgiven him that innocence, the innocence he had to hide and you had to pretend not to see, even if it was naive and foolish. It was all the innocence the kid had left. But if Slater could read Rory's mind he would also have seen the dangerous part, the part about the Captain's daughter. If Slater had known about that, everything would have turned out differently—because Slater had his own ideas about that girl, which he kept to himself, the same as Rory did. Neither would have shared such dreams with another man.

Rory noticed the boss brooding but kept to his work. In that country there was no time to study other men's thoughts. You had to let them alone. After a while he boiled a pot of coffee and brought Slater a tin cup hot enough to burn his lips. "The outfit wouldn't run out of here and they wouldn't let the Captain hang you," he said. He wanted Slater to know that.

Slater blew steam off the coffee and waited for it to cool. "That depends on who wins the war." His eyes were kindly but unsmiling.

"There ain't going to be any war."

Slater nodded as if he agreed, then shook his head. "Even if I leave, you can stay if you want to. You're old enough to decide for yourself."

Rory knew he'd stick with Slater, even if it meant running away. He didn't even know the girl's name. "What would I do here?"

"Work for the Captain, I reckon. That's about all anybody can do around here."

5.

The Captain's outfit was part of the legend still being told to this day. A few men, like Charlie Crow, were experienced trail bosses who could be trusted to drive a herd a thousand miles and come back with their shirts on their back. The rest were drifters, rustlers, convicts escaped from work gangs, most of them up from Texas or New Mexico. They cut their teeth on the big cattle drives, sampled the whorehouses and poker tables of Dodge and Ogallala, and found their way north pursued by posses and lynch mobs. Men like Murtaugh, who'd been a rebel sharpshooter in the war, Gutiérrez the homesick Mexican with his red sash and his leather hat, and Vickery, who rode with Quantrill during the war and the James gang afterwards. The ones who lived through their first winter became his regular outfit, some of them, eventually, ranchers in their own right, though on a much smaller scale, remaining his vassals and familiars.

The Captain ruled over them with seemingly effortless mastery, bitterly earned. His family had owned most of a county in east Texas before the war but ended it penniless, landless, dead. The Captain, sole survivor, drove a makeshift herd of wild longhorns through the same treacherous country where Slater nearly went mad a few years later, across the Brazos and the Concho into the shimmering emptiness of New Mexico. A Comanche raid turned his life around—he could never go back to Texas, or even stay in New Mexico. He remained in Santa Fe just long enough to entice Jacinta into marrying him on the promise of a cattle kingdom, escaping north with what was left of his pride. It was that pride—and Jacinta's own—that sustained them during the next years. Jacinta knew (and told him) that he'd been born to rule, had a right to rule, by the strength of that pride, and the men who gathered around him knew it too, and submitted to his sway, these untamed, independent men who before they joined him could hardly hold a job or stay out of jail. In him they found the mettle they lacked in themselves, and that basin, where he led them after years of wandering in Colorado and Wyoming was the kingdom he ruled not for his own sake but for theirs.

When Slater arrived he cobbled his outfit together from the Captain's rejects. Any roughneck cowboy the Captain scorned, folks would tell him, ride out north and look for Slater, he'll hire you—and Slater did. Before long he ran a prime crew of misfits, the kind nobody else would turn their back on. Ex-convicts, army deserters, horse thieves, murderers. Dealing with those boys, Slater had the magic touch. He knew men the way some men know cattle or horses, knew their flaws and what was best in them—and that was a point of pride, one of his only vanities. The men loved him not for his pride but his humility. He never raised his voice, never threatened or bullied them, just told them what to do and they did it. They were as loyal to him as if they'd sworn an oath in their own blood. He was quiet, brooding, almost mournful in his patience. Was there a story there, the men wondered, some crime or defeat that drove him to this desolate outpost? They all had stories behind them, usually the same story, involving a woman and a gunfight and the strong arm of the law—some, had they not fled to that dead-end oasis, would have found eternity at the end of a rope. The first man Slater hired, and later made his foreman, seemed cut from different cloth. His name was Buckminster and he came from Ohio, an earnest, clean-shaven fellow with black hair and crystal-blue eyes that seemed fixed on the great beyond. Buckminster swore no oaths and took no strong drink. The other men questioned him endlessly about his past. He had no story to tell, he assured them. Just a younger son without prospects who came west to seek his fortune. Some glimpsed the shadow of a troubled soul in those crystal-blue eyes.

Slater's men were part of the legend too. Most had nicknames—
Moondog, Polecat, Crazy Ike—and they did their best to live up to
them. Crazy Ike stood six feet six, broken teeth glinting behind his
flat bloodless lips. In the bunkhouse at night he'd drink whiskey till
he roared and wrap himself in a bear skin to sleep on the floor,
sometimes, in the winter, for days at a time. He'd come down from
the mountains where he handled dynamite for the mines and carried
a blood-stained two-headed axe instead of a gun. Moondog, another
giant of a man, was a cowboy philosopher with a beguiling smile and
the dripping eyes of a mad dog. In his past life, it was said, he'd been
an ordained preacher of a renegade sect. He'd been known to howl
like a coyote and once fought off a pack of wolves with a bowie
knife. Then there was his friend Polecat, so named for his sulfuric
odor and his nonchalant but deadly way of dealing with other men:
circling them, sniffing them, scrutinizing them, and on rare
occasions letting them have it right between the eyes. You didn't
want to be around when Polecat got his back up.

There were others on both sides who would all, when the time
came, earn their places in the legend. They still talk of a young fellow
in Slater's outfit, name of Ferguson, who generally kept to himself.
He was an expert horseman, adept at handling the cattle, though a
little too gentle for the task. He had fair hair and a pleasant voice but
what he's mostly remembered for is a fine set of teeth and a fancy
Mexican belt buckle, silver inlaid with turquoise. The men in Slater's
outfit never forgot that belt buckle or those teeth.

Elena would often see Ferguson on his pinto mare scouting for
strays when she rode out to check on the mustangs by the clay butte.
He'd wave and flash his toothy smile but since he was in Slater's
outfit he never stopped to talk to her. She contented herself with the
society of the mustangs and the ritual of approach and avoidance
they'd worked out together. As she edged closer the wild horses

turned as one, tilting their ears to take in her crooning invitations, and just as they began to back away she'd lift up her carrots or apples and charm them into standing still long enough to eat out of her hand. Susannah, proud to be her favorite, would push to the front and nibble more than her share until one of the older mares nudged her aside. One day Elena was alarmed to find Susannah limping. A clump of cactus spines had lodged in her right foreleg just above the unshod hoof, leaving the area swollen and inflamed. The next morning Elena packed her saddlebag with carbolic, bandages, tape and a pair of needle-nosed pliers that were used for fence work. After an hour of coaxing she was able to lift the mustang's leg and remove the spines. Susannah whinnied ungratefully and trotted away.

Sometimes it wasn't Ferguson she saw scouting for strays, it was Rory, but he kept his distance, didn't wave or smile at her the way Ferguson did, and in a small way that broke her heart, as if she and Rory were secret friends because of that time they'd met in town, though they'd barely looked at each other then, just long enough to snag each other's interest. But no, she didn't really know him, didn't know him at all, and that made the leaden sky seem heavier than usual and the range colder and the mountains farther away.

After the roundup Slater put the Captain's ultimatum to a vote. There were other ranges, better ranges, he told his men, where they could move their operation, but out of stubbornness and pride they voted to stay in the basin. If Slater had voted he would have voted to leave, but he stuck with his men, proud that they would not be taunted by evil. And he still had his eye on the girl, the Captain's daughter, unlikely as it seemed circumstances could ever bring them together. For the time being, the Captain gave no life to his threats. His men shouted taunts and threats at Slater's, pelted them with stones, fired shots over their heads. A few of Slater's calves disappeared and were found with their throats cut. It was all for show, most likely Vickery's doing, to curry favor with the Captain. In the saloon the men observed an uneasy truce, even played cards together, bought each other drinks.

Over the next weeks Slater moved his operations farther out, seemingly away from the Captain's domain but in fact encircling it. He'd built up his herd to the point where he could sell half of it and use the proceeds to expand even further. The point of sale would be the railhead a hundred miles north, across a badland the men called the valley of bones. "That land ain't just bad," Polecat said, "it's evil. Not a drop of water for fifty miles. Nothing but rocks and blinding heat that'll fry your brains and drive the cattle crazy."

They huddled around a fire in front of the bunkhouse, watching sparks climb the wind into a starless sky. "Crazy cattle don't bother me none," Crazy Ike grinned. He split a log with one savage swipe of his two-headed axe and kicked the pieces into the fire.

"Abe Tatum's rustling gang's up there," Buckminster said. "Escaped convicts, half-breeds, deserters, lying in wait like a brood of rattlers. They'd just as soon kill you as look at you."

Rory spat into the fire. "I don't know about you boys, but I ain't afraid of a few desperadoes. They got nothing on this bunch."

Among the men there was muttering, shrugging, shaking of heads, askance looks at Rory and Slater. They didn't appreciate Rory's fledgling bravado, didn't like him pretending he was one of them when he'd done nothing to earn it. The kid, they called him, meaning the boss's kid. He even used the boss's last name when he needed a last name—his real one nobody knew, if he even knew himself. If he'd been anybody else they would have thrashed him for his arrogance and presumption, taught him a lesson he still needed to learn. If he played the show-off with the Tatum gang he'd get them all shot.

Slater could feel the sparks flying but he held his tongue. He wouldn't put up with any complaints about Rory. You had to cut him some slack, was his attitude. You respect me, you'll respect my boy. The same went for Rory's friend Ferguson, because he was young and quiet and respectful. Ferguson, with his big smile, was the other one they called the kid. The plan, when they drove half the herd north, was to leave him behind to look after the other half.

"If I was a worrying man," Slater said, "I'd worry about the Tatum gang."

More muttering, shuffling, now with an undertone of approval and assent.

"Though I'd worry about the Captain more," he added.

"And if I was the Captain," Polecat said, "and he is a worrying man, I'd worry about us."

The men laughed, Rory and Ferguson laughed, but Slater didn't laugh. He and the Captain both knew that the day would come when their conflict would reach its inevitable conclusion. Each of them represented something to the other that was impossible to ignore or overcome.

6.

The Captain stood on his wide front porch, his wife beside him, surveying the vast emptiness that sprawled before him: dry speckled rangeland, patches of grass around rutted swales of hard-baked dust, fantastic pinnacles of cloud reeling in an endless sky. He had built his empire of cattle and men on this patch of dirt, planted a family to perpetuate it—a foolish son, a daughter still innocent of her destiny—and all of it was based on the authority of his pride, his manliness, his courage. Slater knew that was a lie. How long would he keep the secret to himself? The Captain had to conceal it from the men, and his children, not out of shame—he had no shame—but out of pride, to hold his sway over them. With his wife it was different: he dominated her, if at all, through her complicity. She was the moon to his sun, a creature of darkness whose luster borrowed his. The secret was as much hers as his, and she was the more ruthless in protecting it.

He had a weakness for fine cigars, brought up from New Orleans once a year by a Creole trader. His wife joined him in smoking them on the porch as they watched the basin fade into night. The dogs cringed around him in supplication, watchful, creeping forward, beating their tails on the deck if he glanced in their direction. The air stood deathly still.

"He's been given his warning," the Captain said. "He'll leave. He's not a fool."

Who's the fool? Jacinta wanted to ask. "You said yourself he'll spread the story around before he goes."

"I've looked into his reputation." He let the smoke curl around him, savoring the aroma. It was one of his few pleasures, the only one he shared with Jacinta. "He's a man who keeps his own counsel.

Plays his cards close to the vest. If he planned to tell that tale, he'd dangle it in front of me. Angle me to buy his silence."

"He might or he might not."

"Anyway, nobody would believe it." A short, half-hearted laugh. "Let him talk."

You were a coward then and you're a coward now, Jacinta thought. She held her tongue: she would not shame him, dare him, goad him to action. He had to do this himself.

"And there's another thing," the Captain said. "If we got rid of Slater we'd have to get rid of the boy. Rory, his name is. Slater's probably told him everything. We couldn't trust him not to talk."

"Him too, then?"

The Captain tossed his head like a horse refusing the harness. "No, he's just a boy."

It's a ghost town now and in a way it always has been. All the men who went there brought ghosts with them—dead or deserted wives, lunatic sons or daughters, men they'd killed in fights or shot in the back—and most of them encountered others after they arrived, ghosts who found a voice in the wind that howled around them on the range or whistled out of crevices or makeshift graves or heaps of gnawed-on bones. After a few years in the basin the Captain's troubled gray eyes told you, before he ever opened his mouth, that he heard those voices and lived in dread of them. His terrors took him back to east Texas after the war, to the ruined plantation and the insane patriarch who led him into the desert and threw him to the Comanche devils. On his first cattle drive as trail boss they cornered him in an arroyo, whipped that fish hook scar into his lip and made him watch as they scalped three of his men and goaded him to flee, leaving behind a fourth man who still lived. The Comanches mutilated that man—his name was Johnson—but kept him alive as a witness to the Captain's perfidy. Johnson crawled into

San Antonio two weeks later, just strong enough to point to the gash on the Captain's lip that would forever brand him a coward and a betrayer. He faced no legal jeopardy but the opprobrium of men who, knowing what they knew, would never again submit to his domination. He fled west under a new name, found a wife in Santa Fe, new men to rule, and struck north into an unknown country. For a long time he imagined that he could beat back what haunted him from his past, just as he beat back every other hostile force. Then Slater arrived, like a revenant sent to punish him for his sins, sharing his secret but never confronting him or threatening him with it. That silence made him realize that what haunted him was part of his fate and he could do nothing about it.

Moondog, the ex-preacher, was a philosopher of the fatalistic sort, who took no delight in the world except in foretelling its doom. His best friend was Polecat, a man without a philosophy of any kind who never believed a word Moondog said. He was stubborn and superstitious, a dreamer of hopeless dreams and grandiose schemes to make up for a lifetime of bad luck.

One morning the two friends rode out toward the vermillion cliffs looking for strays. The breeze brought a whiff of brimstone and they squinted through a thicket to find its source. Along that escarpment hot springs could burst out unexpectedly from cracks in the earth, bringing water that was as sulfuric and corrosive as acid.

"You think you can cheat death?" Moondog asked Polecat.

"It ain't cheating when the cards are stacked against you. You do whatever you can to win."

A patch of mist hovered over the brush. "Hey, lookee here," Polecat said. "Must be a hot spring."

They pushed their way through the thicket of moldy, broken cane to a sinkhole about eight feet across and six feet deep, filled to the brim with sulfurous water that simmered just below the boiling point. The bleached cadaver of a calf bobbed in the water like a boiled egg, horns and hoofs and a few bones juddering on the bottom, hide mostly eaten away, ribcage and skull held in place by sinew and rawhide leather. A greasy scrim on the surface rippled back the purple sky.

Polecat stared into the steaming hole wondering if his bad luck had finally run out. "What in hell?"

"It's that stray we couldn't find last week," Moondog said. "Must have stumbled in there and boiled up like a pot of soup." He pointed to the bare segmented tail, the empty eye sockets, the drooping ears curiously preserved in the brine. "Nothing left of it but bones and a little fat skimming the surface."

Sort of a sweet smell, Polecat noticed, once you got close to it.

Elena discovered the sinkhole the day after Moondog and Polecat found it. She gasped at the sight of the bucking calf: skinless, dismembered, exposed. Butchered and eaten before it could be slaughtered. The smell made her sick.

She had climbed off her sorrel mare and knelt to peer into the sinkhole. A man rode up behind her and for an instant she imagined that he would push her in. She scrambled backwards, away from the edge, and when she stood up she recognized him. Her heart raced. "You're Rory," she said, and wished she hadn't said it.

Her embarrassment surprised him. "That's so." He tipped his hat politely. "We met once in town."

"Really?" For some reason she felt compelled to deny having met him. "I don't remember that."

He nodded as if he believed her. "Shame about that calf. Must've burnt its mouth trying to get a drink and stumbled in."

His eyes were on her, not on the calf. She felt awkward, excited, cornered. Naturally she said the wrong thing. "We're supposed to hate each other."

"I ain't much for supposing," he said. "Or for hating."

"Me neither."

His smile was too wide for a cowboy who hardly knew her. "Anyway, how could I hate a pretty girl like you?"

Her eyes darted away. She didn't like being told how pretty she was by a man who had no reason to think she'd like it. "Don't start supposing it could be any different," she said.

"No, I don't guess it could be. You being the Captain's daughter and me being so low class and ignorant and all, and a orphan to boot."

An orphan? She hadn't heard about that. "Then Slater isn't your father?"

"Would that be a point in my favor? Well, if so, then no he ain't. He fished me out of the Rio Concho like a crawdaddy. Does that help my case?"

"What case is that?"

"The case for not hating me."

He seemed to be roping her in and that made her uncomfortable. "I don't hate you and I hope you don't hate me," she said. "I only said that because our fathers—or whatever Slater is to you—probably think we ought to hate each other just because they do, and I don't go along with that. Though of course there could be other reasons for not liking each other, or at least for one of us not liking the other. If we actually knew each other."

The cowboy grin was back, with its insinuating familiarity. "Well," he chuckled, "I want to say flat out that I think you're a right pretty gal who has a nice way of talking, though maybe a little argumentative, and who probably has a nice smile, if she'd ever stoop to show it, and a kind heart inside, and I hope we do get to know each other better. Right now I got to mosey because there's work to do down at the camp. Adiós!"

He tipped his hat again and trotted away without another glance in her direction. If he had cast such a glance, he would have seen a slightly less pretty face flushed with anger and embarrassment, eyes blazing, lips muttering a riposte suggesting that he could no longer safely suppose she didn't hate him.

The Captain awoke in the gray morning light, breathing hard, his heart pounding. His lower lip burned where it had been whip-slashed over twenty years before. He fought back an image of Slater staring at it, lingering on it longer than he should have, a dawning in his eyes. He hurled himself out of bed to escape the night that was still inside him and staggered into his boots. For the rest of the day he tasted anger and bitterness and thwarted domination.

At dusk he found Vickery tending a fire behind the barn. Scrap lumber, old fence posts, broken furniture from the bunkhouse, piled together over a heap of dry brush and ignited with some lamp oil and a match. The foreman sat on his haunches warming his hands over the fire. They talked over the day's business and then the subject of Slater came up. "He'd be so easy to get rid of," Vickery said, his eyes glistening like beads on an abacus.

It was true, the Captain agreed without saying so. He'd bred a pack of shameless lowlifes who'd shoot any man you could name without a second thought. "I'm no murderer," he said.

"You've done worse things than kill a man whose life is worth less than a dog's."

He looked away.

Vickery's pale face pulsed with the firelight, shades of red and orange wavering in his eyes. "And you've said yourself that there's no good or evil in this basin."

"Have you seen any sign of them?"

Vickery clicked, then started to laugh. "Only evil."

"Even so," the Captain said, unsmiling, "murder is unworthy of me. Doubly so to have it done by somebody else."

Vickery smirked at his vanity. "Slater is building, expanding, adding to his herd. He'll grind you into the dust if you don't get rid of him now."

The Captain walked away, but his foreman wouldn't relent: he followed him around the barn with one argument after another, impossible to refute. It was like arguing with the devil.

"Stop it," the Captain finally said. "It's wrong to assume Slater will win this war. He needs to sell five hundred head this summer and to do that he has to drive his herd a hundred miles north to the railhead, where the prices are rigged like the tack on a mule train. He'll be lucky to be able to feed his men on the trip home."

"Assuming he even reaches the railhead through that badland," Vickery laughed. "I heard a couple of the fellas talking—I won't mention their names—about the Tatum gang they used to run with up there."

"That'd be Barlow and Nickerson."

"You know all about it then."

The Captain knew all about the Tatum gang. It was a large-scale rustling operation carried out by a rout of thieves, murderers, deserters, men with a price on their heads, renegade Indians and white men dressed as Indians, that would overwhelm a drover on his way to the railhead, stampede his stock away, then round it back up and sell it to the commission agents. "Barlow and Nickerson rode with Tatum until he scared all the cattlemen away. Thank the devil they work for us now."

"So they do," Vickery smiled. "And what harm could it do for them to ride up there and let Abe Tatum know that Slater's on his way with his herd?"

What harm indeed? As the Captain drifted down to the saloon that evening reflecting on his conversation with Vickery, he spotted Slater's foreman Buckminster, who frequented the place even though he didn't drink. The two outfits usually kept apart, but Buckminster chatted up the Captain so often, the Captain wondered if the man was a spy, sent to salt his mind with falsehoods or collect information to pass on to Slater.

"Sometimes I wish I'd never signed that contract with the Army," he told Buckminster that night. "Two thousand head to be delivered by the end of this month."

"At what price?"

"Well," he hesitated, as if reluctant to go on, "it was a fair price when I struck the deal."

"We'll get a better price at the railhead," Buckminster boasted. "Beef's high up there right now."

"Sure it is," the Captain said. "But in a couple weeks it'll be back down to where it was last summer. Ora Haley's moving in with a lot of prime stock."

"Well, we won't be waiting around that long."

"When you riding out?"

"Couple days. Soon as the weather clears."

In this way the Captain learned the timing of Slater's upcoming cattle drive, which, through Vickery, he passed on to Barlow and Nickerson, knowing they'd ride north and relay that information to the rustler Abe Tatum. He'd resisted Vickery's worst temptations—he'd have no hand in killing Slater, whose life was now in Abe Tatum's hands—and by drawing that line he'd retained his authority over Vickery. He could not let his foreman tempt him. But what to make of Buckminster? Was he a spy, a turncoat, or just a strutting fool who couldn't hold his tongue? No, he was no fool, the Captain decided, at least not that kind of fool. His innocence was just his own form of cunning. Something lurked in those crystal-blue eyes that wasn't what he wanted you to see.

7.

What went on in that basin they call a legend now but it wasn't a legend then, just the thankless life of some poor cowpunchers in a place they wished they'd never heard of. Today the story's been told and retold so many times in so many bunkhouses and bar rooms that nobody expects it to be true. You can talk up the good parts, lie about the bad parts, chalk up the violence and the killing to adventure or bad luck. If only you'd known that at the time. If you'd known you were living a legend you might have lived it differently or not lived it at all.

The land had no names on it when the Captain arrived but those left by the Utes, or the primeval race the Utes called the Old Ones. Those names vanished with the Indians and in due course new names—Disaster Falls, Disappointment Draw, the Vale of Tears— took hold to celebrate the white man's folly. You spent your life out on the range, and snow and hail and driving rain was no excuse not to be there. You knew your job and you knew each other, as far as you can ever know a cowboy. In that lonesome basin you could strut and fret like you knew a helluva lot more than you did. You broke your back to make a buck and pissed away every dime on the poker table. In the saloon you swapped lies and boasts and challenged any man to call you a liar.

The Captain talked to the cowboys in the saloon sometimes, never boastful, never bullying, always a little mysterious. It was about the cattle, the horses, the land, and later, about Slater. He never talked about his past or his family. And though you saw that log house with the big front porch every day you never knew what went on inside it. What loving words they spoke, or words of bitterness or hate, what discord or silence they wrapped themselves in when the world was locked outside. Old Zeke, the grizzled mountain man who was too ancient to do anything but cook, used to bring their food in from the cookhouse and serve it to them. He heard a few choice words and passed them on in the bunkhouse. To the cowboys it was like reading hieroglyphics but it left a picture in their mind. The family gathered, time held at arm's length: the Captain and his wife standing fast like a king and queen on a chess board waiting for an unseen hand to decide what to do with them. Nobody thought they had a happy marriage. The men knew the truth about Jacinta long before the Captain did.

Some of the men thought they'd been put in that basin for a reason. To be tested, to be punished, maybe just to die and sift into the dust. Like as not it was just to find out what the reason was. In that case nobody succeeded, except maybe the Captain himself, in his last moments.

Elena had known a strange excitement and confusion since her meeting with Rory at the sinkhole. He'd left her feeling embarrassed, insulted, annoyed at his cowboy arrogance which assumed that she'd want to get to know him better. She'd started the conversation hoping they didn't need to hate each other and ended it thinking maybe that wasn't such a bad idea. Still she couldn't stop thinking about him and what she'd say to him the next time they met. Maybe she'd give him that nice smile he seemed to think he deserved and tell him he should save his sweet-talk for his horse. Yes, that was it. She hoped she'd see him again just so she could tell him that.

There were times when she wished the encounter with Rory had gone differently. Times when she felt helpless, trapped by circumstances she couldn't control or understand. The deadly rivalry between the Captain's outfit and Slater's preyed on her mind. Why were they fighting over this barren wasteland? Wasn't there enough land to go around? And the atmosphere of hostility and dread they all lived under—wasn't her father to blame for that?

She threw herself into ranch work. Feeding the horses, brushing lice off the cows, roping calves and hauling them in to be branded—whatever needed to be done. The men stood in awe of her, and not just because of who she was. More because of the easy way she worked with the animals and her skills with a horse and a rope. She could do just about everything they could do, and that was humbling, a little unnerving. They dreaded the day when the Captain would send her out with a castrating knife. It embarrassed her when Vickery tried to single her out for special treatment. "Now boys," he told the men one morning as they gathered in front of the barn, "we all got a job to do but not everybody's created equal. You need to go easy on the young lady."

She hated being called the young lady or any kind of lady, but she held her tongue until Vickery left to fetch the Captain. She followed him and caught up with him by the corral. "If you do that," she said, "I won't be able to work with the men. You know that, don't you?"

"Do what?" he asked, all innocence.

"Treat me different because I'm the boss's daughter."

"Well, that's what you are, ain't it?"

"You know I am. And you ought to know that my father wants me to learn how to run the ranch and that means doing every kind of job."

"Well, I hope it won't come to that."

"What do you mean?"

"This is rough and dirty work. I sure hope you won't have to spend your life doing it."

Working around the ranch, she heard things she wasn't supposed to hear. About eliminating some of Slater's men:

Moondog, Polecat, Crazy Ike. Vickery's idea, apparently—was he really intent on having them killed? And if so, what would happen to Rory? When she heard the name Hortter, an unfamiliar name, she asked Luke if he knew him. Luke clammed up, but he couldn't keep a secret, he was too proud that he knew it. Hortter was a rustler, he told her. Caught red-handed on their land with one of their calves, and the men strung him up on a gatepost. Oh yes they held a trial first but of course he was guilty, knew what his end would be, there was never any doubt of that. Spent his last hour on earth blubbering like a baby.

That night at supper Elena helped Old Zeke carry the food in from the cookhouse and serve it to the family. Jacinta never cooked, served meals or lifted a finger to help. It mortified her that her only servant was a toothless mountain man who slept in the barn and smelled like a mule. She liked to talk, mostly to Luke, about her girlhood in Santa Fe and the military achievements of her ancestors. The Captain cut up his steak with a razor-sharp knife he carried on his belt.

When Jacinta stopped to take a bite, Elena asked her father about what she'd heard the men saying at the corral. "This feud with Slater," she asked him. "What started it?"

Jacinta eyed her sharply, amazed at her impertinence. Wasn't the answer obvious?

The Captain took his time answering, as if he had to concentrate on chewing his steak. "It's not a feud," he said. "Feuds are petty things, fueled by spite or revenge. This is a war."

"What's the difference?"

"A war has a higher purpose. It's about important things, the only important thing."

Elena hung on his next word, the solution to the riddle. Power, wealth, land? They were all that mattered to him.

"Honor," he said.

She opened her mouth, speechless. Incredulous that he would go to murderous war over such a hollow notion.

"I wouldn't expect a girl your age—or even a grown woman—to understand that."

"No," she said, confessing her ignorance. "It's only men who find honor in killing." Surely he couldn't blame her for agreeing with him. "Hanging Hortter from a gatepost—was it honor that drove you to that?"

She saw a rage in his eyes she'd never seen before. "I don't know anybody named Hortter." His voice was careless, impersonal. "You say he was hanged. Who was he?"

"A rustler, they say."

"Then he got the justice he deserved."

"Remember how this started," Jacinta cut in, hoping to keep Elena from going any farther. "It was that man Slater's insulting behavior, his challenge to your father, in front of his wife and children, in the middle of town where everyone could see it. What man could tolerate such insolence? Certainly not your father, who has built his life on honor and pride."

The Captain waited for her to finish. "And unlike a feud," he said, still talking to Elena, "a war doesn't go on forever. It has a beginning and a middle and an end."

"When does it end?"

"It ends when one side is destroyed. There's a winner and a loser."

He stood up, wiped the knife on his napkin and tossed the napkin back on the table. "That's how this one will end. And I mean to be the winner."

Jacinta did not share the Captain's bed but slept in her own room. On one side of her canopy bed stood a shrine crowded with votive candles and carved statues of saints, on the other an ancient loom she'd inherited from her superstitious aunt in New Mexico. She seldom left the house, never without the Captain, though often she stood at her bedroom window peering over the range in the vain hope that something might have changed. The men feared the sight of her, her air of restrained frenzy, the obsidian eyes buried deep beneath her dark eyebrows, her thin lips twitching with the memory of prayers or curses. Old Zeke had seen the shrine in her room with its graven images, and when he told the other men in the bunk house, Gutiérrez, the boy from Chihuahua who everybody loved like their own son, crossed himself and said she was a witch, weaving spells and prayers to Santa Muerte. Our Lady of Holy Death.

She called Elena into her room that night and sat her in front of the loom. In it was an unfinished tapestry, woven with impossible landscapes, chimerical beasts, angels and shrouded skeletons, trailing into a cedar chest where it vanished like time into eternity. Her heart racing, Elena felt herself teetering on the edge of dread.

"You shouldn't provoke your father like that," her mother said.

"I didn't mean to provoke him."

"Asking him about Slater, as if Slater were his equal. Of course that would provoke him. And then mentioning Hortter—"

"You know about Hortter?"

"A man in his position has to make hard decisions, for the sake of the outfit, and his family. Yes, for us."

Jacinta lifted the folds of the shawl and fluttered them in front of Elena, who glimpsed the dazzling figures as they sprang to life and flitted away. What were they supposed to represent?

"This is for your wedding," Jacinta said.

"I'm not getting married," Elena said.

Her mother smiled knowingly. "I was younger than you are now when I married your father. I was stubborn, like you. Rebellious. It couldn't last. There was no place my rebellion could take me except to the convent, which is a living death."

"I'm not like you."

"No, but you'll do the same thing I did—sacrifice yourself to some man's pleasure and pride. I pity you but you have no choice. It's what every woman must do."

"It doesn't have to be that way."

"Yes it does. You'll find that out soon enough. What other future do you imagine for yourself in this place?"

Elena glanced at the tapestry, hoping to find a better destiny written there, but all she saw was darkness, inchoate shapes, indeterminate colors. She still hadn't met a man, including her father, who wasn't vain, arrogant, cruel. She doubted she would ever love any man enough to marry him.

"You may love him or think that someday you will love him," Jacinta said, "but after years of suffering you'll realize that your only hope is what you hate most about him. That's what you feed on: his pride, his domination, his heartlessness—all the things that make him powerful among men, the things that make him do what disgusts you. You'll want that power as much as he does—it's the only thing that will save you—and you can only achieve it through him."

Jacinta had laid bare the tragedy of her own life. Elena wanted desperately not to repeat it. With a dose of her father's heartlessness she said, "There's too much pride in your heart, and in his. What is it but selfishness?"

Her mother backed away, cheeks blazing with anger or embarrassment or both. "You think he does all this for himself? Out of selfishness?"

"Why else?"

"You don't understand him. He never thinks about himself. He does it for us, and for the outfit." She held Elena in her baleful pitying gaze. "You have no idea how he suffers."

8.

The roundup was completed. Cows goaded from the draws with their bleating young, yearling heifers frisking on the flats, young steers marked with Slater's brand, wrestled into the dirt for a trail brand to seal their final journey. Five hundred head culled out for delivery to the railhead, the rest left behind to be minded by Ferguson.

Rory felt lucky that Slater took him along on the drive, the first he'd ridden with such a large herd. Let Ferguson, though a couple years older, stay behind with the heifers and the calves and the pregnant cows—that was one of Slater's rules, he refused to drive pregnant cows and club their calves to death along the trail—and Rory wouldn't risk being seen by Elena doing less than a man's job. Why did he care what she saw or what she thought? When they'd met by the sinkhole all she seemed to care about was whether she ought to hate him or not. But he was still tingling with the thrill of that encounter, whether he wanted to admit it or not. He pictured her bright eyes, her sleek black hair, the flush that darkened her cheeks as he turned to ride away. In spite of himself he wondered if she liked him, realizing the question was absurd. How could he judge what a woman might like, when he'd hardly known any? More troubling was what she thought of other men. Slater, who'd seen even less of her than he had, made a flattering remark about her and Rory's mind raced with a violence that surprised him, and it raced faster when Buckminster said something disrespectful and laughed with two of the men. Rory thought of Ferguson with his bright smile and his fine horsemanship and wondered if he would stop to chat with her when the rest of them were out on the trail. That would have angered him too if he found out about it. None of this he understood. It was all new to him. But for whatever reason he wished Elena could see him on that trail with the other men, doing a man's job.

Three days north they tripped down an escarpment into a badland that dated to the beginning of the world or its end, whether past or future could not be divined. They had been warned about that valley of bones but the sight of it snatched the breath from their gaping mouths. Men cast bets on whether Armageddon had arrived since they'd left the bunkhouse and the odds ran in its favor. Here lay a fantastic landscape of sandstone spires that tuned the wind like organ pipes, groaning and shrilling in tones that were beyond the human ear but could turn a cow to bawling and prancing with mad eyes and a lashing tail. Men too were stirred to frenzy. Crazy Ike shouted into that diapason wind until he was hoarse, pirouetting in dizzying loops around the strays and stragglers to keep them from being spirited away by the wind. Then came the thirst, not a drop of moisture for fifty miles, the cattle wild, stumbling, their tongues hanging out, and when at last they smelled water they stampeded toward it, the men battling to slow them down, cut them into smaller bands, drive them sideways lest they leap into some mirage—and then came a roaring cavalry of deserters, outlaws, renegades, the Tatum gang thundering out of the rockscape, whooping like Comanches, filling the sky with lead and gunsmoke. Turned in mid-stampede, the cattle spiraled, their horns snagging together as they staggered counterclockwise in a deafening maelstrom of dust.

In the melee Rory recognized Barlow and Nickerson from the Captain's outfit leading a dozen others he didn't know, Abe Tatum shouting orders behind them. Few cowboys packed side arms in those days, but those rustlers did, along with rifles and shotguns. They fired in the air but didn't shoot to kill. Slater's men struggled to stay on their mounts, which were rearing and screaming in panic. Some of them had rifles or shotguns on their saddles, but Slater ordered them to hold their fire. They raced in circles trying to keep the cattle together, but the terrain was open there, a bench land above a dry creek bottom, and the herd broke into frightened bands that ran off in all directions.

Some of the men chased after them but most stood their ground, squinting through fifty yards of dust. The piping wind howled out of the rocks around them. Rory raced up to Tatum, shouting insults, but Tatum smirked and turned away, keeping his rifle low across his saddle.

"Get your boy out of here!" he yelled to Slater. "I don't want to see him get hurt."

Slater called Rory back and Rory glared at Slater, humiliated to be treated like a child. He loped back and stood behind the others, next to Buckminster and Moondog.

"Let's all of us get out of here," Buckminster shouted. "Come on, boys."

Crazy Ike galloped forward flailing his axe like a sickle and the rustlers fled before him. They could have shot him easily enough but the unwritten law of cattle theft was to avoid bloodshed. Nobody wanted to be the first to fire on another man. That could set off a conflagration that would kill them all.

But death can find a way even though not in the shape of a bullet. The sight of Barlow and Nickerson—recognized from the Captain's outfit—infuriated Moondog, who puffed up with rage and roared like an avenging berserker. He leaped off his horse, unarmed, and ran toward Barlow and yanked him off his saddle, throwing him head first onto the stony ground. Barlow rolled over, bleeding from the mouth, and Moondog tossed him again, smashing his head against a pillar of red sandstone that jutted out of the plain like a grave marker.

"Stop it you son of a bitch!" Nickerson roweled his horse toward Moondog, lashing at him with a whip. Moondog caught the whip in his hands and tore Nickerson off his mount. He hit the ground hard and bolted away to the jeers of Slater's outfit, leaving Barlow crumpled on the rocks, staring stupidly into the sun. If Barlow had gone there (as some thought) with the intention of killing Slater, then death, jealous of its privileges and priorities, had blocked his way. The bullet meant for Slater never left his gun. Nickerson was powerless to help him.

Moondog stood alone, all the rustlers' guns leveled at him. He showed his teeth, ready to tear them apart at the least provocation. His hands dripped blood from the bite of Nickerson's whip.

"Go ahead and shoot if you think you can finish me off before I break your necks," he said. He turned toward a man—probably a renegade Comanche—with painted face and braided hair and white man's clothes. "How about you, you son of a bitch? How'd you like your eyes plucked out and shoved down your throat?"

The wind moaned in the rocks as each man waited for his next heartbeat. Rory felt his horse sagging under him, swaying, as if the ground was about to give way. His head was as light and wispy as the clouds in the sky.

Then something unexpected happened, which was talked about long afterwards. Slater spurred his mount forward, right up to Tatum, and leaned forward to speak to him in a low tone. Nobody in either outfit could hear what they said. After a minute or two they both nodded crisply and Slater turned and cantered back.

"Put your guns down," Tatum told his men. "We don't need no more killing."

"No shooting," Slater said. "Moondog, come back here and get on your horse."

Some of Slater's men had hung back with Buckminster. Slater counted three casualties among the rustlers—including Barlow, who was dead—and only one on his side, the luckless Polecat, who had been whipped in the face as he ventured too close to Nickerson. By the time Tatum called a retreat and the marauders galloped away, most of the cattle had scattered across the broken land, leaving only a waft of dust to mark their paths.

Slater's men rounded up what stock they could find, about half the herd by nightfall, and drove them the next day to the railhead and sold them to the commission agents. The rest they left to be salvaged and sold to the same agents by the rustlers. All those cattle would be reunited in the same slaughterhouse in Chicago, at roughly the same price to the ultimate purchaser.

The ride home began in a morning thunderstorm that trailed them back through the badland, washed and slick and treacherous. After the rain stopped the men rode muttering and mutinous, heads down, as if they'd seen a curse emblazoned in the sky. In their bones they felt the dark rumbling that throbbed around them, the wind's low moan tolling through the rock. Rory felt bitter eyes on him, the eyes of diminished men who'd been made to stand down from a fight. They were ashamed of themselves, all but Moondog, who'd killed a man and was proud of it until the greasy aftertaste of death choked and silenced him and the others felt the catch in their throats that reminded them how close they'd come to coughing out that taste on the red rocks.

When they stopped to water the horses, Polecat, whose whip-sliced cheek dripped pus, curveted up to Slater and challenged him with his eyes. He said nothing but the challenge was clear. Slater calmly stared him down.

"The Captain sent Barlow and Nickerson up here to steal our stock," Polecat said. "We should have killed them both."

"One was enough," Slater said.

"I ain't done with Nickerson," Polecat said.

"No, I don't guess you are. But as long as you're riding with me you'll do as I say. Moondog did right backing off when I told him to. So did Rory. That's the only reason we're still alive."

The men grumbled and cursed under their breath. A few shook their heads or spat on the wet ground. They didn't like hearing Moondog and Rory praised in the same breath. Moondog was one of them, Rory a headstrong fool who could have got them shot.

"The boss is right," Buckminster said. "Now let's get these horses watered so we can move on."

Slater was grateful to Buckminster for backing him up. Buckminster was good with other men, a diplomat, some called him, and a peacemaker. He had the knack of reasoning with even the toughest customers. "You're a right good foreman," Slater told him later, when nobody was listening. "You're smart, you're loyal. I'll always have a place for a man like you."

"I ain't planning on going anywhere," Buckminster said.

"I appreciate that. You stick around and there'll be something in it for you."

He acted surprised, wide-eyed as a child. "What've you got in mind?"

"You stick around and you'll see," Slater said. "It'll be worth your while. There's enough in this country to go around. Enough land, enough cattle, enough horseflesh. I got Rory to take care of too."

Buckminster tried to stifle his resentment. He didn't appreciate Rory's privileged status, or his recklessness, but as foreman he had to walk a fine line. What he said next wasn't on the right side of that line and Slater didn't like it.

"What's Rory ever done?" Buckminster asked.

"He's like a son to me," Slater said. "That's what he done."

In spite of his privileged status Rory sulked all the way back to the ranch. Rode apart from the others, barely talked to them even when they talked to him. Looked away from Slater, his face a mask of stone. He was embarrassed, humiliated, angry, mostly at Slater for calling him out when he yelled at Tatum. He was the only one with the stones to tell the rustlers to get the hell out. Some of the men called him brave, others scowled that he almost got himself and the rest of them killed. Slater waited until they were home so they could talk without making a show of it.

They stood in the corral after unsaddling and combing down their horses. It was after sunset but the sky was wide and clear, the storm a distant memory. The wind scoured their teeth with dust. "I was proud that you told that son of a bitch what he needed to hear," Slater said. "But glad you stopped when you did."

Rory kept his eyes down. "You made me look like a fool."

"No, I made you stop looking like a fool before you got shot full of holes."

"Tatum wouldn't have shot me."

"He didn't want to shoot you but he would have done it if you dared him to."

Rory turned to face Slater, the anger flaring inside him. "You ain't seen me draw. I can—"

"Listen to me, Rory," Slater cut him off, clamping a grip on his wrist. "If Tatum had fumbled his rifle, everybody out there would've been shot. You got no right to put the men in danger. What Moondog did was even worse, killing that man Barlow who worked for the Captain. We ain't heard the end of that."

Rory yanked himself free and glowered at Slater. "You'd never fight back, would you? You're afraid of the Captain too."

"Afraid? You think I'm afraid?"

"What else do you call it?"

"I call it sense. When you're outnumbered, you got to back off. That ain't the same as being afraid."

Slater was right about the Barlow killing. News of it traveled fast and triggered a lynch mob atmosphere in the saloon. Men from the Captain's outfit taunted and threatened Slater's crew when they walked in, egged on by Nickerson, who mocked Polecat for the scar he'd whipped on his cheek. For a week Moondog did his drinking in the bunkhouse out of tin cans brought back by Crazy Ike. One night when the Captain was there, the mob surrounded Buckminster demanding that he call out Slater for letting Moondog kill Barlow.

"Barlow was riding with Tatum's gang," Buckminster said. "He deserved what he got."

Nickerson slapped the bar and lurched toward Buckminster, swinging a whisky bottle by the neck the way he would have hefted an ax.

"And Nickerson," Buckminster said, "is damn lucky he ain't in the ground next to him."

Eight strong hands gripped Buckminster's arms while Nickerson smashed the bottle on a table and brandished its jagged stub in his face. A few inches closer to his throat and he would have bled out like a slaughtered calf. Or six inches higher and his clean-shaven face, which women found handsome, would have been torn to shreds, his eyes stripped blind. All those things Nickerson could have done. He certainly had it in him to do that to a man, especially a vain man like Buckminster, who kept his hair trimmed and dressed in a fitted suit and vest when he went into town.

"Say your prayers you son of a bitch," Nickerson grinned as he twirled the bottle edge closer.

Unexpectedly the Captain stood up and stepped into the crowd, which parted before him. "Buckminster's right," he said. A hush had fallen over the room. "Coddling rustlers is not how I do business."

He glared at the men pinning back Buckminster's arms. "Let him go."

Within a few days Nickerson had vanished from the basin, nobody knew where to. That happened sometimes—men came and went like lone crows. They showed up, worked for a while, then disappeared. Ferguson hadn't been seen since Slater's outfit came back from the cattle drive. Nobody thought much of it.

One evening Polecat and Moondog rode out to the geyser hole where they'd found the stray calf a few weeks before. In that seething pool they found a human skeleton, its parts bound together with wire like a hay bale, wrists twisted behind it, the skull, wide-eyed in wonderment, harnessed to a corked gallon jug that bobbed in the shimmering moonlight, holding the skeleton upright in a pair of whitened leather boots.

"I'll be damned if that don't look like Ferguson's fancy Mexican belt buckle," Polecat said in a faltering voice. "And Ferguson's fine set of teeth."

They remembered the stray calf they'd discovered there—poor critter must have stumbled in before the roundup. Drowned and boiled and melted to slime in less than a week—a strange misfortune, but that's all it was, plain bad luck. That isn't what happened to Ferguson, unless it was blind chance that trussed him up with barbed wire and looped that jug around his neck.

Under the darkening sky they watched for odd rises of mist where a similar end might await them. Was the whole basin pitted with traps where a man might be dangled to his death? For all they knew the earth, just beneath the surface, might be encircled by a chthonic necropolis, a way station to hell where the dead stand upright, exhaling brimstone into moonlit skies.

"What ate the flesh? I wonder," Polecat said. "And the brains and all. Nothing could live in that sinkhole, could it?"

Moondog crouched and peered over the yellow rim into the hole, where tiny corkscrews danced in the moonlight.

"Worms, I reckon."

9.

Often in the morning Elena rode out to the clay butte to bring treats to Susannah and talk to her while she petted and brushed her down. Sometimes she'd spot Rory—at least she hoped it was Rory— slouching on his palomino just below the rim of the red sandstone mesa to the north. He seemed to be watching her but never came closer than half a mile, as if wary of the reception she'd give him. She pretended not to care whether she saw him or not.

Before Slater drove his herd north it was Ferguson she'd seen in the high country. After that she never saw him again. She thought nothing of it until one morning, stepping into the barn to bring out her sorrel mare, she heard men laughing and joking as they broke up bales of hay with pitchforks to feed the horses. She knew one of the men—his name was Bob Wallace and he always had a twinkle in his eye. "Hey Vickery," he called out to the foreman. "You ain't seen that Ferguson boy around here, have you?"

Vickery wasn't one to appreciate a joke. "No, I ain't."

"I could swear this pinto mare you been feeding was his." Wallace smacked the horse's rump and the other men laughed more.

"Keep your hands off my horse," Vickery snarled.

"Sort of has a brimstone smell about her, don't she, boys? Like she just crawled out of a sinkhole."

Vickery grabbed the pitchfork out of Wallace's hands and raised it in front of his throat. "Unless you want to end up like Ferguson, you better keep your mouth shut."

A sinkhole? Did Vickery mean the one where she'd talked with Rory? A calf had fallen in there, she remembered. Was that what had happened to Ferguson? It never occurred to her that this could have been anything but an accident.

She rode out to the vermillion cliffs that afternoon and picked her way through the thicket to the sinkhole where she'd met Rory. To her astonishment there he stood once again, his face an image of hatred and fury that shocked her. His eyes reared up from the steaming pool to meet hers. "Come out to inspect your father's evil handiwork?"

"I don't know what you mean."

"Like hell you don't."

Peering into the hole she saw the skeleton tangled in the wire, bobbing under the corked jug. The Mexican belt buckle, the whitened leather boots, the unmistakable smile. She dropped to the ground, faint with nausea. It was yellow and rock-hard where the bitter water had bubbled over the brim.

"Don't tell me you didn't know about this," Rory said.

She hesitated, struggling to understand.

"Why else would you come out here?"

"I...heard something," she said. "But I didn't expect this. I didn't expect to find anything like this."

"Your father did this. Tied that boy up and threw him in there and watched him die."

"No." She couldn't bear to hear her father accused of that. "It was Vickery. I heard the men taunting him about it. He's got the pinto mare in our barn."

Rory stared back in disbelief. "Don't you get it? Vickery does what your father tells him to do."

They both stood silent, afraid to go on. There wasn't much between them beyond vague wishes and baseless hopes, which counted for nothing in that basin. But whatever they had, neither wanted it to end this way.

"Why did they do it?" Elena asked.

"One of the Captain's men got killed when we ran into them rustlers up north. Barlow. You heard of him?"

She nodded grimly, never having cared for Barlow. "I heard that one of your men killed him."

"It was self-defense."

"Isn't it always self-defense?"

The hatred flashed back into Rory's eyes as he glanced at what was left of Ferguson. "This wasn't."

She turned away, unable to endure what she saw in those eyes. She wanted to like him but when he aimed his fury at her all she could think about was fighting back. "My father had nothing to do with it," she said.

"How do you know that?"

"He's not that kind of man."

Rory cocked his head and gave her a long look-over, like he might have given a recalcitrant horse. "If I wasn't so damn mad I'd almost think that was funny."

Elena's cheeks flushed with some combination of emotions it would have taken a month to sort out. His anger had shaken her with a melancholy sense of loss and now his mockery stoked her disappointment into something like despair. She felt like crying but choked it off, unwilling to concede such weakness. "You think a lot of things are funny that aren't," she said. A strand of black hair blew over her face and she flicked it back.

"Maybe that's the only way I can keep from going crazy in this hell-hole."

She'd never heard any of the men talk like that. "What hell-hole?"

"This basin we all seem bound to fight over until we kill each other off."

"Why do you have to do that?"

"Just how it was meant to be, I guess."

He stepped back from the edge of the sinkhole. The mist steaming off it had left his boots wet and slimy. She pointed down to the sulfurous water bubbling up around Ferguson's bones. "When you said hell-hole I thought you might have meant this."

He shook his head and turned away rather than to look down. "How long have you lived here?" he asked her.

"Twelve years, I guess. About as long as I can remember."

"Ferguson was my best friend in the outfit. The only one close to my age."

His anger had faded and he must have felt the need to explain it. Probably as close to an apology as she would ever get. "I've never known a girl my own age," she said.

"It can be awful lonesome out here. But look"—he pointed to the red rocks along the rim of the mesa, blazing in the afternoon sun—"it can be beautiful too."

That was strange talk coming from a cowboy, Elena thought. Beauty wasn't something they talked about or even noticed. "It was a hell-hole a minute ago," she said.

He mustered a smile. "I guess I must be kin of the devil if I can see the beauty in it."

There was somebody else on that mesa the devil might have recognized as one of his own. When Elena and Rory rode out together from the sinkhole, Elena startled, pulled up on her reins, almost lost her balance. Hearing her gasp, Rory turned to see her staring at the face of the mesa where moments before he'd showed her the sun pouring out its beauty on the lifeless rocks. She held her eyes fixed on a man who stood near the base watching them. "I thought that was you at first," she said, breathing deeply.

"Couldn't very well be me, could it? That's Vickery."

"What's he doing here?"

"He's keeping an eye on one of us," Rory said. "Maybe both."

The loss of Ferguson spelled the end of Rory's boyish innocence. From that day forward he experienced a kind of melancholy he'd never known before. Without Ferguson he was much younger than any of the other men. They treated him with disdain because he was favored by Slater. To them he would always be the boss's kid, scorned when he made a mistake, resented when he did something right. Their heartlessness frightened him, though sometimes he found himself trying to imitate it. He found it a perfect mirror for the endless loneliness of the basin. You could peer across it from the nearest rise but there was nothing to see but miles of broken plains and the rims of dry washes and gullies until your eye lit on some hazy butte or mesa that was probably a mirage.

He sat by himself on a log by the cold fire staring into the half-burned logs when Slater sat down beside him, smoking one of his cheroots. "The men are pretty heated about Ferguson," Slater said.

"It was Vickery that did it."

"Are you sure that's Ferguson's horse he's feeding?"

"That's what I heard."

Slater hesitated, but decided not to ask him where he heard it. "They want revenge but I can't let them kill the Captain's foreman. That'd be a declaration of war."

"Might clear the air."

"Clear it of us, anyway. They outnumber us three to one."

"What are you going to do then?"

"I don't know. If Vickery did it I won't let them kill somebody else in his place."

Slater struck Rory as oddly dispassionate, as if innocent until proven guilty was the law of the plains. How long could the men be expected to tolerate that? The cattle drive up north had left them with a bitter aftertaste. Half the herd lost and now Ferguson's murder was a festering wound that only more bloodshed could heal.

Yet Slater hung back, as if he could overrule the custom and practice of fate. Why? If Rory had known his secret thoughts about Elena, the pieces of the puzzle might have fallen into place.

Elena found her father leaning on the top rail of the corral, supervising some men breaking a yearling colt they'd led out from the barn. "Go easy," he told one of the men. "That colt's got a lot of spirit we want to hang onto." She leaned next to him and watched the men trying over and over again to saddle and mount the colt. If they'd left it to her the horse would have been eating out of her hand by now.

"I was out to that sinkhole yesterday," she said, "out by the vermillion cliffs."

"What were you doing out there?" the Captain asked.

"There's a man in there, or what's left of a man. Do you know Ferguson in Slater's outfit?"

"Young fella?"

She nodded. "Uh-huh."

"That's a shame. Must have fallen in."

"Then before he fell in he must have tied his hands behind his back and wrapped himself in barbed wire."

"Like I said, it's a shame."

"You don't act very surprised."

He wheeled and glared into her eyes. "You think I knew about this?"

"Vickery's keeping Ferguson's pinto mare in the barn. He knows about it."

"Well, whatever happened, I had nothing to do with it. I doubt if Vickery did either."

He sounded like he always did: serious, honest, authoritative. But she knew he was lying, just like Rory said he would. What did she think he would say? Maybe she was supposed to know how he made his living, how they all made their living. Maybe that's why her mother said she fed on what she hated most about him, the pride and domination and heartlessness that made him powerful among men. She thought of Ferguson's bones stewing in that sinkhole, the sulfuric slime which had been his flesh bubbling over the toes of her boots.

She gulped back her disgust. "You said this wasn't a feud, it wasn't just killing for spite or revenge. You said it's a war, which I guess makes you think it has a higher purpose."

"That's right."

"Ferguson wasn't a soldier in any war. He was just a kid they sent out to round up some stray calves."

The Captain whistled to Luke and sent him into the barn to fetch Vickery. "Tell Vickery I want to see him."

Vickery sauntered up to the corral with a wad of tobacco in his mouth, spitting it in the dirt. "Captain?"

"Elena says you've been feeding a pinto mare in the barn."

"That's so, Captain. I found her wandering around on the range, saddle and all. Wish I knew who she belongs to."

"Elena says it was Ferguson's. One of Slater's men."

"Well, if Ferguson shows up to claim her, we're going to have to charge him board. We been feeding that horse for a week."

Elena hated the sight of Vickery. His burn-scarred cheek, his sneering upturned nose, the spastic clicking that his sharp eyes dared you to notice. "Ferguson's dead," she said.

"I'm sorry to hear that, more or less. To tell you the truth, one less of Slater's low-lifes around here don't bother me much."

She turned away from Vickery and asked her father: "Can't you put an end to this killing?"

"The only killing going on is what they done to us," Vickery said with an eye on the Captain. "First Barlow, then Nickerson—you think he just up and vanished? Then Crazy Ike comes into the saloon and tears the place apart. We're two men down. Slater ain't lost anybody until now."

"Please tell me the killing will stop."

Vickery broke in again. "We done all we can. It's up to Slater to stop it."

The Captain studied her face, his brow darkening. "What were you doing out at that sinkhole anyway?"

"I can answer that," Vickery said. "She was meeting her sweetheart out there. Slater's boy Rory."

"He's not my sweetheart."

There was fury in the Captain's eyes, and scorn. And—because she was his daughter—disappointment. "So that's why you're so keen on stopping the killing," he scowled, "unless the killing's done by them. Did he put you up to this? Talking to me like this?"

"No." She would not let Rory be insulted. "If he had something to say to you he'd say it himself."

The Captain met that with the blank stare, held just a little too long, with which he usually silenced his wife. "I don't want to hear about you going anywhere near him again."

"I'll go where I please."

He flicked a horsefly off the back of his hand and turned away with an instruction to Vickery. "Keep an eye on her and let me know whether she does what I said."

There were other men besides Rory who kept a place in their hearts for Elena: Bob Wallace, who'd often amused her with his songs and jokes; a jovial German named Herzog who claimed to be the youngest son of a count; and Charlie Crow, Vickery's second in command, a quiet Texan who'd been driving cattle since the age of fifteen. But these men, for all their attainments, were common cowpunchers. The Captain had made up his mind that his daughter would marry a rich cattleman, a man with a substantial herd that could be consolidated with his own. He knew Luke would never be able to manage the ranch. By training Elena in the arts of ranching he'd ensured the perpetuation of his domain, provided that she married the right man and had some sons. There were only a few suitable candidates and he would select one soon. After Vickery portrayed her chance meeting with Rory as a lovers' tryst, he realized that this decision couldn't be delayed any longer. At the supper table he waited until everyone had finished eating and laid a hand on Elena's wrist when she stood to leave the table. "Stick around," he said. "There's something we need to talk about."

"What is it?" She was surprised, uneasy.

"I told your mother about your rendezvous with Slater's boy. She agrees you need to steer clear of him."

She glanced at her mother, whose face was white and immobile, like polished bone. "It wasn't a rendezvous," Elena said.

"Unless you want him to catch the same fever that Ferguson caught."

Her eyes blazed. "You admit it, then. You admit that you—"

He slammed his fist on the table. "I admit nothing. And I won't be spoken to that way. You listen to me. You'll have nothing more to do with that boy because starting tomorrow you're going to be too busy picking out a husband."

"I will not."

"A suitable husband. Not some drunken cowpuncher that Slater pulled out of a river."

"I'm not interested in picking out a husband."

The Captain hefted his hulking frame over the table and glared down at his daughter. "You'll have your choice among the biggest ranchers in three counties. That ought to be enough even for a princess like you."

He stormed upstairs, leaving Elena alone with her mother and Luke. Luke huddled with his head down, rolling his eyes toward

Elena to see how she was taking it. Jacinta, lips thin and pale, seemed to be engrossed in some inner calculation. Her black eyes gleamed in her bone-white face, sharp but distracted. "I don't blame you for what you're doing with that boy," she told Elena.

"I'm not doing anything."

"It's your father's fault for letting that man stay in the basin too long."

"That man? What man?"

"Slater. This wouldn't have happened if he'd listened to me. How long has it been? Six months? Almost a year? He's gone weak. He won't stand up and do what needs to be done."

It was as if she were talking to herself, muttering, shaking her head. As if she'd forgotten Elena was sitting beside her, Luke across from her.

"Mother?" Elena said. "What are you talking about?"

Apparently she'd finished her calculations and seemed pleased by the result. "You needn't worry," she said to Luke. "I'll get it done if he won't. And you, Elena. I've told you what you need to do. You're not a girl anymore. Your father's right about that. You need to marry a suitable man. A man who's proud and ruthless or you'll be nothing, your whole life will be nothing."

Jacinta retreated into her room, leaving Elena and Luke to clear the table. They scraped the garbage into a pot for the dogs and took the dishes outside to wash them in the tubs by the cookhouse. They were both quiet. Elena angry at her father, disturbed by her mother, whose mental sickness (that's what the Captain called it) had been growing worse in recent months. Luke waiting for the right moment to stake out his ground in the debate about his sister's need to marry.

"I don't know why they think they got to do this," he said. "Maybe you don't want to get married."

"I don't."

"Then why are they trying to force you to?"

"They don't want to see what they've built go to ruin. I can't blame them."

As soon as that came out of her mouth she realized it was the wrong thing to say. She'd been grateful for Luke's sympathy but it wasn't sympathy, it was irritation at the slight—worse than a slight, a judgment on his capabilities—their father had implied in entrusting the future of the ranch to her, when by all rights it should have been his. What she'd said had only added to the insult.

"When I'm running this ranch I won't need no husband of yours telling me what to do," he said.

"No, Luke. Of course you won't."

"Probably even if you do get married you'll live a long ways away. Your husband'll have his own ranch to run."

"That's right."

He tried to look resolute and proud but his eyes were moist. "You won't leave the basin, will you, Elena?"

"No, I won't. I promise."

By midsummer the rival outfits had settled into an uneasy stalemate. Shots were fired, curses and threats exchanged. Calves caught on the wrong side of an invisible line were butchered and left for the wolves to glut on. It was an illusion of peace, the balancing of enemies in a brief embrace like two rutting elk with their antlers locked. The Captain had grown moody, distracted, indecisive. Jacinta peered into his darkness and saw Slater biding his time. She feared that in some occult way her husband needed Slater. That Slater, through his silence, was holding him on a string. But Slater, unknown to Jacinta, was caught in his own entanglement, the strings held by his men, who refused to leave the basin, some of them—Moondog, Polecat, Crazy Ike and others—relishing the prospect of a bloody reckoning with the Captain. Did the Captain sense that danger? Was that why he refused to do what needed to be done?

Elena was sick at heart. All her life she had taken the greatness of her father for granted, as everyone did: he was a leader of men, a dispenser of justice, a bringer of order to the basin. Now for the first time she saw him for what he was. He had all but confessed to killing Ferguson and threatened the same treatment for Rory. Her sickened anger took in the entire basin, as if it was some fallen land, corruption everywhere, not only in her father's eyes but in the soil, the dying grass, the cattle doomed to slaughter. She had lost her innocence. She longed to escape from her appointed destiny as a pawn in the deadly game being played on this checkered landscape. Her father and the men he wanted her to marry looked on her as breeding stock, a prize heifer selected to bring forth a new generation of men to rule the basin. Her mother whispered encouragement in his ears, dire blandishments in hers. How could she escape to walk her own path? She wouldn't find an ally among the grizzled brutes her father would push on her. Rory was her own age, a free spirit like she wanted to be, but he was dirt poor and all but kin to Slater— an impossible match. And was there any reason to think he'd be any different? Even if he was—even if his sense of humor and his kindly nature set him apart from other men—the Captain's final warning couldn't have been any more blunt. If she didn't stay away from him he would end up like Ferguson, swaying on the bottom of a geyser hole.

The wind blew hotter and drier with each passing day, but imperceptibly the hours had begun to die away. Surely some revelation was at hand.

Part II

10.

On that range, every day of every year, the work of man was the breeding of flesh out of flesh. There was no lord of flies who spawned the generations but the brutal coming together of male and female and the parting of new life from old. Children heard the bawling and bellowing on the range long before they were allowed to witness it, and they knew that it was born of blood and filth and that the earth could not remain alive without it. And struggle as they might with each other, the men knew that their herds of longhorns would soon be worthless unless they were upgraded with blooded stock: Angus, Hereford, shorthorn. On the open range, where cows mated indiscriminately, the state of nature was never more than one generation away.

On the Fourth of July a pair of cattle traders named Blythe and Gregson came through with a small drove of mixed-breed longhorns they were taking north. They were small, shifty men who talked in chiseled phrases and wore soft felt hats of a type nobody had seen before. They introduced themselves to the Captain and he invited them to supper. The men drank whisky and picked their teeth with bowie knives, but out of politeness they avoided talking cattle until the meal was finished. Then Blythe told the Captain about a six-year-old prize Avileña Negra bull brought to America by a Castilian grandee named Matamoros who'd fallen on hard times. "That bull is as black as the pit of hell," Blythe said, "with a roar like a chorus of demons. He's twice the weight of the longhorns you're running here."

"And why do I need to know about this beast?" the Captain asked.

"Señor Matamoros is offering him for stud on an exclusive basis to any man who will pay his price. If that bull sired even a tenth of your herd, Captain, you'd have an advantage your competitors could never overcome."

"But surely the stud fees..."

"The bull will be on lease for the entire breeding season."

For some time after the strangers left, the Captain sat mulling their proposal, which first intrigued and then fascinated and finally excited him, like a great temptation. Jacinta had crossed herself when Blythe said the bull was as black as the pit of hell and roared like a chorus of demons. Now she sat with her eyes down, muttering to the saints she'd been taught to venerate when she was a girl. Those saints had deserted her when the Captain brought her to the basin— "There are no gods here and no saints," he'd told her, "no good and no evil. The Utes had their gods, who fled when the tribe was driven out. It's ours now, to make of what we will."—but she clung to their memory and prayed for their help. There was evil in the basin, she knew, but this bull was beyond any iniquity in her own heart, or his, it was evil itself, unmitigated by human weakness. Such were her imaginings—the result, the Captain would have said, of her loneliness or her superstitious upbringing, or possibly (though the Captain would not have said it then) of her mind slipping into madness.

He ignored her hesitation to leap on the opportunity offered by the bull. "This is too good a chance to pass up," he said. "With that blooded bull in their veins, my herd will be invincible."

Jacinta raised her wary eyes to meet his. "Don't you have other drovers to think about?"

"I'd have the bull for the whole breeding season. I can share him with whoever I wish."

"Put him out on the range?"

"No, keep him in my stock pen. Reward my friends and punish my enemies."

"You heard the man," Jacinta muttered. "That beast is from the pit of hell. His voice is a chorus of demons."

"He will be Slater's undoing," the Captain nodded.

She crossed herself and lowered her eyes. "No," she said. "Yours."

"Enough of your superstitions. Luke will go and fetch that bull. It's time he started doing a man's work."

Luke leaped at the chance to fetch the bull. The beast could not be driven but had to be carted in chains like an elephant. Luke took two of their best men and a heavy, ox-drawn stock wagon a hundred miles north to the railhead where the enormous black bull stood bellowing in a reinforced pen. They chained his neck and his crooked white horns and all four legs and ran a rope through the ring in his nose and still could hardly drag him into the wagon without toppling it. He roared indeed like a blasphemous choir when he found himself bound behind a despised team of oxen. The men regaled him with tales of the harem he would soon be lording over, but he would not be appeased. Luke whipped his snout and still could not stop his infernal raging. When after six hard days' travel they made it back to town and unloaded him, still chained, in the Captain's stock pen, he hurled himself toward the yoked oxen, writhing and bellowing, determined to drive the eunuchs from his sight. Luke whipped him on his muzzle and ears until he cringed away with his mighty head down and the black fury in his eyes fixed on his tormentor.

Elena had watched from her bedroom window as the corral beside the house filled with heifers going into their first heat. In the morning she'd slip out to hand-feed them, searching in their wide eyes for some glimpse of understanding of what necessity had decreed for them. They groaned and wailed, inconsolable, jostled each other, ran at the fence. She pictured herself in their place, marching to the stock pen to face in one terrible moment the embrace of the bull, the giggles of boys, the goadings of cowboys and the bitter confirmation of what she already knew about life on the range.

The morning after Luke came back, Elena rode into town with him to inspect the bull. Still chained, he chuffed in a stall like a champion on display. The wide brow and curved white horns, the massive, drooping head, the cunning, half-closed eyes. A taut blackness that spelled the negation of every earthly thing, like a mirror in darkness. The roaring silenced by fatigue, or by guile, until Luke came in sight, when it rose to a howling pitch.

Luke was proud, boasting, eager to show his fearlessness and mastery. He invited Elena to touch the bull. "It's all right," he said. "You can touch him. He's chained up."

She reached out and touched the bull's writhing neck. The hide felt rock hard and throbbed with a fleshly power she had never felt before.

"He can't hurt you," Luke said. "Look."

He pulled on the rope and slapped his whip on the bull's snout, and although the animal stamped and snorted, it couldn't kick or even turn its head. It was, as Luke assured her, harmless.

11.

The arrival of the Spanish bull marked a turning point in the hostilities between the Captain and Slater. There had been casualties on both sides, a slow burn of provocations and retaliations, challenges issued and lessons taught. Death kept its distance, unwelcome but expected in the course of things. What no one desired or foresaw or grasped, when it came, was downfall and destitution.

One morning in the middle of July, around the time of Elena's birthday, a big yellow cur appeared at the ranch, as tall as a mastiff, its agate eyes blank as a slate. When it snarled at the Captain he closed it in a stall and whipped it until it rolled over and licked his hand. None of the other men, except Vickery, would go anywhere near that dog. The other dogs quickly accepted it as their leader. Where had it come from? At the saloon all the men professed ignorance—and it infuriated the Captain that such a beast could exist in the basin without anyone knowing how it got there. But with that whipping he'd made it his dog, nobody else's, just as he'd done, one by one, with the men. As a proud man it was his right to rule them but that dominance gave him little satisfaction, no more than the obedience and affection of the cur—it was unworthy of him, his very success debased and weakened him. Still he favored that yellow cur over all his other dogs, and it favored him.

The thin grass which had flourished in May and June wilted in July's scorching heat. By the end of a rainless August it would be tinder for a prairie fire. The cattle had to browse every square inch to stay alive. The Captain's men drove in the yearling heifers, a dozen at a time, to breed in the stock pen with the Spanish bull. In the meantime they had plenty of other work to do. They brought in boys from town to help cut and bale hay in the one field where the grass stayed green all summer, stowing it in lean-to sheds at the bottom of a dry canyon called Disappointment Draw. That hay field was a kind of false paradise. Below it the terrain dipped through a narrowing gulch called the Vale of Tears toward the basin's southern rim, then tipped down a bare canyon wall to the river a thousand feet below.

In the middle of August, word spread that the Captain, having finished servicing his own herd, would put the prize bull up for stud, free of charge, to any drover in the basin. Men found that offer surprising, which it was, and unselfish, which it wasn't. With cows breeding freely on the range, it was in everybody's interest to upgrade the stock. Slater doubted if his herd was meant to be included, though without it the Captain's project was doomed to failure. If he and the Captain could cooperate on this, he reasoned, it might be an opening to peace. Yet Slater was awkward with words. If it took more than a few of them to find common ground with the Captain, he would fail, and so he sent Buckminster to approach the Captain as his ambassador. He liked Buckminster, trusted his honest face and crystal-blue eyes where he'd never glimpsed the least hint of guile or betrayal.

Buckminster set off on the six mile ride in the midmorning heat and arrived in town just after noon. The town was full to bursting with ranchers and cowboys and yearling heifers eager for their first affair. Each rancher was allowed ten heifers, herding them into a corral beside the pen where the bull waited to take his pleasure. Those heifers must have known what they were there for. In the corral they pranced and frolicked, but when the cowboys led them, one by one, into the bull's pen they put aside their childish ways and got down to the serious business of seduction. The cowboys laughed and cheered them on, the ranchers beamed like proud fathers at a wedding, small boys clung to the fence snickering and shoving each other out of the way. Luke strutted around shouting orders until the Captain made him stop. The bull still hated Luke: it stamped and roared every time it heard his voice. Some who knew Spanish cattle—such as Gutiérrez, who came from Chihuahua—had their doubts about the bloodlines of that bull, wondering if it wasn't of the savage toro bravo breed the Spanish had brought to Mexico for bullfighting, but knowing the Captain they kept those thoughts to themselves.

The Captain officiated from a high seat overlooking the bull pen, the lesser ranchers paying him not in coin but in obeisance. Buckminster rode up on his tall black mare and tipped his hat. "Captain."

"Buckminster," the Captain nodded. Unlike Slater, he saw through Buckminster's honest mask to the forked shadow that wavered inside, which he knew was kin to his own. "What can I do for you?"

"Slater would like to know if he can bring some of his heifers to be introduced to your bull."

"Why did he send you? Why can't he come over here and ask me man to man?"

"Well, sir—"

"Don't 'sir' me on your mission of disrespect."

"I beg your pardon."

There was no begging and no pardon. The Captain said, "Is he too good to ask me himself?"

Buckminster held his gaze, unblinking and apparently sincere. Then he stepped closer and lowered his voice. "He didn't confide me his reasoning, Captain, but I think it's this. He can't afford to lose face in front of the men. They already think he's gone soft. If he asks you himself and you refuse him, they might run him out of the basin."

The Captain answered with a sly, soundless chuckle. "I wonder why you'd tell me that. It's almost as if you're inviting me to do it."

"That ain't so."

"You're a bright fellow, everybody says. Is that what you want to see happen?"

"No, sir."

"There's that sirring again that I told you I don't like. You know why I don't like it? Because you aren't the least bit humble and you know it. You're an arrogant son of a bitch and you've got big plans for yourself, don't you? Maybe you see yourself taking over Slater's operation after I run him out."

Buckminster let his face convey that he was shocked. A slow kind of shock, still open to question. In fact it shocked him that the Captain could see through him so easily.

"Don't even try to deny it. And I'll tell you something—I could live with that result. I see you as the kind of man I could do business with."

"I don't want to get crossways with Slater."

"No, that's the last thing I'd want to see." The Captain lowered his voice as if they were already conspirators. "You stay square with Slater. Just tell him to come back tomorrow and ask me himself, and we'll see what we can do."

Luke slouched up to the Captain as Buckminster walked away. "What did Buckminster want?" he asked his father.

"Slater sent him over to ask for a few squirts from the bull. Seems to think I'm some kind of pimp."

"Most of the men hate Buckminster."

"The man's a snake. Hard to imagine what Slater sees in him."

"They say Slater prides himself that he knows men, the way some men know cattle."

The Captain had to chuckle, being subject to the same point of pride, though all he knew of men was what was worst in them. "That may be true as a rule," he said, "but like all vanities, it has its fatal flaw. There's two men Slater doesn't know: Buckminster and himself."

The Captain's temptations flattered Buckminster's vanity and led him down a path he'd already started to envision for himself. A man with big plans for himself. A man the Captain could do business with. That business might even include inviting him into the family as his son-in-law. He'd noticed Elena by the stock pen, watched her trot off astride her saddle, her hips wide, her back lean and straight, her black hair fluttering like the horse's mane. She was nineteen, ripe for the picking. He wasn't the only man in the basin with designs on her, but he fancied that his prospects were better than most. His wholesome good looks, his crystal-blue eyes, his moderate habits, had fooled Slater and in his past life had fooled many a girl. But he buried these thoughts behind his plain, guileless face when he reported back to Slater. "The Captain didn't say yes and he didn't say no," he told Slater. "He wants you to ask him yourself. You do that and I think you'll get what you want." He knew he was lying, just as the Captain had been.

"Did he say that?"

"In so many words."

The next morning they rode into town side by side, Moondog and Polecat in the lead with loaded shotguns across their saddles, Rory shambling behind them like a circus rider on his palomino, his old Colt rifle dangling in the scabbard beside him. That rifle, he knew, was just for show. If things got ugly it wouldn't do him any good at all. But there was no reason to expect any unpleasantness. Buckminster said the Captain's tone had been encouraging.

When they came within sight of the stock pen, the bustle around it wavered like grass in a dying wind. The Captain, down from his high seat, stood talking to Luke and some of his hands, all wearing side arms, horsewhips slung on their belts. They turned as one to face the approaching riders.

Rory spurred his horse forward as Moondog and Polecat closed up around Slater. There were only five of them, counting Slater, who was unarmed, against the muttering, hair-trigger crowd, which had frozen in place. At its edges men could be seen slinking off, women too, hurrying children away behind their skirts. Elena perched on a railing on the far side of the corral, her eyes on Rory, which surprised him. The last time he went looking for her she'd galloped away. Even now, though she stared at him, her expression was solemn, distant, disapproving.

When Buckminster saw Elena's face—he assumed she was looking at him—he knew he'd made a mistake leading Slater into this trap. He should have kept Slater away from the Captain until his future was secure.

"Let me talk to him," he told Slater, hoping to avoid a disaster.

"No," Slater said as he dismounted. "I got to do this myself."

Rory saw the crowd part as Slater walked toward the Captain, followed by Buckminster. Moondog and Polecat hung back on their mounts, shotguns level across their saddles. Rory stayed behind them, where Slater had told him to stay. He wanted to climb down and walk with Slater but he knew that would only make him angry.

The Captain's men stuck out their chests and stepped in front of Slater and Buckminster, hands above their waists. The foreman Vickery laid the heel of his right hand on the pearl handle of his Colt .45. Luke struggled between fear and bravado, as if he might either run away or shove a gun in Slater's face.

The Captain greeted Slater with an air of surprise that fooled no one. "Slater. To what do I owe the pleasure?"

He spoke in a polite, proprietorial tone, as if inquiring about Slater's health or his opinion of the weather, signaling that his response would be a matter of indifference. As if it was just another hot, lazy afternoon on the range. Behind him Slater saw the bull mounting a heifer with the same detachment.

"I reckon you know, Captain," Slater said. "I heard you're putting your bull out to stud for other ranchers."

"Did you hear that you were on the invitation list?"

"That's why I thought to ask."

Luke shuddered forward, his face dark as blood, and opened his mouth but the Captain yanked him back before he could speak. "Go ahead and ask."

"All right. Can I bring some of my heifers down here?"

At a stroke the Captain's indifference flamed into contempt. "The other ranchers have clothed their requests in courtesy, befitting a man of my standing and theirs. What I hear from you rings more like a stark demand for something you have no right to expect."

"I'm unschooled in courtesy," Slater said, "but I ask you, with all respect, to consider my request and do what's right."

The Captain winced, almost as if he'd been slapped. "What's right? Then do you think you're entitled to my bull?"

"Captain," Buckminster said. "Yesterday—"

"Never mind yesterday. Let him answer."

Slater stayed calm—insultingly calm, in the Captain's narrowed eyes. "It would be right to show me the same regard you show every man," he said. "I'd do the same for you."

The suggestion of equality—a conciliatory gesture to any other man—pricked the Captain as the ultimate challenge to his pride. It was as if he'd been crouching and now he rose to his full height. "Are we on an equal footing, then, you and I? Exchanging favors like two cowpunchers sharing smokes on the trail?"

"No, sir. We're just a couple of men trying to make a living in this hard country."

The Captain's eyes darted over the crowd and his men pressed closer, clicking the hammers back on their revolvers. Moondog and

Polecat, still mounted, gripped their shotguns but kept them down, as Slater had instructed them to do. Rory saw what he would later remember from that day. The Captain looming in front of Slater's weathered hat. Luke's dark face and trembling lips. The black rutting bull and the terrified heifer embracing in their ancient dance.

With an upward nod, the Captain ordered his cowhands to step back. He noted with satisfaction that Buckminster, like all men, was a coward. His face was talc-white and his lips were drawn tight. He would be easy to control.

"Is that what we are?" he called out, playing to the crowd. "Just a couple of men trying to make a living in a hard country?" He aimed a sneer at Slater. "You're nothing, Slater. Nobody. Now get the hell out of here."

The cowhands howled out hoots and catcalls and stamped their feet. The bull glanced up from his work and roared.

Slater's eyes had lighted on the whip-scar on the Captain's lower lip. The lip recoiled as if set to flick them off, like a horse twitching a fly off its eye, but they stayed fixed on their target. In a desperate motion the Captain tried to bat them away, his hand brushing his lip but to no effect. Slater kept his eyes fixed on the scar. He wanted the Captain to know he recognized it.

The Captain reacted with fury. "Let me put it this way, Slater," he said. "I'd see the whole race of cattle go down to extinction before I'd let my prize bull mingle with your tainted herd."

Slater allowed himself the slightest of smiles, invisible to all but the Captain. How could the others see it? This was between him and the Captain alone.

12.

That night Slater's men in their brotherhood of suppressed rage crouched around a smoldering fire, passing a gallon jug of whiskey that would soon be empty. Their mood was as bitter and black as the night wind. Each had brought an unacknowledged part of himself to that basin, a shadow that lingered even in the dark of night. The demonic chorus of the bull's roar echoed in their souls. They did not, as Buckminster expected, turn on Slater at his show of weakness. They were the sort of men who could endure every hardship but humiliation. The Captain had mocked Slater but each of them—except Buckminster, in his secret alliance with the Captain—took it as a personal insult aimed at himself.

Slater stared at the dying fire, its spent fury still flickering in his eyes. In that light he saw the source of the Captain's impotent wrath: a trail camp in west Texas, three cowhands scalped by the Comanches. To expunge that image the Captain would have to kill him. For the second time at the Captain's hands Slater had been mocked by evil. The insult echoed in his mind like a gunshot across a canyon. The Captain had no idea who he was dealing with. Slater was a man with danger caged inside him like a wounded bear.

"I swear to god," Crazy Ike said, hoisting the whiskey jug, "or to the devil if there ain't no god in this basin—I'll break that son of a bitch's neck, and every one of his men I can lay my hands on."

"Be careful, Ike," Slater warned him. "That's the whiskey talking."

"Then give me more of it and let it talk."

"An oath like that can't easily be forgotten," Slater said, shaking his head.

"Let it be my fate, then," Crazy Ike said, "and damn the man who tries to stop me."

"I want Vickery for myself," Polecat said, reaching for the whiskey, "and that boy Luke—I swear I'll kill them first."

Slater spit into the fire. "Enough of these ungodly oaths. You won't be carrying them out as part of my outfit." He stood up and walked into the darkness. A match flared in front of his face as he lit a cheroot.

The men heaved and grumbled, champing and gasping like spent horses, their voices heavy with mutiny. Those oaths could not be taken back or ignored. They had chosen their fates and no one could stop them. The burden, unspoken, was that Slater was a coward. It wasn't about the bull, it was about Slater and whether he could stay on as head of the outfit—and whether the outfit could stay in the basin—unless they fought back, and fought back hard.

Moondog tried to weave a solution. "The way I see it, all we need is the use of that bull for a few hours. That's what this is all about, ain't it? No need to push it any farther."

Rory knew that wasn't what it was all about, they all knew that. It was so Slater could save face, so they could all save face.

"What are you saying?" one of the men asked.

"Let's just go back and take that bull."

"Take him?"

"Take him and put him to work," Moondog laughed.

They kept their eyes on Slater to divine his reaction. All they could see was the glowing tip of his cigar. The heifers bawled and bleated in the darkness.

There was no man in that country, maybe on the earth, whose thoughts were as hard to read as Slater's. They were slower and denser than other men's, more circuitous, taking in a wider view of the terrain as they plodded along like a mule train drawing a heavy load. But once they got where they were going, no force could turn them back until they'd done what they set out to do. In fact he didn't care what the men thought of him. He was thinking of Elena—he'd noticed her sitting on the rail when they arrived at the stock pen. Then she disappeared. He hoped she hadn't witnessed his being mocked by her father.

"I'm thinking," he said in a quiet voice, stepping back toward the fire, "that somebody ought to go back over there and fetch that bull."

The men cheered and scrambled to their feet. They passed the jug around and each of them—except Buckminster—drank his fill.

Buckminster had kept silent during this debate, staring at the fire. Now he raised his eyes and faced Slater. He was risking everything, but everything was at stake. His ambitions, his position with the Captain, his hopes for Elena. "Let's not get carried away," he said. "Is this really a good idea? It's like a declaration of war."

"The declaration happened this afternoon," Slater said. "But the war ain't started yet. You boys want to fight back, this is the way to draw our line in the sand. Otherwise we pull up stakes and clear out of here tomorrow."

"You ain't coming with us?" Moondog grunted.

"No, I ain't," Slater said with an edge in his voice. "I don't want this to be about me. You men need to do this yourselves if you want to do it. But first you got to understand something. This is staking out new terrain. It's like riding into a canyon where nobody's ever been before."

That quieted them down. Slater kicked some dirt on the fire, smothering the last embers. "One more thing," he said. "Don't take your guns along, or if you do, keep them strapped in your saddles. Don't even put your hands on them unless you're fired on. We ain't a gang of murderers."

That was false and they all knew it. Almost every one of them— all of them except Rory, in fact—had been baptized in the blood of men. Was Slater of the same confession? Nobody wanted to call him a liar and find out.

"No shooting," he repeated. "I don't want any man killed over a damn bull."

Slater's camp stood north of the hay field, on Seven Mile Ridge at the head of Disappointment Draw. In some forgotten age, when water still flowed in the basin, a deep wash had been scooped out between Slater's camp and the Captain's ranch, as if heaven had decreed their kinship. The men called it the sand wash. It was bone dry and thirty feet across, like a giant hollow flume. In one direction you could follow it almost into town, in the other down to the hay fields and, if you ventured too far, through the Vale of Tears to the canyon rim. Lately Slater had added a new barrier—barbed wire—to keep his cattle from wandering onto the Captain's turf. The Captain declared war on any attempt to fence the range and on moonlit nights his men raided Slater's fence line to cut the wire and topple the cedar fence posts. Slater had responded by digging a trench ten feet out from the fence line, concealed under thistle and brush, to trip up the fence cutters' horses and hurl their riders into the fence. In case that didn't stop them, he had his men hew dozens of sharpened palings about four feet long which they mounted in the trench, pointing upward, turning it into a man trap.

The night of the raid a half moon rose above clouds that swirled like white water over the range. Under the scudding shadows Slater's men saddled their mounts in high spirits and packed them with ropes and chains. They downed the rest of the whiskey and pulled on their spurs and chaps and rawhide gloves and rode into the moonlight, tracing a path through the sand wash toward town. There'd be no shooting, but they packed guns in case they were fired on. It wasn't exactly a prank or a frolic, but neither was it, in Rory's mind, the beginning of a war. Something madcap about it, a freebooting expedition out of a storybook. They meant no harm, at least Rory didn't. Teach the Captain a lesson, that was it. Teach him a lesson for humiliating Slater.

Buckminster rode along with the others but not to vindicate Slater's honor. He had lured Slater to his humiliation and there was no going back from that. No mystery about the Captain's purpose: he'd goaded Slater's men into this foolish mission to make them worthy of the punishment he intended to inflict. Too late to prevent it from happening. Buckminster could only distance himself, turn it to his advantage. There were other opportunities once you acknowledged that Slater was a dying animal—and they didn't all involve serving the Captain. He hung back in the sand wash, his horse shambling silently in the dust. Then when a cloud covered the moon, he disappeared over a rise.

The other men pressed on. As they passed near the Captain's ranch they yodeled like wolves and heard the Captain's dogs yipping and howling in tormented alarm. The Captain, in his pride, claimed dominion over every living thing in the basin. All had their place under him, even the wolves—he refused to let his men hunt or shoot them, even when they ravened down from the high country to taunt and torture his dogs with the lure of freedom and rapacity. That night when the dogs cried out, Slater's men howled like wolves, and the dogs whined and cried piteously. The wolves hated the Captain and his groveling dogs.

The men came up out of the wash past scrubby mounds of bunchgrass and sage and made their way silently to the edge of town. Keeping to the shadows they passed behind the saloon and rode single file to the Captain's stock pen, where the exhausted bull lay twitching in dreams of conquest. The men joked and snickered but they worked hard at keeping quiet. They tied their horses and climbed into the corral, and before the wide-browed bull was awake they'd entangled his neck and shoulders in lassoes, hobbled his legs with a chain, and ran a rope through his nose ring. Struggling to stand up, he let loose an unearthly roar that echoed from one end of the basin to the other.

Buckminster had hitched his tall black mare in front of the saloon and sent two drunks inside to fetch Vickery. The Captain's foreman came through the swinging doors, bullwhip coiled on his belt, just as the bull roared. Wheeling toward the cattle pen he saw only darkness and the shimmering clouds. He scowled at Buckminster. "What in hell's going on?"

"They're taking the bull," Buckminster said.

"What do you mean? Who's taking it?"

"Some of Slater's men."

Vickery squinted suspiciously. "Slater ain't here?"

"He don't know about it."

Vickery was clicking like a roulette wheel. "Get out of my way." He shoved Buckminster aside and stalked toward the cattle pen.

Buckminster followed him into the moonlight, his clean-shaven face glistening as white as the sand. "They'll be gone before you get there."

They were gone already, Vickery realized. He could hear whips cracking, horses stamping, the bull's roar receding. It was hopeless trying to stop them by himself.

"It's just for one night," Buckminster said. "They'll bring the bull back in the morning."

Vickery seemed ready to explode. He turned on Buckminster with his hand on his whip, his fingers edging down over the haft. "Why are you telling me this, you son of a bitch? Why ain't you over there with the rest of them?"

"I just want you to know we ain't enemies, you and me."

"The hell we ain't."

"Even if this flares up into something," Buckminster said, "the two of us don't have to be on opposite sides. We got a lot in common, you and me. We know how to run an outfit without taking orders from some boss who don't even own the land."

Vickery's eyes narrowed and he lowered his voice. "You talking about Slater and the Captain?"

"You could suppose that if you want to. I never said it."

Buckminster unhitched his horse and mounted it. He set his feet in the stirrups and pulled back on the reins to turn the horse around.

"And what else would you be supposing?" Vickery asked.

"Well, the Captain'll be none too pleased about his bull being taken, even for one night. Supposing he starts a war over it, just out of spite—and that's what it would be, spite, because he'll be getting the bull back in the morning no matter what. You want to get killed in that war? I sure as hell don't."

"Now what are you supposing?"

"That unlike Slater and the Captain, the two of us could address the situation like reasonable men."

Vickery made a sound that might have been the smacking of lips. His eyes shone like a coyote's under a pale moon. "You sound like a traitor to me."

"Tomorrow you keep your eyes open and maybe you'll find out. If something ugly starts, don't take any shots at me until you find out whose side I'm on."

When they'd surrounded the bull in his pen it was as if they'd surprised a monster in its labyrinth, drawing that roar that made the earth tremble. Suddenly Rory knew what Slater had meant by staking out a new fate for yourself. Nothing would be the same after this. The Captain would bellow in his turn and the sky would open up and the sand would run like water. There was no going back now, the men in the saloon were probably on their way over with guns and whips and ropes. All Slater's men could do was throw themselves on the bull, chain his legs, lash his neck and shoulders, avoid his deadly spiraling horns until they could hitch him to their terrified horses. He would kill every one of them if they gave him a chance. Still roaring he fought them every step of the way as they dragged him out of the stock pen and into the sand wash. After a quarter of a mile they stopped when Buckminster rode up beside them.

"Where'd you go?" Rory asked him. "We thought you was with us."

"I rode over to the saloon to see if they were coming after us. They heard the roar but they're all too drunk to care."

The Captain, scanning the sky on his wide front porch, had no inkling that a new fate had been staked out for him. It was a mild summer night, a slight whiff of smoke in the air. The gauzy moon fluttered behind shifting clouds, shedding just enough light to darken the edges of the earth. The basin in its emptiness seemed beyond the reach of destiny.

When he'd heard the bull roaring in the cattle pen, he was only mildly alarmed. He was responsible for that bull, obliged to return it in good health to Matamoros. He never suspected the outrage that Slater's men had committed, or its bitter fruit. He asked Luke and Elena to ride down to the cattle pen to investigate. As they headed toward the barn to fetch their horses, he told Luke, "You better take your gun, just in case." Without being asked, Elena slipped her Colt .45 into her saddle bag.

The two of them trotted toward the cattle pen and found it empty. Luke dug in his stirrups and pulled up on his reins and his horse reared and almost threw him. His eyes were wild.

"What are you doing?" Elena asked.

"They stole the bull!" His gun trembled in his hand, pointing upwards, as if he might shoot the sky.

"Don't be stupid! Put that away!"

He slipped the gun back in its holster, and then he turned his horse around and galloped into the sand wash toward the raiders. He circled in front of them, shouting furiously as if he could fight six men and a two-thousand pound bull. Elena raced behind him and at the top of a low rise she looked down, fearful yet contemptuous, as women always are of men toying with violence. Rory felt her fierce eyes tearing into him.

"What in hell are you doing?" Luke shouted. He stopped his horse a foot in front of Buckminster and Polecat, bristling with desperate authority.

The men laughed. "What does it look like we're doing?"

He reached for his gun and Buckminster slapped a grip on his wrist. "We're not armed."

He eased it back in the holster. Moondog and Crazy Ike were still laughing at Luke. He was just a boy with peach-fuzz on his chin trying to act like a man. Rory glanced back up at Elena, smiled and shrugged as if to tell her not to worry. Nothing bad was going to happen.

"Take that bull back where it belongs," Luke said, struggling to keep his voice from cracking.

The bull bucked and roared when it heard Luke's voice, and the men had to strain to hold it back. "Seems this old boy wants to eat you alive," Moondog said. "What'd you do to him anyway?"

They peered at the boy as if they expected an answer. He was playing the man but he was almost in tears imagining what his father would say if he let them steal the bull. "You know you can't do this."

"We'll bring him back in the morning," Moondog said pleasantly. "We just want to let him have a little fun with our heifers."

"Take him back to the pen."

Every time Luke spoke, the bull bucked and lurched toward him with its head down, stamping the ground, trying to charge him even with the chain around its legs. Polecat reached down to release the chain. "You better go on your way, son, or we might just let him loose."

Luke trotted up the rise where Elena waited, seemingly in retreat, and the men, laughing and jeering at him as he rode away, resumed their efforts to move the bull forward. With the chain released, the bull could move his legs more freely but they thought they could control him with the lassoes around his neck and shoulders and the rope threaded through the nose ring.

Elena lost sight of Luke as a billow of clouds blocked the moon, relieved that he'd given up the fight, which surely their father and his outfit would finish. She could hear his saddle creaking, his reins jangling. She thought she heard him crying and she drew nearer.

"Luke? Are you all right?"

But it was too late. Without a word he pulled out his revolver and opened fire on the men below. They ducked and scattered, some racing away on their horses, others rolling on the ground to take cover. The bull bellowed and slipped its bonds, charging off into the night. Some of the men tore after it, cursing and shouting.

Luke spurred his horse and raced toward home to alert his father. Elena remained still, trying to understand what had just happened. Peering down through the dim light, she saw a man writhing in the dirt.

She bolted down into the sand wash and jumped off her horse with her gun in her hand. The man lay on his side, facing away from her, moaning as he pressed his hand over a wound in his shoulder. She leveled her Colt .45 at his head and turned him over with her foot. It was Rory.

"Thank God it's you," he said, trying to smile. He'd decided to take the friendly approach, break the ice a little, in hopes that she wouldn't kill him.

"Save your prayers for when they might do you some good," she said.

"You going to shoot me?"

"I've a mind to. Stealing cattle is a hanging crime."

He laughed out loud, which was not only painful but the wrong thing to do. It implied disrespect. He could see her hand shaking, which wasn't a good sign. Her trigger finger might be shaking next. "You've got to understand, we ain't stealing that bull," he said. "We're just borrowing him for a little moonlight romance with our heifers. You'll get him back in the morning."

"How do I know that?"

"You've seen him in action. He's a fast worker."

He pulled up his knees and tried to stand up without leaning on his wounded left shoulder. She toppled him with her boot and rolled him over on his back. "Stay down," she said, steadying her gun in front of his face. "I mean it."

You never really know a girl, he reflected later, until you've stared down the barrel of her Colt .45. In that definitive moment he peered up at Elena—her finger on the trigger, the high-cocked hammer in front of her face—and asked himself, was there a spark of affection in those eyes? The hint of a smile in those tight, bloodless lips? Enough encouragement in those eyes, in that smile, to stake his life on? Looking up that long barrel, he couldn't be sure. Her face was as stony and disapproving as it had been that afternoon.

"I thought we got it settled a long time ago that we don't hate each other," he said. "I found out that doesn't include not galloping away when you see me coming. But it does include not shooting each other, don't it?"

"I wouldn't assume that if I were you."

"My pals'll hear the shot. They're still somewhere around here."

"No, they ran away and left you to die."

That was harsh and she immediately regretted saying it. She felt her face flush and worried that she might lose control, start crying or start shooting or both. Her throat tightened. "Though I hope you won't."

"Now we're getting somewhere," Rory grinned. "If you hope I won't die, then kindly lower your gun and refrain from shooting me." He sat up and held out his hand, wet with blood from his wounded shoulder. "And stop this bleeding or I'll be dead before you have a chance to think about it."

She knelt down to examine the wound and ran to her saddle bag to fetch the knife and first aid supplies she kept there for the mustangs. With the knife she cut off his shirt, then cleansed the wound with carbolic and wrapped a clean dressing over it. "This'll do for now," she said, "but you better get that bullet out before another day goes by."

"You think I'm going to let one of them butchers in my outfit take a knife to me? Why can't you do it?"

"My father'll be out here in a few minutes with a dozen men and he'll probably hang you."

"Okay, you can do it tomorrow. Where can I find you?" His lips were pale, his breathing shallow, and for an instant she fancied that it wasn't the loss of blood or the shock of the gunshot that put the fever in his eyes but the thought of seeing her again. There must have been men in his outfit who could remove a bullet, but wasn't it the height of self-deception to imagine that Rory, that any man, could be such a fool as to exploit an occasion like this to cozen a woman into a rendezvous?

"The usual place," she said, her face warm. "Out by the mustangs."

She tore his shirt into strips and wrapped them around his wound. As she bent around him, he felt the warmth of her breath and the softness of her breast. A few strands of her hair brushed his cheek.

"I feel like I've died and gone to heaven," he murmured, leaning closer.

She lurched backwards and again he found himself staring down the barrel of her Colt .45. "That can still be arranged."

"Now Elena—"

"Except the heaven part."

At gunpoint—which is an awkward position to be in when you're trying to sweet talk a woman—he picked up his hat and staggered to his horse. As she helped him onto the saddle, they could hear the pound of hoofbeats approaching. "That's my father and his men," she said. "Most likely coming to hang you."

"Well, then," he smiled, "I guess I'd better be on my way."

She seemed frightened, on the verge of tears. "This didn't happen. You never saw me out here."

"No, but I'll never forget you." He tipped his hat and spurred his horse forward. "Adiós, amiga! Much obliged."

13.

It hardly rained at all that summer. The bunchgrass withered and burned in the dust, leaving the cattle gaunted and sick, near to madness for lack of food and water. The temperature hovered in the nineties for weeks. Horses foundered and had to be shot. The men too suffered. Cracked bloody faces, eyes scratched with grit, red as the badland cliffs. Fights broke out, stabbings, whippings. A few men died. The rest were bitter and despairing, as if they could read their future in the cracked earth. Until that summer none of those men ever thought about the future. Either they didn't expect to see it or they didn't much care what it was. It would show up when it had a mind to, and nothing they did could change that. Like as not it wouldn't be good. The basin seemed a timeless, permanent place, carved out of rock. It would always be the same.

But anyone, if he thought about it, could have foreseen bad times ahead for the Captain. He wasn't the man he used to be. He seemed hollowed-out, distracted, tormented by some idea he couldn't leave alone. One hot night—it must have been a couple weeks before Slater's cattle raid—the Captain and Vickery sat in the saloon downing whiskey after whiskey until for both of them the room began to waver and blur. The Captain pointed to the mirror facing them behind the bar, the big mirror that had to be carted across the badland on a special spring wagon to keep it from shattering, which in the smoky light made the men standing behind him look like ghosts, their shrunken doubles flickering overhead in the crystal chandelier. He let out a gasp: "What's Slater doing here?"

Vickery could see where he'd pointed—astonishingly, at his own reflection. "That ain't Slater," he said. "That's you, Captain. Don't you know what you look like?"

Another man might have laughed—it sounded like one drunk teasing another—but Vickery never laughed. Plenty of men in that room heard what he said, though, and they never forgot it, after what happened.

The wildfires started the night of the raid in the west canyon about ten miles away. The days had been scorching hot up there, almost hot enough for the air itself to kindle the fragile bunchgrass and dried-out sagebrush that stitched that land in place. The flames jumped quickly to the scrub pines and juniper that clung just below the rim and from there down the draws into the badland, where, to look at them raging there, you'd have to believe rocks could burn. It was lightning that started the fires, lightning without rain, which was common at that time of year. The rains would come later, when thunderheads rolled in from the northwest, scouring the burn scars into mud that would sluice down into the draws and flood the badland. Then you'd smell the dead wind and the sickening sweetness of ozone, but for now all you could smell was smoke, you tasted it too and choked on it, high white billows drifting south over the basin and filling it down to the ground until you lost sight of the ridges and headlands and mesas that closed it in and you forgot it was a basin. It seemed to be the whole world gone up in smoke.

When Luke raced frantically through the arching gateway crying out about the theft of the bull, the Captain seemed reluctant to take it seriously. He mustered a few men and led them down to the sand wash, but the bull and its abductors had disappeared. He found Elena alone there and brought her home, deferring the counterattack until morning when his forces would be fresh and eager for battle. Luke failed to mention that he'd fired into the crowd and run away, Elena that she'd nursed Rory and helped him escape. They both sensed their father's desperate impotence, his shock at being caught unawares, his vacillation between stony silence and towering rage.

Back in the house Jacinta was weaving in her room. Luke skulked off to his bunk without a word. Before she retired Elena noticed flashes of fire in the high country ten miles to the west and the first drifts of smoke infiltrating the basin. The Captain shrugged when she told him about it. He sat up sipping whiskey, playing solitaire, listening to the eight-day clock ticking on the wall behind him. There was no reason to have that clock, he decided. Its only purpose was to mock him, to remind him of an external order that had no applicability to him. It would tick for six more days, as long as God took to create the world, and then it would stop forever. He would have wound it backwards, to the beginning of time, if time could have been undone. Smoke seeped into the house, invisible as the night itself. Outside stalked predators, thieves, spies, traitors. He blew out his lantern and studied the lingering glow until it disappeared, leaving only himself, alone in darkness deeper than any he'd ever seen. It was as if his own shadow had engulfed him and obliterated everything else but the ticking of that clock. He sat alone in the darkness and the night wore on. Then came dawn, a leaden dawn of smoke and impenetrable light. He stared out the window waiting for sunrise. But the smoke had blocked the sun so completely that there wasn't a sunrise, just a blind man's fancy of one behind a curtain of white. The world had changed utterly.

At seven o'clock the Captain stood tall on his high front porch, with his family and his closest lieutenants, as on a rampart surveying a doomed battlefield. Himself in the center, Jacinta to his right. Luke on his other side, Elena beside Jacinta, and behind them the foreman Vickery and Charlie Crow, his second in command They peered out at the men, not just the cowhands but the reapers, the wranglers, the blacksmiths, gathered before them on the packed-earth yard and under the archway, restless, breathing the smoke that tasted like fire. The men hefted their guns and whips, muttered and cursed in a rumor of war. Even the horses in the corral stared curiously, tipping their ears forward to hear the Captain's commanding voice. The big yellow cur lay curled at the Captain's feet.

"You all know why we're here," he said, careful to find the right words. He fixed his eyes on the pale patch of sky where the rising sun should have been. "This day hasn't started, may never start, from the looks of things. And we may never see it end if those fires don't stop."

The wind whistled its incredulous response. The mesas and the badlands had burned before, and would burn again, before the world ended.

"They say they didn't steal that bull," the Captain told his men. "They say they only borrowed it. Whatever they call it, there'll be the devil to pay for what they done."

The men answered with one voice (though each spoke in his own words): The devil to pay. And they wondered, Who'll pay him? and in what coin?

"They need to be taught a lesson," Luke declared.

A lesson, a lesson, a lesson, echoed through the crowd.

"We will teach them that lesson in due course," the Captain said. "I brought that bull here and I intend to return it to its owner safe and sound."

"They need to be punished," Luke said.

"I say hang 'em," Vickery said.

Hang 'em, hang 'em, hang 'em, came the echo.

"I'll have the bull first," the Captain said, "my satisfaction later. There won't be any hanging."

"What'll there be then?" Luke demanded.

"Diplomacy, if you're capable of it. I want you to go over there and bring that bull back without shooting anybody or getting shot. Can you do that?"

Jacinta's bone-white face darkened, her fierce eyes gleaming even in the sunless dawn. Her cheeks were hollow, her mouth half-open, lips dry. All night she'd sat at her loom, divining the future in the mad colors and figures she wove in her endless tapestry. "No," she muttered. "Not Luke. You can't send Luke over there to do your begging for you."

"Hush," the Captain whispered.

She raised her voice: "We need to get rid of Slater once and for all."

The seething crowd agreed. The Captain reached for his revolver and fired it in the air. A few of the men tried to back away and he fired over their heads, lower each time, and when they stopped he aimed right at their faces, one after another, as the blood drained out of them and they prayed to be spared. He held them like that for a few seconds and said, "If any of you sons of bitches thinks you know better than I do and wants to take me on, I'm ready and waiting for you."

They stopped in the silence of dread as he turned to his wife. "Now let's see if Luke can do the job I gave him."

"No," she murmured. "Not Luke."

Luke stood stock still, afraid to look at his father or the men in the crowd. On any other day they would have mocked him and treated him like a child. He stuck his hands in his pockets to keep them from trembling.

The men drifted back to the bunkhouse as soon as the Captain's fury had passed. They finished breakfast and waited for Vickery and Charlie Crow to come out with their orders for the day. The foreman, who'd stood behind the Captain on the porch, had done some thinking since he'd talked with Buckminster the night before. He didn't trust Buckminster with his slick clothes and his back-east ways but the man was on to something with his proposal for a joint mutiny. The Captain's behavior that morning showed that he was losing his grip and when that happened the wolves would start to circle. If he joined Buckminster, would the men go along with him? He couldn't be sure. But if Buckminster wanted to get rid of both bosses, let him think he was in the game. They'd start by eliminating Slater and before the wolves circled in on the Captain, he could make sure they found Buckminster in their path.

Now he sidled up to the Captain, his burn scar glowing red as an open wound, his tongue clicking even before he started to speak. "Luke can take a few men and get that bull," he said, "but that ain't enough to punish Slater for what he done. We got a army here we can take over there behind the butte and let him think we're just coming for the bull, but instead we'll go after his herd and drive it down the Vale of Tears and over the cliff."

The Captain faced him disdainfully. "That I would not do."

"Why not? This is your chance to get rid of Slater."

"I wouldn't kill a thousand head of cattle—even Slater's cattle— just to spite Slater."

"Then kill Slater and keep his cattle," Vickery smirked.

Elena felt her knees weaken. "You can't do that."

"If I kill Slater," the Captain glared back at his foreman, "it'll be man to man. I won't shoot him in the back, or have somebody else shoot him for me."

"If we kill the whole outfit, who's going to know?"

Shaking with anger, Elena tried to push her way between Vickery and her father. "Get out of here!" she yelled at Vickery. He stood firm without pushing back at her. Charlie Crow shared her anger but held his tongue.

"Elena, go inside the house," Jacinta said.

The Captain ignored them all and turned to Luke. "Get the stock wagon ready to go. Take six men. I don't want any gunplay. Bring that bull back alive. That's all I'm going to say about this." He pivoted like a general who'd delivered his final orders, stepped down off the porch, and disappeared into the smoke.

Vickery sent Charlie Crow to the bunkhouse to get the men ready for work. Then he edged toward Jacinta and spoke in a low voice. "We can still do this," he said. "The Captain don't need to know."

The smoke smothered Slater's camp like a churning river of dust, reeking of scorched sage and pinyon pine and bitter prickly pear. The visible world was long forgotten by the time his men woke up, gagging and wheezing in their bunks. You could have told them they were dead and buried and toiling in hell and every one of them would have believed you. Their high spirits had faded as they staggered home in the dark. Lashing the bull immobile in the corral, they crawled into bed just sober enough to dread the morning's reckoning. Rory followed an hour behind them and they never missed him or suspected that he'd been shot. At dawn the heifers they'd lined up for servicing were bawling and prancing, as skittery and sore as the men. The bull stamped the dirt, dipped his head, tried to break free even when a heifer was led in for him.

The men couldn't bear to light a fire in that smoke so instead of coffee they drank water with whiskey in it and called it tea. Moondog was the first to address the issue that was on everyone's mind. "I think we ought to take that bull back before they come to get him," he said. "The old boy's about done with his work here."

"Not after what they done to us," Crazy Ike said. "They come up behind us in the dark and tried to shoot us in the back."

"That was just Luke," Moondog said. "You can't go by him."

Crazy Ike spat a mouthful on the cold ashes of the last night's fire. "They can come and get him, see if we shoot back. Let them beg."

Slater wished he'd never let them go on that raid. "I'd say take him back if I thought that would end this," he said. "But I doubt they'll be satisfied with getting him back."

"What do you think they'll do?"

"I expect we'll be hearing from them. In this smoke they could sneak up on us before we knew they were within pistol range."

To hide what was left of his bloodstained shirt, Rory had put his jacket on when he returned to the camp. Now he stood off by himself, weak and a little feverish. He wasn't about to let any of the outfit dig around in his shoulder wound looking for the bullet. And he didn't want any of them to know about Elena.

The only one who acted suspicious was Buckminster. He sidled up with his tin cup of whiskeyed water, blowing on it as if it were coffee. His blue eyes looked gray, almost white, in the smoke. "That girl was there last night with her brother," he said, peering over his cup.

"She didn't shoot, though. She tried to stop him."

"She tell you that?"

"No, she didn't tell me anything. I was watching her."

"I thought maybe she told you after the rest of us got chased away."

Rory felt a knot of anger tightening in his gut. "I ran after the bull. Never found it, though."

"You must've run the wrong way," Buckminster smirked. "Because there he is. Me and Moondog brought him in."

He wanted to choke Buckminster if that's what it would take to shut him up. Instead he said, "Glad you did."

"Got your eye on her, do you? Well, so do other men."

"What are you talking about? What other men?"

"Just keep both eyes open and you'll find out. That gal gets around."

The Captain called his crew the outfit from hell, and if they weren't exactly from there, no one doubted that's where they would end up. There was the Irishman O'Rourke, who'd smash the face of any man who crossed him with an ash cudgel the size of his leg. Gutiérrez, admired for his bravery and viciousness, who packed razor-sharp knives in niches in his boots. John Riley, the blacksmith and the only black man in the outfit, a mountain of a man who scarcely needed hammer and tongs to do his work—with his huge hands he could twist iron into any shape and wrestle a stallion into submission.

Such were the men Vickery chose to send with Luke to reclaim the bull. Three, not six as the Captain had ordered. "You can't carry your guns down there," Vickery told them. They sat their horses under the archway that opened the Captain's compound to the road, while Luke, wearing a flamboyant red shirt, hitched the oxen to the stock wagon. "If there's any gunplay that bull won't last thirty seconds, Slater's gang'll shoot him just to spite us. So take your guns along, but keep them in the wagon until the bull's out of the way. And then you can wipe them sons of bitches off the earth for all I care."

Charlie Crow found Elena combing Susannah in her stall in the barn. "Miss," he said (he could never bring himself to call the Captain's daughter by her first name), "there's something you should know, or your father should know. Something Vickery probably won't tell him."

"What's that, Charlie?" She liked Crow, appreciated his loyalty, his occasional confidences, and the way he stood up for the men when Vickery abused them.

"Well, it's like this. Vickery's sending the men out to fight with Slater."

"Sure, I know that. It's what they do every day."

"No, I don't mean what they usually do. This is different. He's sending them out there to kill Slater and his outfit and destroy his herd."

She studied his leathern face, which he held slightly turned away. He was still young—probably under thirty—but as weathered from fifteen years of sun and dust as an old saddle. She knew he hated Vickery and was loyal to the Captain, but something burned in his eyes that was more than spite or mere duty. She remembered what she'd heard Vickery say to her mother. "You can't mean that," she said.

He turned to face her. "I'm afraid I do."

"Are you going out with them?"

"I'm not made for war, miss."

"All right, I want you to stay here this afternoon. I've got some work I want you to do with the horses."

The day was a shadowless twilight that spanned the horizons, the air thick with smoke, pluming up in places as if from fissures in the earth. The hot August sun hovered unseen. Men coughed and sweated, choked on their words. Horses milled in the corral, snorting and whinnying. Dogs panted and loped in circles, noses to the ground. All of creation seemed to be on edge as the fires raged invisible in the canyons and headlands to the west, scouring down to the dust and the hard rock of the earth.

The Captain paced anxiously on the wide porch, surveying what could be seen of his kingdom through the smoke. His anger rose as he watched Luke and the others depart for Slater's camp with the ox-drawn stock wagon. He frowned at his foreman Vickery. "I told Luke to take six men with him," he said. "He only took three."

"We decided he didn't need six men. It's a mission of peace."

Had his son overruled him? Or Vickery? Retrieving the bull was a mission of honor, not of peace. He had wanted six men as a show of strength. This was not a supplication.

"They went unarmed," Vickery told him. "We don't want any shooting around that bull."

He swallowed down his anger. "Good."

The whole day had seemed wrong. After a night without sleep, a day without a sunrise, strangled in its cradle. A disobedient day, fighting him every inch. "Where are the rest of the men?" he asked Vickery. "I don't see them anywhere."

"Hard to see through this smoke, I guess."

"My eyes are burning. They've been burning all day."

"The men are out there, doing their jobs." Vickery pointed toward a swirling patch behind the bunkhouse. "Look, there's Bagley and Snyder and Viklund, you can see them just riding out to water the heifers. And over there"—he swiveled toward the sand wash that led into the range—"there's Ortiz and Quire... ah, they just disappeared in the smoke."

"I can't see them," the Captain said.

"Then listen. You can hear them, can't you?"

The Captain shook his head.

"The smoke muffles the air so." It was Jacinta, who followed by Elena had stepped outside a moment before. "Where's Luke?"

"Luke's gone to fetch the bull," the Captain said.

Her step faltered. "What? I told him he was not to go."

"He went because I told him to. If he can't do a man's job he shouldn't be on this ranch."

"Father," Elena said, "the reason you can't hear the men is that they aren't there."

"Hush," her mother said.

"Where are they then?"

"They've ridden off to kill Slater and destroy his herd."

"Elena, go inside!" Jacinta hissed. "You don't know what you're saying."

The Captain had never been so angry at his daughter. Did she imagine that his orders were just so much wasted breath that the men could ignore and disobey? "They wouldn't do that," he insisted. "I forbade it."

"You've got to believe me. Vickery sent them out with those instructions."

Suddenly it dawned on the Captain that Elena could be right. "Is any of this true, Vickery?"

"Of course not, Captain. I'm afraid the young lady's imagination has run off with her. Three of the men rode down to Slater's with Luke—you saw them—but for the rest of them it's just another day on the range. Same goes for me. I better get out there, they're waiting for me."

"I heard you and Mother talking," Elena said. "You said you were going to kill them and the Captain didn't need to know—"

"Go inside, Elena." Jacinta seized her arm, yanking her toward the door. "Stop this right now and go inside."

Elena tore herself away and ran down to the corral. Without looking back, she saddled her sorrel mare and raced out toward the high meadow behind the clay butte to wait for Rory.

Rory waited until everybody was busy with chores before he rode out to look for Elena. The usual place, she'd said. Out by the mustangs. He'd seen her out there sometimes, in the high meadow back of the clay butte, bringing sacks of food to the wild horses, riding one of them bareback in a wide circle around the ridge. His left arm and shoulder throbbed with pain and his breath faltered. His horse balked at the smoke, tried to run away from it but it was everywhere. The trail faded about fifty feet ahead and beyond that there was nothing. The sun had never appeared but he could feel its heat trapped in the smoke. There was no air, only smoke. No shadows flecked the gray wilted earth.

Elena waited for him in the usual place. Her sorrel mare, hobbled and lost-looking, wandered in a tight circle around her. Elena stood coaxing Susannah to come forward for a handful of carrots, but the mustang herd, disoriented and distraught, milled in a wash below the ridge. She waited anxiously for Rory but almost hoped he wouldn't come. She dreaded what she had to tell him. It would be a day of terror, of bloodshed and betrayal. A day without a dawn which for some would end before dusk. Would he believe her? She felt like a prophet condemned to disbelief.

When he trotted up on his palomino she helped him climb down. His face was as gray as the shrouded sky. "Morning," he nodded, attempting a smile.

"You look pale. Did you get the bullet out?"

"No, I was hoping you could that."

Without a word she reached in her saddle bag and pulled out her surgical supplies—carbolic, needle-nosed pliers, a needle and thread—and a half-full bottle of whiskey she'd stolen from her father's cupboard. She spread a blanket on the ground and made Rory sit down.

"I brought this in case you needed it." She handed him the whiskey. "Start drinking."

"This ain't going to hurt, is it?"

She showed him the pliers and stuck the handle of her quirt in his mouth. "Bite down on this."

"I guess I better take a drink first."

He gulped three fast swallows and felt nauseated. She made him lie down. She opened his shirt and pulled it back. The wound was purple, almost black, purging blood and pus. His whole left arm and shoulder were bruised and swollen. She poured carbolic over the pliers and on the wound. She knelt on his elbow and leaned her other knee on the opposite shoulder. He tried to raise his head. "Keep your head down. Yes, this is going to hurt."

Digging out the bullet was easier than she'd expected, like pulling a cactus spine out of a mustang's fetlock. Rory bit down on the whip handle and tears ran out of his burning eyes. The pain left him breathless, drenched in sweat.

She took her time stitching and bandaging the wound and when she finished she said, "You lie still and don't move. I've got to tell you something that's going to upset you."

His face reddened under its wind-scoured hide. "I thought we were getting along pretty well, not hating each other, at least, maybe even liking each other a little—"

"It's not that," she said, blushing. "It's worse than that."

His color had come back from the whiskey and the pain and his racing heart. "What then?"

"They sent Luke over to fetch back the bull."

"We expected that. He can have it."

"There's another gang that'll be going around the back of the ridge. They're going to stampede your herd down to the rim and drive it over the cliff."

"Slater won't let them do that."

"They're going to kill Slater. Kill all of you."

Rory choked back his anger. "I never thought the Captain would stoop so low."

"It's Vickery. Charlie Crow told me. My father doesn't even know about it."

"Why didn't you tell him?"

"I tried to and he didn't believe me. I've never seen him so angry—at me, for telling him the truth."

Rory wobbled to his feet, drunk with pain and dread and disbelief. "I've got to tell Slater."

"You need to rest," Elena said.

She gripped his elbow to steady him, not to hold him back, but he pushed her hand away. "I ain't resting when they're about to shoot us and drive our herd off a cliff."

"At least let me fix that bandage." She leaned close to adjust the bandage and there were tears in her eyes.

"Why are you crying?" he said. "Does it look that bad?"

"No, your arm's going to be all right."

"Then why are you crying?"

"Just sympathy, I guess."

He smiled. It was his first smile of the day, and he knew it would be his last. "That's sweet," he said. "Really sweet."

Those were his last words, before he climbed one-handed on his palomino and vanished into the smoldering sky.

Behind the curtain of smoke Buckminster watched him ride away. Having trailed him from the bunkhouse, he'd tied his horse in a draw and stolen closer until he had them in his sights, though still out of earshot. Elena hovered over Rory, nursed him, helped him up, though she never kissed him. Seeing her there reminded Buckminster how much he wanted her. One way or another he'd get what he wanted. If necessary he would take it, as he'd done before— back east, where some fathers and brothers, adept with axes and scythes and mauls, lay in wait for his return. But not just now, not today. By the end of today, if all went well, Elena would be his for the taking.

14.

It was a day of anger and terror rising in the smoke, of bravery and cunning betrayal, stampeding herds and screaming horses. If you were there you'd never stop talking about it, but most of what you'd say would be wrong. Boasts, delusions, and outright lies—that's all you'd know, because there wasn't a man in that whirling chaos who could see through the fog of war. And a war is what it was, a range war but a war all the same. Fought, like most wars, by men who would've called themselves friends if they'd met in a saloon. Men who for no particular reason signed up with different outfits and for that reason alone wanted to kill each other. Men whose names you'd know, whose faces you'd recognize—sunburned, friendly faces become stiff and hollow, impersonations now of the men who wore them, mere masks. Faces unrecognizable in the terrible anonymity of death. They rode and died for Slater or the Captain and that was all they had in common. Each had his own talents, quirks, failings—those would go down to death with them and be forgotten. Nobody talks about them now.

Slater made the decision to divide his forces as soon as Rory told him what he'd learned from Elena. Of course they would come for the bull, he expected that, but this new threat—to kill him and destroy his herd—was beyond imagining. There was no law on the plains—he knew that—especially in that basin remote from all things civilized. But isn't there something beyond law, or before it, some part of nature itself that makes us men and not beasts? "I can't believe the Captain would do that," Slater said.

"Elena says he don't know about it," Rory said. "It's Vickery that's doing it. Charlie Crow told her."

"Vickery's a killer," Buckminster said. "He'd do anything."

Slater thought long and hard before he spoke. "Okay," he said. "Here's what we're going to do. Moondog, Polecat, Crazy Ike—you three stay here with the bull."

"We ought to kill that bull," Crazy Ike said, wiping the drool from his mouth. "Roast it up and have a dinner fit for the gods."

"No, I don't want no killing. They come for the bull, you hand him over. No shooting—stash your guns out of the way. But don't let them burn the barn down or do any other mischief. And protect the horses and the heifers we've got down here. Everybody else'll come along with me to protect the herd. If it's a war they want, that's what they're going to get."

They laughed and cheered at that, as men do when they march off to war, as though war is a laughing matter. Some would go down to a painful death before they'd see another day.

"And Buckminster"—Slater took Buckminster aside, lucky to have a foreman he could trust—"there's something I want you to do. You don't have to, it could be dangerous."

"Sure," Buckminster said (so loyal, Slater thought, he didn't even ask what it was before agreeing). "What is it?"

"Elena said the Captain don't know about this. I want you to go to the Captain and tell him what's going on. If he knew about it, I think he'd stop it."

"Will Vickery let me get through to him?"

"I don't know. That's why I say it's dangerous. Will you do it?"

The ox-drawn stock wagon churned through the dust, Luke driving, O'Rourke, Gutiérrez and Riley on horseback beside him. They marched through the sand wash and across the clouded range toward Seven Mile Ridge, invisible in the smoke. Luke arched high over the oxen with his whip, eager but fearful of what awaited them at Slater's camp: the ferocious bull and the ordeal of chaining him in the wagon and driving the frightened team back to the Captain's stock pen. They struggled out of the wash and squinted up the ridge toward Slater's camp, where they glimpsed the ink-black bull in the corral, with only three men guarding him. The first order of business would be reclaiming the bull, the second, Vickery had decreed, the death of those men. Why did they need to die? Luke asked himself. He'd have no part of that. The others would probably obey Vickery, and those three men, whoever they were, would end the day facedown in the dirt. It would all be over in a few seconds, and forgotten quicker than that, as soon as their blood had soaked the earth. But he faltered in the silent clutch of dread: Where were the rest of Slater's men? In the bunkhouse sleeping off their night of cattle stealing? Or waiting in ambush for his wagon coming to reclaim the bull?

The three men waiting at the corral were Moondog, Crazy Ike and Polecat. Moondog with his canine teeth filed to a point, Crazy Ike maddened by the shrapnel lodged in his skull. Polecat, unlucky man, with a scar on his cheek where once a Comanche tomahawk had found its mark. They'd stashed their guns in the barn behind a pile of tools and construction debris. A pitchfork, an ash-handled sledge hammer, Crazy Ike's double-headed axe, its haft more than four feet long. Boulders, fence posts, long sharpened cedar palings, coils and tangles of barbed wire. The oxen drew closer under Luke's whip, and the horsemen dismounted and raised their empty hands.

"We're unarmed," O'Rourke shouted. "Nobody wants to hurt that bull."

Crazy Ike wished he could shoot them, but Slater had been clear: Don't start a bloodbath. And you couldn't shoot an unarmed man, even out here—they'd hang you for that. Luke climbed down from the wagon and walked toward them, his hands free, no iron in his belt. He looked scared, his eyes darting this way and that, as if he expected an ambush. "We're here to take the bull," he shouted.

The bull bristled and snorted and pawed the dirt. It hated Luke, you could tell that. "I dare you to come and get him," Moondog yelled back.

The Irishman O'Rourke was the mouthpiece, did the talking for all of them. "You've only borrowed him, we're told. It's time to pay back the loan."

"That bull don't want to go with Luke," Moondog said. "He prefers it here."

"That's right!" Crazy Ike laughed. "He prefers it here!"

"We'll be the judge of that," O'Rourke said evenly. "You have no claim on that bull."

"You said last night you only needed him for a few hours," Luke said.

The bull stamped his front legs and roared. But for the shackles on his hind leg he might have smashed his way out of the corral. Luke stood where he was.

"I can't blame you if you're afraid to take him," Moondog said. "It would take a man to get him out of here."

"What about three men?" O'Rourke asked, glancing at the others. The Mexican with his black glinting eyes. John Riley, a bull of a man with the hands of a giant.

"Well, that would depend, wouldn't it?" Moondog smiled to show them his teeth. "On who the three men are?"

Polecat stepped forward in his sheepskin chaps, fleece-side out, as if he stood astride a pair of fighting rams. Crazy Ike shambled up beside him, almost as tall as the giant Riley, but magnified by his insanity. When he looked at Riley, this blacksmith who'd been some white man's property, he longed for his two-headed axe, honed razor sharp to split him in half.

The six of them stood eye to eye, stock still, staring like antelope on a hillside. Breaths caught and held. Hearts in their chests pounding.

Then and later, nobody could say how it started. A lowered hand, a raised knee. A careless twitch or shove. Then Crazy Ike threw a punch at John Riley. The giant toppled backwards and O'Rourke kicked Crazy Ike in the knee. Crouching, Gutiérrez reached into his boot and came up with a glittering six-inch blade. Without raising it above his waist, he slashed it at Polecat, that unlucky man.

Wallace, Quire, Galogly, Bagley, Viklund, Herzog. They were no saints—nor was the rest of the Captain's outfit—but they were men and not just flesh and bone. Each had his own pride, his own joys, his own way of laughing at the world, and rough as he lived he knew a few gentle ways which in some other place might have endeared him to a woman or a child. They all had mothers, they'd been to church at one time or another, they'd fallen in love, usually with a whore, so it couldn't last, but a woman nonetheless. And that morning as they milled on their horses out of sight of the Captain's ranch, waiting for Vickery to come out and lead them in the attack on Slater, they peered into the smoke, restless, distracted, pensive as much as they ever were, some with minds as vacant as the ashen sky, others jittery with unwelcome intimations of what lay ahead.

There's one man in every outfit who talks too much. In the Captain's that was a nervous little hostler from South Texas with a mouthful of crooked teeth named Quire. He was a whiner, a worrier, a dime store philosopher, and no matter what the occasion, he couldn't stop talking. Not that anybody paid him any mind. They let him flap his tongue just to fill up space on those empty plains and when they'd heard enough they told him to shut up. That morning waiting for Vickery he was agitating for peace. "I don't know as I understand this wrangling between Slater and the Captain," he told anyone who would listen. "It ain't just a clash, it's a curse. They're coiled around each other like two rattlers in a pit and sooner or later one of them's going to swallow the other. And for us hired men, which side we landed on is blind chance, but we got to stand and fight for our side, come hell or high water—and how likely is high water in this basin, where every drop sinks into the earth? So it's hell, is what it is, and we're the damn fools who signed up for it."

"Shut up," Galogly said. A melancholy Irishman, a man of few words and dark thoughts, he had a taut, expressionless face. Some said he'd spent time in prison in Illinois.

"Speaking for myself," Quire went on, "I don't want no part of it. I've no love for the Captain and no hatred for Slater. I'm just a man who needs work. I don't even remember how I got here."

"Shut up," Galogly repeated with a little more emphasis.

"I just might do that. The whole situation leaves me speechless."

A Texas cowboy named Bob Wallace who always had a joke or a song or a story to amuse the others said, "Quire, the day you're speechless is the day they put you in the ground."

"That'll never happen," Bagley said—he was a big-headed man with a booming voice that was about three octaves lower than everybody else's—"because he won't shut up long enough to die."

"If we'd a known you being speechless was even a possibility," Wallace told Quire, "we would've started this war long ago."

Wallace laughed at his own joke and some of the men laughed with him but not Viklund. Viklund was a dour Swede who prided himself on his good looks, which was pure vanity in that deserted basin. He washed every day and shaved twice a week, even in winter. The men teased him mercilessly but he never stopped his girlish preening. "I never signed up for a soldier," he said, running his fingers through his blond hair. "I left the old country so I wouldn't have to fight."

Herzog, the jovial German they called Noblesse Oblige, had donned a pair of white kid gloves for the occasion and tucked a pearl-handled revolver into his belt. He seemed to relish the impending conflict as if it were a duel on the field of honor. "Slater's crew are all cowards like Viklund here," he said—smiling at Viklund, who bristled at the insult and turned away—"It will be over before lunch and we can get back to work."

Time passed slowly in those moments when there seemed nothing more important than jokes and insults and Quire's habit of flapping his tongue, nothing noteworthy about those moments or that day in their lives, though later they wished they could have clung to them. It was a day hardly worth noticing and of which there would be no remembering. A few ravens grumbled in the glaucous sky and floated away. For them it was a day like any other.

Then the men heard the dogs, the Captain's dogs frolicking around Vickery's piebald gelding as he drifted toward them through the smoke. The big yellow cur trotted in front of him, not frolicking but dead serious, as though it knew their reason for being there.

Slater and his outfit had ridden north, leaving just the three men behind to defend the camp. They skirted Seven Mile Ridge and trailed down into the big flat, ten miles across, where the herds grazed on sparse bunchgrass under a glaring but invisible sun. You couldn't see more than fifty yards in any direction but the cattle were out there, grumbling in mournful tones like ships lost in fog, the two herds commingled in places and indistinguishable except for their brands. For the most part the Captain's herd grazed to the west and Slater's to the east, a division marked in part by a mile-long stretch of barbed wire and the trench just west of it, armed with inverted palings, hewn sharp and fire-hardened, that would spear the guts out of any man or horse unlucky enough to fall into it. Slater was alarmed by Vickery's plan to stampede his herd south into the Vale of Tears. The smoke stung the cattle's eyes, made them frantic—at the least surprise or threat they would panic and charge ahead until they found their doom. All he could do was scatter them out on the broad plain so Vickery would have to divide his men into small platoons to round them up. That would help even the odds, he reckoned. Still, if Vickery set his plan in motion it would be a grim and murderous day on the range.

"I've a mind to call it off," he told Rory. They sat their horses overlooking the flat from a low rise speckled with sage. "Let them take our cattle. We can go north, try to find a way out of here."

"The men won't obey you," Rory said, and Slater knew he was right.

"They'd probably shoot me themselves," he said.

The outfit had hauled their ordnance down to the flat in a four-mule wagon—rifles, shotguns, side arms and boxes of ammunition for each, as well as axe handles and machetes, coils of barbed wire and armfuls of fire-sharpened palings. This weaponry they unloaded at strategic points—on tops of ridges, at rock outcrops, behind the rims of arroyos and gulches—where they would take their stand. They parked the wagon behind a wind-blown dune and made it their headquarters, hobbling the mules in a nearby draw. They rode out to scatter their herd east and drive the Captain's in front of what they judged would be the line of attack, then they gathered at the wagon and settled down to wait. Rory stood lookout—though he could hardly see beyond shotgun range—while the rest of the men crouched around the wagon, smoking, teasing each other, playing cards or tossing dice in hopes that this would be their lucky day, all sweating and sweltering in the trapped heat of that foul August morning.

Rory kept his eyes on the fence line, the Captain's cattle drifting in behind it as far as the trench, blocking the view, he reckoned, of any man or horse riding in among the cattle from the west. His shoulder throbbed where he'd been shot but he still had the use of his arm. An ex-Confederate artilleryman named Hank Crenshaw, who liked to say he cheated death at Gettysburg, stood behind him, talking about gods he didn't believe in. "They're out here on a day like this," he said. "Inside every man, spirits urging him on or to run away—his pride, his shame, his lust for violence, his fear."

"Ain't nobody out here but us at the moment," Rory said without turning around.

"You don't think so? Look at those wolves."

He pointed and Rory saw them, on a hump of hardened sand about fifty yards away: a small pack of wolves, no more than six or eight of them, pacing in circles, tongues lolling, smiling, all of them, at some private joke only wolves would understand. The other men noticed them at the same time.

A cowhand called Jameson stood up with his rifle and took careful aim.

"Hold it!" Slater said, grabbing his wrist. "You want to give away our position? Them wolves'll clear out of here when the shooting starts."

The sight of the wolves tightened their throats, kindled dread in their bones. "You afraid?" Crenshaw asked Rory in a low voice so the others couldn't hear. "When the shooting starts, men are going to die."

"You got a fate, is what I think," Rory said defiantly. He thought by saying that, by believing in fate, he could absolve himself from fear. "When your time comes, it comes. Ain't nothing you can do about it."

"Sure there is," Crenshaw said. "At any given time—like right now—there's always two fates you could have, both just as likely. Turn right or turn left, fight or run, shoot at the man in front of you or let him get away. You always have a choice."

"What if I choose the wrong one?"

Crenshaw faced him with a shrewd smile. "It's your misfortune and none of my own."

Five miles away Vickery's army lurked like living shadows half-hidden in the smoke, waiting for their foreman to lead them in the attack. Vickery was just leaving the ranch, the Captain's dogs moiling around him, when he saw the shade of Buckminster drifting toward him through the haze. The dogs snarled and bayed, the yellow cur reared for attack, but Vickery called them off. The two men stared at each other for a moment, blinking against the bitter air, neither moving his hands, as Buckminster's horse shambled to a halt. "Where do you think you're going?" Vickery wanted to know.

"Slater sent me over here to talk to the Captain."

"The Captain ain't home. You can talk to me."

"Okay," Buckminster said. "Slater knows what you're fixing to do. Elena talked to Rory."

Vickery turned his head to one side, showing Buckminster his burn scar, and spat. "You going to try and stop me?"

Buckminster ventured an ironic smile. "Like we talked about last night," he said, "you and me don't need to be enemies."

Vickery took his time answering. "You say you know what we're fixing to do. If we ain't enemies, does that mean you'll go along with it?"

"I'll even help it along if you and me go into it as partners."

"Partners? What would that partnership look like?"

The tempter had him hooked, his audacity piqued, asking for the details. "When it's all over, I'd be running Slater's operation and you'd be running the Captain's."

"Which means Slater and the Captain got to be out of the picture."

"That's right. A few others too."

"Casualties of war?"

"It's a sad thing. Happens in every war."

Vickery coughed and glanced away, covering his mouth with his fist. He was impressed by the grandeur of Buckminster's vision.

Even on those pitiless plains where often as not a man's life meant
less to him than a whore's caress or a hand of poker, he'd never
imagined a scheme so grand as the one Buckminster seemed to be
suggesting. "Who are the others you mentioned?" he asked
carelessly.

"Well, Luke for sure, and Charlie Crow."

"Why Crow?"

"You can't trust him. He'll stick with the Captain. And not the
girl. I'm keeping her for myself."

A wry smile, unfamiliar on his face. He twisted up his mouth
and spat. "She won't like you."

"She'll come around. There's other girls didn't like me at first."

"What about the missus?"

"Send her back to whatever hell she come from."

That brought a low warning laugh. "You don't know her. She's
a she-devil."

"OK, I'll take care of her then." No hesitancy now, even in the
face of a she-devil. "In a war," Buckminster said, "one side kills
people on the other side, and vice versa. You don't kill people on
your own side. That would make you a traitor, and who would trust
you after that?"

"But you ain't a traitor if you let the other side do it."

"We're singing out of the same choir-book, don't you think?"

In a few minutes Buckminster and Vickery had sketched the
outlines of a deal, swapping casualties, divvying up the spoils before
the war began. Buckminster would eliminate the Captain, Luke,
Jacinta, and Charlie Crow, keeping Elena for himself. Vickery would
kill Slater. Each would kill the boss of the other's outfit, clearing the
way to take over his own, and of course both herds would be spared.
Vickery and Buckminster would make peace as soon as they were in
control of their outfits. "Oh, and one more thing," Buckminster said.

"That boy Rory's got to go—he's Slater's heir—and I can't be seen shooting him. You got to do it."

"Such a shame," Vickery said.

As Buckminster cantered into the mist, Vickery could have shot him in the back, and he considered it. How did he know this blue-eyed dandy wasn't just spying for Slater, setting him up for the kill? On the other hand, there was no harm in playing along with him for now. He liked half of Buckminster's proposal: the half that eliminated the Captain and his wife and son and gave him everything they owned. The other half—control of Slater's operation—would come his way too after the dust settled, if Buckminster turned his back on him again. Treating with the enemy is always risky, but for the time being, Vickery decided, he would pretend to stick with the deal. If he'd been a gambling man (which he wasn't, being a strict Presbyterian) he would have put his money on Buckminster biting the dust long before he did.

Rory heard the dogs first, long before anyone could see them. They must have been running ahead of Vickery's gang, though how they knew where to find Slater's men was anybody's guess. The barking and baying crossed north and south, came closer, crossed again. The wolves stopped circling and sat on their haunches, sniffing for the dogs, a race they despised as low-born slaves of men. A scattering of ravens appeared over the wolves, rattling out of the sullen sky. Ravens will peck out a calf's eyes, a man's too if he can't defend himself or if he's dead—all the men knew that. Now the men blinked in the smoke, their eyes moist and red, and the ungainly black birds hovered over them, croaking patiently, and their purpose was not lost on the men. They waved their guns and axes and palings as if the ravens were the enemy host and not, like the wolves, an indifferent chorus of onlookers, eager only for flesh to glut on.

When the dogs reached the fence line—possibly because they smelled the wolves—they fell back and waited for the horses to bring Vickery's men forward. By this time pale silhouettes of cattle were thick along the trench like crook-horned monsters and the trench was blocked from being seen by the first riders and their mounts, who rose like charging phantoms in the haze, scattering the cattle away from the trench to clear a misty path. When the riders saw the barbed wire they pulled up, too late to stop their horses from stumbling into the trench, rearing and screaming and hurling the riders into the fence or, the less lucky ones, onto the sharpened palings that lined the trench. Bob Wallace, who owned a guitar and was known on the range as a singer and jokester and storyteller, fell stomach-down on a paling and as he rolled over (slowly, with an agonized cry for mercy) his entrails spiraled out around him in the dust. All movement stopped—men, horses, cattle, even, as it seemed, the ravens—in shock at that sight, or as if the men on both sides (who all knew and liked Bob Wallace) took time for a silent prayer or wished they knew a prophet who could read those entrails and tell them what their own fates would be.

15.

At Slater's camp even the bull was astonished at how quickly the fight erupted. Polecat's sheepskin chaps and heavy belt saved him from Gutiérrez's first knife thrust. Still he was astonished and infuriated by the attempt. This was not his destiny, to be gutted by a nineteen-year-old Mexican in a red sash and a leather hat under the choking sky. He'd never had anything but bad luck and he'd always figured he would die on these plains, but not this way. He grabbed the Mexican's wrist and twisted the knife out of his grip and it tumbled in the dirt and he kicked it away.

The boy staggered backwards and dipped his hand in his boot, his cunning young eyes peering under the brim of his hat. "You're going to die, gringo," he spat. "Your fancy chaps won't save you this time." A new knife flashed out of the boot and Polecat heard it whistle past his ear. He dodged into the barn and grabbed a coil of barbed wire left over from the fence-building, a twisting, treacherous spiral of loose wire which he lashed at the Mexican's legs, toppling him backwards. Gutiérrez squirmed in the biting wire as his adversary reeled him in like an eel in a net, dragging him back to be skewered on one of the cedar palings, as long and sharp as a spear, which had been hewn to spike the man traps. Polecat almost felt sorry for the boy, he was so young. Was this the death he imagined for himself? To gasp out his life writhing in shit in a cattle yard, his leather hat still snagged in place by its rawhide thong?

But the Mexican dodged away and hurled yet another knife at Polecat, piercing his right shoulder above the armpit. The wound was deep, painful, spurting blood. "You're a dead man," Gutiérrez laughed, and Polecat, swooning, wondered if he was right. His mind winged back, unaccountably, to his first day on the trail so many years ago, that glimpse of the late winter light over the Texas plains, the misty rain, the smell of wet trail horses and jumpy longhorns headed to slaughter. The same age the Mexican was now, that's why he thought of it. Just a kid.

In agony he pulled the knife out. Gutiérrez grabbed the paling in both hands and ran at him, aiming to pierce him through and pin him to the barn like a bearskin hung up to dry. Polecat twisted around and lunged the knife at Gutiérrez, but the Mexican knocked it to the ground. And when he bent down to pick it up, Polecat threw himself on his back and wrapped his hands around the rawhide thong that held his leather hat under his chin and pulled back on it with every ounce of strength he could muster until the boy stopped thrashing and gagging and gnawing the dirt.

The black giant Riley had lumbered back to the wagon to fetch his hammer and tongs, heavy, deadly tools that could crush a man's knees and shanks and leave him scuttling like a crab for the rest of his days. Moondog ran at Riley with a sledge hammer fetched from the barn, clashing it against the blacksmith's clanging tongs, and the two of them battered back each other's blows, dueling against the bite of iron death. Fate hovered over them, the fate that all men share, pondering which man it would favor on that smoky August day. Both worthy men—neither deserved to lose that fight.

O'Rourke ran from the wagon waving his ashen cudgel at Crazy Ike, who stood ready to attack with his two-headed axe. Crazy Ike's nickname was no exaggeration, no figure of speech. Since Shiloh, more than twenty years now, he'd answered to no one but the crooning inner voices that commanded violence and mayhem. "Let's call an end to this," O'Rourke said with a smile. "We've got no dog in this fight. Let the Captain and Slater fight it out and when they've killed each other I'll stand you a pint." He could reason with any man, that had been his experience, from County Meath to Chicago to this desert wasteland where men reasoned with their fists. And any man who wouldn't yield to persuasion would know the agony of the ashwood smashing his face.

Crazy Ike glared at the smooth-talking Irishman, twirling the axe above his head, his bloodless lips pulled taut. He hated a man who tried to substitute a bargain for a fight. "Afraid to fight, you cringing cur? I'll split you in half like a Irish potato."

He wheeled and hurled the axe and O'Rourke dodged sideways, the axe spinning past him into the dirt. "Ah, you'll have to aim better than that, you clumsy ape." O'Rourke stood his ground and they locked eyes, the unblinking gaze of death still choosing its victim. Crazy Ike, mad dog that he was, loped back into the barn and scooped up an armful of the hewn palings, fire-hardened cedar, each four feet long, and hurled them one after another at the Irishman. One stuck in his thigh, another in his shoulder, but he paid them no mind. He charged forward like a bull at a matador oblivious to the stakes trailing out of him. Swinging his ashen club he smashed the berserker's forehead, broke his nose, blinded him with blood. But even after meting out such punishment he was no match for Crazy Ike. The frenzied killer embraced him, lifted him up, and threw him headlong on the ground, snapping his neck, then lifted him again, limp, breathless, bleeding from the mouth, and pounded him into the dirt, again and again, until his face was flattened and unrecognizable and he was no longer that man, that fair-haired breaker of horses from County Meath, but a bloody mass of random flesh.

When John Riley the blacksmith saw what had been done to O'Rourke, he turned his back on Moondog and rounded on Crazy Ike, who stood silent, motionless, darkly mindful of his madness and the devastation he had wrought. For an instant it seemed that the two might talk, not to bluff or bargain but to commiserate before the life breath blew away from one or the other of them. But it was not to be: that moment flickered and passed and in another instant they were hell bent on their heartsick work. On an impulse Polecat, unlucky man, leaped between them just as the blacksmith, bellowing like an ox, lurched forward with his arms high and threw all his weight behind his hammer, the ruthless hammer which had beaten pig iron into plowshares, wheel rims, pump handles and a thousand sizzling horseshoes—it came down on Polecat's forehead and split his skull down the middle, and his brains and eyes and his tongue and half his teeth burst out in an explosion like a muffled gunshot. No time for a choking groan or a spasm in the dust, no last glimpse of the barren sky. His limbs went slack and he collapsed in a pile of putrefying meat and offal. And Riley, wielding his tongs, twisted the pulped head off its stem and tossed it in a pile of cow shit beside the corral.

Enraged beyond endurance, Riley had not finished his grand and grisly work. Cruel fragments of his past whirled in around him like suffocating dust, beguiling his vision. The headless Polecat became the Georgia sergeant who ordered him to forge his own shackles, his hammer the hammer he refused to do it with, his whip scars a testament to his defiance.

Crazy Ike stood where Riley had left him, eerily sane, but frozen speechless at the carnage he'd just witnessed. Wondering if he could survive a fight with this man, wondering if this was any way to die, or to kill. Pictures from his own past flashed in his astonishment: the card shark whipped senseless in Amarillo, the brawling mule skinner crushed in Ratón, the foreman in Cripple Creek, an arrogant Yankee hurtling head first down a mineshaft. Lessons learned that could have no bearing on John Riley.

Riley lurched toward Crazy Ike swinging his tongs, aiming to tear his head off as he had done Polecat's. "Wait, damn it!" Crazy Ike shouted, and Riley hesitated, no longer than a heartbeat— whether through surprise, compassion or a pretense of composure—and in that moment Crazy Ike, now more cunning than crazy, crouched and grabbed the shimmering coil of barbed wire that Polecat had left on the ground. He whipped the wire around and snagged Riley's ankles and brought him down hard, caught in the wire. Without hesitation he dragged him tangled in the wire to the chestnut mare he'd left standing by the wagon. He wound the wire around the saddle horn and whipped the horse and the horse bolted forward. Riley bellowed out threats and curses but the chestnut mare knew his voice, he was the blacksmith who'd wrestled her in place, hammered iron into her hoofs, cursed and bellowed at her too. She reared and galloped away, dragging the writhing blacksmith across the broken ground and down into a sharp, rocky ravine until his curses stopped.

Moondog watched them go, shaking his head sadly. "That was a man," he said to Crazy Ike.

One by one the horses' shadows rose in the haze and their riders took on human form as they came toward the trench, slowly now, following Wallace's death agonies—Bob Wallace the singer of tales, who'd ever been quick with a kind word—and when they found him, wide-eyed, surprised by death, they stood a moment studying his tangled guts for an augury of things to come, learning for certain only that he would sing no more. Vickery dismounted and vaulted over the trench and stood at the fence line, angry but unarmed.

"Slater!" he called out. "Let me see your face."

Slater strode forward, his men closing up behind him. They stood looking down from the rise where they'd set up the wagon. "Here it is if you can see it."

"I'm unarmed."

"What do you want?"

"We're giving you a chance to clear out of the basin with your outfit. Those men you left to guard the bull are dead—all three of them—and your camp's a smoldering heap of ashes. You go up into the badland and we won't trouble you no more."

The news about the three men in the camp, lies which they accepted as true, hit Slater's men like a wave of sickness. Moondog, Polecat, Crazy Ike—all dead. Their own lives were worth nothing alongside of that. In their mouths were no words, only the coppery taste of death. Their breath already reeked of it. Even Vickery's men—who'd seen death in Wallace's astonished eyes—couldn't swallow for tasting it. They were the Captain's men, loyal to the Captain, but none had signed up to die for him. They might have been on the other side of that fence, standing with Slater, or somewhere else altogether, still strangers to the terror that choked them now, the fear, the certainty, of headlong death.

"What about the herd?" Slater shouted to Vickery.

"The herd stays here in lieu of the lease payments you never made."

"I never had a lease."

"The Captain's doing you a favor pretending you had one. You been warned plenty of times."

Slater had talked to Buckminster when he returned from the Captain's. Elena was wrong, Buckminster told him—the Captain had ordered Vickery to provoke a confrontation with Slater, but not like this. "The Captain never said to take your herd," Buckminster told him now. "That's Vickery talking. He's trying to get it for himself."

"What's your answer, Slater?" Vickery demanded, head tilted like a deaf man's.

"My cattle ain't going anywhere," Slater said. "My men neither."

The men sent up a cheer and a torrent of insults aimed at Vickery, who stood motionless as if to repel them. The yellow cur had skulked up beside him, aping his stance, head tilted, snarling, while the other dogs cowered in supplication to the wolves. Then

Vickery motioned behind him with his left hand in the air. His men obeyed, as soldiers always do, dismounting and leaping across the trench with tools in their hands to cut the barbed wire. Slater's men, their shotguns and rifles within easy reach, could have mowed them down between the trench and the wire, or on the wire as they tried to cut it, and had they been as men are now they would have done it. But in those times when men still had their self-respect there were limits to what they would do.

Instead they left their firearms behind and surged down to the fence line and beat back Vickery's men with palings and axe handles and whips, pressing so close to them (as Slater had ordered beforehand), and so quickly, that Vickery's men could defend themselves only with their fists or by using their guns as clubs. Potter opened a welt on Viklund's cheek with his whip, Hank Crenshaw broke Galogly's arm with an axe handle, Rory leaped on Herzog, the German who claimed to be an aristocrat, and wrestled his face into the dirt. Others of Vickery's men fell back, their clothes tangled in the wire, stumbling to avoid the trench, their horses rearing and screaming behind them, the dogs yowling but cringing back—they fought with their fists, their heads, their rifle butts, but they couldn't repel the attackers, and many of them, finally, turned their backs and disappeared into the haze. And it might have ended there if Vickery, who'd backed away from the fence line when the assault came, hadn't raised his .45 and calmly shot Crenshaw (who just a week before had taken five hundred dollars off him at the poker table with a straight flush) between the eyes.

Again the silence of grim death rang in their ears and its taste welled up in every throat. A few racing heartbeats passed in that silence and they all knew without reckoning the price of Vickery's wickedness. His men turned and tried to run as wrath descended on Slater's outfit and they lost all pity and restraint. They leaped on

Vickery's men with ruthless axe handles and keen cedar palings and flaying whips and tore them down to death.

Rory knew all the men who died in the fit of rage triggered by Crenshaw's murder. Galogly, the taciturn Irishman, whose arm Crenshaw had smashed with an axe handle, couldn't defend himself when Jameson leaped on him and clubbed his brains out with the butt of his own rifle. The pacifist Viklund, gushing blood where Potter had whipped his face, stood motionless as if defying any man to make him fight, and Finnerty, who'd been Crenshaw's best friend, set upon him with an axe handle and pummeled him until he clawed the dust. And then Rory himself had his baptism in blood. He saw Herzog draw his pearl-handled revolver from his belt and swivel toward Slater, and Rory picked up a paling and hurled it at him like a spear. It caught him in the throat and he rattled out a strangled scream as blood spurted over his clutching hands and his limbs went slack. Vickery turned and ran and the dogs and the rest of his men scrambled after him into the haze.

"Don't chase them," Slater called out. "Come on over here."

He led them up the hill to the wagon where he reminded them of the strategy they'd agreed on. Spread out in small groups to defend the herd, staying near the weapons caches. Don't attack them, let them attack and fight back if you have to. Push the herd to the north and west, don't let them stampede it south.

The men stood silent, awe-struck by the killers in their midst. Jameson wild-eyed with Galogly's hideous death, Finnerty bent in half, coughing to disguise his sobbing. Rory, heart pounding, breath wheezing, suffocating in his isolation: suddenly he was a man apart, an intruder in unexplored territory. He had killed a man, speared him like a savage. A jovial German in white kid gloves who'd bought him a beer at the saloon. Watched him die choking on his own blood.

"I saw what you did," Slater told Rory, and Rory looked away. "Appreciate it."

Rory's stomach gave a heave. Appreciate it. Always good to be appreciated.

"After you kill a man," Finnerty told him, "you'll never be the same." He coughed out a laugh. "The next one's easier."

"This ain't over," Slater said, turning to the others. "We're lucky we only lost one man. They lost four. But don't let that go to your head. How many men've they got? Thirty to our twelve? They outnumber us three to one."

Buckminster had stayed out of the fray, something most of the men noticed. They wondered whether Slater had noticed, and how could he not have? The foreman never seemed to get his hands dirty and Slater never seemed to notice. "Maybe they've had enough," Buckminster said. "Four men dead. How's Vickery going to explain that to the Captain?"

"They'll be back," Slater said, "and next time they'll have their guns ready. Here's what we got to do. Cut that wire, let their herd come through and drive it below ours so they won't dare start a stampede."

Rory joined the others in cutting the wire and driving the Captain's cattle east across the trench and into the flat. Then he cantered north with Littlefield and DeGraff, a couple of boys from the Panhandle, to a gully where earlier they'd stashed three shotguns, three rifles and a supply of shells and rounds. A few cattle had drifted into the gully.

"No need to go any further," Littlefield said. "We can stay right here and protect them beeves."

"That's right," DeGraff agreed. DeGraff always agreed with Littlefield, as if he didn't have a brain of his own.

They hollowed out kneeling places just below the rim of the gully where they could sight over the edge and keep their heads down when the shooting started. Littlefield and DeGraff seemed to think it was a joke, a boyish prank like the ones they used to play back home. "Them fellas ain't coming back here after the whupping they took," Littlefield said. DeGraff agreed.

Rory knew better. Slater was right—they'd be back and this time they'd shoot to kill. He loaded a rifle and a shotgun and crouched below the rim of the gully squinting into the smoke, trying not to think about what he was getting ready for. He'd killed his first man that morning. How many would he kill before the day was done? It never occurred to him that somebody might kill him. He was only twenty-one years old. His mouth was so dry he couldn't swallow his own spit. His mind raced. How was he going to tell Elena what he'd done? She'd find out, so there was no point in hiding it. Come right out and say it: he'd killed a man to save Slater. A life for a life, maybe a better one, maybe not. He owed Slater his life but he only owed Herzog the price of a beer.

In the midst of all this confusion Buckminster had disappeared into the smoke. He circled west toward the hollow where Vickery had gathered his men and caught sight of him waiting on the crown of a low rise. Vickery beckoned to Buckminster and Buckminster trotted his horse up to greet him. Too late he noticed Vickery's shotgun braced over the pommel of his saddle. Pointing at him.

"You son of a bitch," Vickery said.

Buckminster didn't flinch. "You think I could have stopped that? You brought it on yourself, sending your men into that trench and shooting Crenshaw."

"What do I get for being your partner?"

"You get what I told you you'd get. I'll take care of the Captain and his family and you can have the ranch. But first you've got to get Slater and Rory out of my way."

"Shoot them yourself," Vickery said. He raised his shotgun inch by inch until it was level with Buckminster's crystal blue eyes.

"If any of Slater's men see me do that, I'll be dead," he said.

"If you don't do it, you'll be dead. I promise you that."

Vickery had to hand it to Buckminster. The son of a bitch didn't rattle easy. You could point a shotgun at his blue eyes and threaten to pull the trigger and he just stared back at you like a dead man. Something about him wasn't right but that was why he was willing to shoot the Captain and his wife, especially the wife—all the other men would have been sure she'd drag them down to hell.

"Listen," Buckminster said, "I want to help you. Forget about the barbed wire and just send your men around to loop down on them from the north. Slater'll be waiting for you with his crew in small groups dug into the draws. He told them not to fire unless fired upon. If you follow me you can get close enough to wipe them out before they fire a shot."

"Or for them to wipe us out."

"Like I said, Slater won't let his men fire until you do. When you see them, sweet talk them into letting you come close. No shooting, no threats. Ride in close enough to kill Slater and Rory before they know what hit them. If you kill those two you won't have any problem with the others."

"You think they'll just give up?"

"I know they will. Every one of them's a coward born and bred."

Littlefield and DeGraff were smoking and swapping dirty stories, giggling when they finished one. Rory couldn't stand the waiting or the fretting it gave him time for. Why had their side so quickly gained the advantage? Because they were in the right, he wanted to say, but no, that was a fairy tale and he knew it. The men in his outfit weren't any better than the Captain's. Righteousness, justice, moral law, whatever it was—if it existed in that basin—was an afterthought, an excuse you made up later for killing somebody. For the first time since Slater had pulled him out of the Rio Concho when he was eight years old, he wanted to run away. Not out of fear (there goes his innocence again, Slater would have said, he's fool enough to think there's nothing to be afraid of), but out of disgust, physical disgust—he could taste it, gagging in his throat—at being trapped in this basin, this life, this brittle, vacant sandstone world.

Slater had dug into a nearby sand wash with three or four men, Jameson with his bunch in a draw farther off. The wolves and ravens had migrated with them, taking up their lookout on top of a low butte half a mile away. By this time a large segment of the Captain's herd had crossed the trench and browsed their way east and south of Slater's. Peering west, Rory saw Buckminster riding toward them, alone, his face as pale as a corpse. When he spotted Slater ensconced in the wash he galloped toward him. "I've been out scouting," Buckminster said. "Vickery's riding in from up there." He pointed northwest, the direction he'd come from. "I was lucky to get back here before they saw me."

Slater never saw through Buckminster's lies, until it was too late. "They're coming, boys," he shouted to the men. "Get ready."

Time hung in the air like the smoke, past present and future aswirl as every man counted his sins and his forlorn hopes and wondered how many more breaths he would take. Five minutes trembled by, an hour or a year by some reckonings in those sandy dugouts. Every man wishing he was someplace else—all but Littlefield and DeGraff, who still thought it was a joke.

Then, still gazing west, Rory saw it: a spectral cavalry floating behind the scrim of smoke, the horses bobbing as if they were treading water, the dogs weaving around them, the men upright, staring straight ahead. Vickery led the way with the Captain's yellow cur, its muzzle up, lips snarled back, bristling for a fight, but the men held no weapons and signaled no intention to attack.

Slater ordered his outfit to stand down. "Don't shoot!"

Vickery waved his hat and his men raised their empty hands in a gesture of surrender. They came forward at a walking pace, the smoke dissolving around them, close enough that Rory could name each man, tell you his life story if he had time. Their eyes were blank, lips taut and pale.

"We don't need to fight," Vickery called out. "Let's talk."

"Stop there and we'll talk," Slater yelled, raising himself over the edge of the wash to answer Vickery.

They kept coming and Slater waited. Rory didn't like it. He didn't trust Vickery or any of those men, they were the Captain's minions, their minds set on killing. They didn't stop and Slater let them keep coming.

Finally Slater shouted, "Stop, I said!" but it was too late. The man riding beside Vickery—his name was Murtaugh, he'd been a sharpshooter in the rebel army—suddenly raised his rifle and shot at Slater and before Rory or anyone could react Vickery's entire force was firing—rifles, pistols, shotguns, whatever came to hand—as they charged forward, yelling and screaming like savages amid the explosions and the pounding and gasping of horses, the dogs baying and running in circles. Bullets whizzed past Rory's head and then above it as he ducked and slid behind the rim of the gully.

"Stay down!" he shouted. "Shoot them if they stick their heads over the edge."

No sooner had he said that when a boy named Kelleher (Rory had played cards with him twice, he was a soft-spoken boy, not much older than Rory, who talked about his parents' farm in Missouri), reared on his mount over the edge, wheeling his pistol toward Littlefield. Rory had his shotgun poised and ready to fire. The shot sprayed Kelleher's leg and his horse's flank, bringing them down toppling into the gully, the man firing wildly, pleading with his eyes, when he recognized Rory, and Rory hesitated. But Littlefield, less forgiving (or perhaps because he hadn't already killed a man that day), blew the top of Kelleher's head off with his shotgun.

Next over the rim came Bagley, a big man with a prophet's voice and a Colt .45 drawn and ready to fire. "You'll die for that," he told Littlefield, and Littlefield had no time to plead, even with his eyes. Bagley dispatched him and wheeled toward the cringing DeGraff and said: "And you, DeGraff" (for the killers on both sides knew each victim's name and the place he called home, even the names of his sisters, who, but for the killing, they might have hoped to marry someday)—and having uttered that name he paused over DeGraff, weighing his words, for a prophet with a gun can easily speak to a man's future. And Rory, who had hoped not to kill again, raised his shotgun and shot Bagley in the neck rather than watch him fill DeGraff's empty brain with lead. And without another word Bagley went down to writhe in the dirt.

Rory retched and almost vomited, his mind spinning with the realization that he would have to die for this nightmare to end. He rode out of the gully expecting to be shot. Dust swirled around him like a mist and he passed as if invisible. The sulfur of gunpowder and the curses of men had fouled the bitter air with the stench of murder. The men raced every which way, shooting randomly, it seemed, flailing at each other with knives and whips and sharpened fence palings. Those men looked different now. They no longer had names or faces or any other mark of individuality. They were soulless fighting machines he could kill or be killed by without conscience or regret, partners in the unholy romance of battle. For in death all men are equal and alike.

The horses screamed, the dogs bayed, the cattle bellowed and stamped the dirt, ready to stampede if they only knew where. Rory raced to the sand wash and found Slater face down, blood drenching the dirt around him, while his men struggled to defend their position. Two were already dead: Potter, who could rope a steer on the run from a hundred paces, and Brubaker, a wild-eyed deserter who talked with a stammer and read his Bible every night. And on the Captain's side there were three: Snyder, the freckle-faced choirboy who drank whiskey for breakfast, lunch and dinner; Ortiz, up from Mexico, always pining for the girl he left behind; and Thibodeau, a proud Cajun who'd never stopped fighting the war, the darkness swirling in his eyes as he clawed the dirt. So many dead, Rory thought, the end must be near.

Long-haired Finnerty, a braggart and often a drunk, stood with his rifle on the far edge of the wash, bellowing out taunts and insults, daring anyone who'd listen to hesitate just long enough for him to shoot them. "Come on, you scumsucking sons of bitches! If you want to die, step right over here!" He caught a glimpse of a man skulking away and landed a round in the middle of his back. The man pitched in the dust.

"You're a bunch of old women, is what you are," Finnerty yelled, "who've never come up against a man. Shoot me if you can, but I'm warning you I'll take you with me."

Gunshots rang out and he dodged right and left as if he could see them coming. More firing and he danced away laughing and hooting. Nothing could touch him until Murtaugh, the Tennessee sharpshooter who'd taken Slater down, fixed him in his sights— Murtaugh who always wore a silver crucifix around his neck, who in his glory days during the war nested on wooded hillsides picking bluecoats off their wagons like pigeons. He aimed and without thinking pulled the trigger. Finnerty's long hair flared out and his knees buckled and his life slipped away on the wind.

On the low butte the wolves pranced and howled, tongues lolling, the ravens drifting above them. A dozen ravens rode the wind to the rocks below. All biding their time. The dogs—save the yellow cur, which stayed with Vickery—slinked toward the butte in supplication to the wolves, as if awaiting their command.

Rory knelt beside Slater, trying to stop his bleeding with a torn shirt. He'd been shot in the left shoulder. "I'll be all right," Slater said, his voice gasping and weak. "Look out for yourself."

Rory scrabbled to the rim of the wash and saw men on both sides drunk with the thrill and horror of battle. Gunfire exploding, horses rearing, frenzied fighting at close range. Slater's outnumbered forces were in retreat, backing into the wash. In a few minutes Vickery's men would command the rim and shoot them all like rats in a barrel.

Then a pair of phantoms breasted the smoke and charged howling into Vickery's men. Two corpses risen from the dead—Moondog and Crazy Ike. They rode like berserkers, slashing and killing everything and everyone in their path with axes, palings, pistols, entangling coils of barbed wire. They were not themselves—hadn't Vickery already announced their deaths?—but accursed spirits belched out of the earth in a visitation that shocked and terrified both sides. Slater's men poured out of the wash as Vickery's army dissolved into the smoke, pounded from the rear until few were left standing.

Rory stayed with Slater, holding his arm up to stanch the flow of blood "That was Murtaugh who shot me," he said bitterly. "Broke the truce and shot me cold."

"I'll get him," Rory said.

Slater's eyes blazed. "No, save him for me. Vickery too."

16.

The Captain stood on his colonnaded porch, the ruler of an island lost in the mist, earth and sky gray as the sea, watching: the mottled range in front of him, unseen, the dusty yard, the empty corrals, the arching wagon gate drifting in and out of view as the wind ebbed and flowed. There were no shadows in that smoke, yet everything seemed a shadow. Not to worry about the fire, he told himself: it would burn itself out, leaving blackened skeletons of trees with no chance of living anyway, ash piling up on the slick kilned earth of a burn scar. The men were out on the range working with the herd—he'd seen Vickery ride out to join them. But something wasn't right—more than something: everything seemed wrong today. He worried about his son. Why had Vickery sent Luke to Slater's camp with only three men, when he'd told him to take six? Slater would return the bull, surely, but if there was any resistance Luke wasn't the one to deal with it, those other men either, O'Rourke and Gutiérrez, hotheads who'd been known to court trouble, Riley a blacksmith who must have been taken along for the chains and shackles they'd need to bind up the bull.

"Where are my dogs?" he asked Jacinta suddenly.

"They ran off after Vickery when he rode out," she said, her inflamed eyes fixed on the invisible horizon, awaiting Luke's return. She stood with her teeth clenched, her thin lips stretched tight: the face of a woman on the edge of an abyss. Luke had been gone too long. How long could it take him to bring back that bull?

"The yellow cur go with them?"

"It did."

The shouts, the screams, the bitter tumult of the battle being fought a few miles away did not reach the Captain's ears, but for a muffled popping that might have been whips cracking or horses kicking in their stalls. A figure on horseback emerged from the smoke and opened the corral gate. It was Elena, returning from the high meadow where she'd met Rory a few hours before. She rubbed her sorrel mare down and led it into the barn, where she found Charlie Crow crouched on a hay bale with his head in his hands. She could hear shooting in the distance. "I'm going to try telling my father one more time," she said.

"It's too late," Crow said without looking up.

She stepped outside and climbed the stairs to the porch where her mother and father stood, her stomach churning. The absence of Vickery and all the hands could only mean that they'd ridden off on their mission of destruction.

Jacinta shot her a menacing glance. "Go inside, Elena."

"I'm going to tell him again," she said. "Maybe he'll listen this time."

Her mother looked as insubstantial as the smoke, her face paper thin, her complexion bloodless. "Go inside, I said."

The Captain woke from his reverie. "Tell me what?"

"Vickery rode out with the men to kill Slater and destroy his cattle."

"No"—he seemed more surprised than angry this time—"I told him not to do that."

"He did it anyway. Don't you hear the shooting?"

Jacinta tossed her head and smiled, openly and shamelessly because she knew it was too late to stop Vickery. "He imagines that he still rules over men," she told Elena.

Elena stood still. "Listen." She pointed northeast where a faint rumble rolled across the plain like some phantom buffalo herd come back from Indian times.

"It's thunder," the Captain said.

"No, it's a stampede."

He stepped forward and listened closely, then his face darkened. "Was this Luke's idea? Did Luke tell them to do this?"

"Luke went to Slater's camp to get the bull," Elena said, "like you told him to. That stampede is north of Slater's camp, though it's moving south."

He grabbed Jacinta's arm and spun her around. "Did you know about this?"

"Let go of me! Of course I knew about it. Every fool in the outfit knew about it except you. You're the only one who doesn't know what has to be done."

"Vickery," the Captain muttered, his wild eyes on Elena. "It was Vickery, wasn't it?"

She nodded. "It was his idea. I tried to tell you but you wouldn't listen."

"Did they kill Slater?"

"I don't know." Turning away to hide her anguish, her sickening fear.

He collapsed on a pine bench and sat wringing his hands. "There's nothing I can do about it now, is there?" He sounded almost relieved, as if fate had no further use for him.

She heard Rory's voice instead of her father's, telling her it was all right, the violence and death that came to the basin that day would pass him by. "Probably not," she said, lightheaded, disbelieving.

The Captain stood up and put his arm around her, steadying both of them against the porch railing. "Did you ever hear the buffalo when they stampeded?" he asked gently, as if Slater was the farthest thing from his mind. "No, I guess not, they were gone before your time. You could hear them miles away like a hundred locomotives, raising dust up to the clouds. They ran like an earthquake, blind, mad, beating thunder out of the earth. They never stopped, they pounded on until all that was left was the dust."

They heard gunshots, angry volleys of them, as the thunder rolled south. It was moving away from them now, toward the Vale of Tears.

The Captain mustered a smile. "At least it's not my herd."

Jacinta wheeled toward him like a bird of prey. "You sent our son out there," she shrieked as he fought her back. "You sent Luke out there to fight that devil."

In a few minutes the thunder would stop, too suddenly, as if the cattle had run off the end of the earth. Elena would wonder: Was it the quiet of peace, or the quiet of death? And the smoke, which all day had been drifting in behind them, blew into their faces from the east.

Rory felt the earth shaking as the thunder of pounding hoofs rolled toward him. He scrambled up to the rim of the wash and saw a sight no man could forget. A couple hundred longhorns from the Captain's herd raced east in a cloud of dust and as they ran they frightened the rest of the herd, a thousand or two thousand strong, into stampeding south toward the hay fields and the Vale of Tears. Buckminster bobbed in the midst of them, whether caught in the flood or driving them on seemed beyond his control. From a distance Vickery saw the stampede forming and assumed that the cattle were Slater's. Well, he thought, he'd carried out his part of the bargain, or the most important part of it, when Murtaugh shot Slater. Surprising how naive Buckminster had turned out, trusting him not to shoot him in the back, even after he'd claimed the girl, when he should have known there wasn't a man in that basin who wouldn't have shot him to get that girl for himself. He wasn't about to shoot him just now. Let him drive Slater's herd wherever he wanted and then go back and kill the Captain and his family, minus the girl, and there'd be plenty of time for recriminations—best to shoot him before he talked about their deal.

But to Slater's outfit there was no mistaking those frenzied cattle—they were the Captain's, marked by his brand on the right flank facing them—and they assumed that Buckminster was driving them.

"Let's go, boys!" Moondog cried out. "Get behind that herd!"

Rory leaped on his horse and galloped with Moondog after Buckminster, both firing their pistols in the air to keep the cattle charging in the right direction. "Where in hell's Buckminster going with this herd?" he yelled at Moondog.

Moondog grinned back at him with mad-dog eyes. "I reckon he means to drive it over the cliff."

When he grasped what Moondog had said, Rory lost his balance and almost fell off his horse. The thought of such an outrage made his head swim with disbelief and disgust. Even after all the bloodshed he'd witnessed that day he was not prepared for this. He wanted to escape into the smoke, but his horse, running alongside Moondog's, was caught up in the chase, enormous crook-horned beasts lumbering on three sides and now behind them as stragglers trampled out of the draws. There was no turning them back, no matter why they'd started. How many were there? A thousand? Two thousand? Racing to be sacrificed, smelling their doom—in their terror they were closing in around him and Moondog. They were no longer driving the stampede but part of it.

When Vickery saw Rory and Moondog—and later Crazy Ike— falling in behind Buckminster he realized his mistake. Buckminster had recalculated his chances and betrayed him. It was the Captain's herd they were driving, and suddenly he knew where they were headed. "Damn it to hell!" he shouted to the remnants of his troops. "Chase them sons of bitches down and shoot every last one of them!" And with the yellow cur belling at his heels he led his men down through Disappointment Draw toward the hay field where the farmhands had just finished baling the hay and stacking it in the lean-to sheds for the winter.

They took a shortcut and reached the hay field ahead of the stampede, which thundered toward him like a runaway train. The bewildered farmhands—mostly boys from town, earning seven cents an hour—stood waiting with their scythes and rakes for the disaster to arrive. The yellow cur held them at bay, ready to leap at their throats if they turned and ran.

"Burn this hay!" Vickery called out. He rode in front of the sheds, shooting into the bales in hopes of igniting them. Some of the boys lit matches and sticks and ran behind him lighting fires, and as Vickery had intended a wall of white smoke plumed up from the sheds and flames blazed around them and when the first wave of frenzied cattle arrived they spread out to avoid the fire and for a while the stampede lost its momentum. But Buckminster, riding wildly in the midst of the chaos, kept driving the cattle south in a narrowing spiral. Rory and Moondog and the others were swept along behind him.

Vickery raised his rifle but lost them in the smoke. He sat his horse in front of the burning sheds with Murtaugh and Quire and the others who were left. The smoke parted, revealing Crazy Ike charging toward them, howling and screaming with his shotgun raised. But before Vickery and Murtaugh could aim their rifles the smoke closed back around them.

"Stop them!" Vickery shouted at the farm boys. The boys ran forward through the stubble waving their sickles and scythes, invisible in the smoke, and before they were seen again the shotgun boomed and death struck them down.

The fire had spread from the sheds to the edges of the field. Reeling in desperation, Vickery galloped south with those few of his men who were still alive. They tried to turn the spiraling herd, but in its panic to escape the flames it surrounded them and sucked them in.

Rory whirled in the same maelstrom, from which, he realized, there could never be an escape. The land pitched downward now—they must have surged into the narrow defile called the Vale of Tears—and in a moment's time they'd be swept across the canyon rim to plunge headlong over a thousand feet of crumbling shale to the boulder-strewn riverbed below.

All at once the sea of cattle parted and the pandemonium of the stampede froze in place, its hellish din muted to eerie silence as if his life, in its last moments, was to be spread out before him and he would be offered one last chance to make the choices he never made, and in that delusory heartbeat he caught a glimpse of Vickery, as white as a ghost, riding with Murtaugh and Quire and he thought he ought to shoot them but he remembered his last conversation with Slater and the instructions not to shoot Vickery or Murtaugh but to leave them for Slater, but it was like something out of a dream, it made no sense at a time like this when they would all be dead before he could draw another breath, and then still within this timeless dream he felt a massive arm slide around his shoulders and he was plucked out of his saddle and laid over the pommel of another and it was Moondog, reputedly a dead man, who had snatched him off his horse and was carrying him to the farthest edge of the rampaging herd. Crazy Ike, another dead man, rode with them and they stopped when they came to a rocky outcrop that shielded them from the torrent, and there they found another man sprawled on the rocks, clutching the reins of a dead horse crushed against the ledge. It was Quire, the man who never stopped talking. He was one of the Captain's men but Rory gave no thought to that. "I never signed up for this," Quire said. "I certainly never signed up for this. I could've told Vickery it would end this way if he'd asked, anybody could've told him that, and I'll tell you something else—" but before he could finish his words, blood spurted out of his mouth and the end closed in around him.

When the last of the cattle disappeared over the rim and the thundering agony of their descent to the rocks below had ended, a mournful silence engulfed the men left behind in the Vale of Tears, clinging to rocks or ancient roots or to the trampled remains of horses or men. The silence echoed with the recollection of what preceded it, the men's minds throbbing, howling, whirling. None dared a groan or a murmur. Had they done this or had they been caught up in a savage convulsion of nature? A bloody sacrifice had kept the world from ending. That was all they knew.

Who was left? Rory, Moondog, Crazy Ike. They were the only ones from Slater's outfit. From the Captain's only Murtaugh was still breathing. The two foremen, if they'd survived, must have been absorbed into crevices in the rock.

Rory rode back to Slater's camp behind Moondog, arms halfway around the giant's waist, leaning into him, still stunned, spent with lingering fear. Crazy Ike followed along on a horse that was blind and stumbling. They still breathed the madness of battle, still vibrated with the thunder of eight thousand hoofs, the lightning fervor of death. There was no talking, no boasting, no grieving for those they'd never see again.

"Vickery told us the three of you were dead," Rory said. "You and Crazy Ike and Polecat."

"Vickery's a damn liar," Moondog said. "He was right about Polecat though."

Slater had arrived at the camp a few minutes ahead of them, stretched out in the wagon bed among the breathless dead—Crenshaw, Littlefield, Potter, Finnerty—plus some of the Captain's men. Many others had to be left behind, guarded by Jameson to hold the wolves at bay. Slater was still alive, pale as the clay butte but still alive. Behind the wagon trudged a file of prisoners, what were left of Vickery's men, roped together with their hands tied behind them. Ravens croaked overhead, wolves loped ahead in a wide invisible circle.

Slater climbed out of the wagon with the help of Rory and Moondog and lowered himself onto the log he used as a seat by the fire. "Is this all that's left of you?" he asked Rory. "Where's Buckminster?"

"I ain't seen him. Vickery neither."

Even after all he'd seen and done that day, Slater was appalled by the scene of carnage spread out before him at the camp. Polecat's head torn off by the blacksmith's tongs. O'Rourke mauled and unrecognizable in the dirt. Gutiérrez's tongue black and hanging out of his mouth like a water snake. Riley dragged to ribbons in the gully. And who was that dead man over there, masked with his own blood?

"That's Luke," Moondog said.

Slater's voice caught in his throat. "Which one of you killed him?"

"We didn't kill him," Moondog said, glancing at Crazy Ike. "We thought about it, after Riley got dragged into the gully. There was two of us left and only one of him. He stood there gawking in his red shirt like the fool that he was. His face looked sick and his teeth was chattering like magpies. We could have shot him, and we would have if he went back to his wagon for a gun. But he knew he was safer without one."

"Then what happened to him?"

After the fight was over, after Gutiérrez and O'Rourke and Riley had all been killed, Luke opened the corral gate and stepped inside. He wasn't afraid of Moondog and Crazy Ike—they wouldn't dare touch him—or even of the bull. He was afraid of his father. Walking away from the fight without a scratch and three men dead. Better men than he—the Captain wouldn't have said that if his mother was listening, he would have waited and humiliated him in front of the men, daring them to take it out of his hide. They loved to rub his nose in all the hurt and anger he had stored up in him, trying to lure it out so they could pounce on him, and his father thought that would make a man of him, though everybody knew he never would be. He wasn't good with his hands or smart with the livestock or with the men either. All he'd ever wanted to do was get out of the basin.

And now he stood face to face with this blooded bull, black as the pit of hell, who hated him, hated his weakness just like his father did, hated his red shirt, hated the sound of his voice. It stood unchained in the corral, studying him with its enormous dripping eyes, snuffling and snorting as he opened the gate, tipping its broad head and its twisted horns, pawing the dirt. He stood still, averted his gaze, tried to swallow his fear. This is what it means to be a man, he told himself. It was another chance, maybe his last chance, to show that he could do a man's work. His father would always be disappointed in him no matter what he did. His mother would cry over him, try to protect him, but he'd never loved her, even when he was a little child. She showed him no respect. His sister was the only one he'd ever loved. He wished she could be here to see this.

He had to get the bull lashed up, bound in his toils, so he could drag it out to the wagon. How could he do that by himself? Moondog and Crazy Ike wouldn't help him, no point in asking them. They stood covered in blood, grinning, nodding their heads to urge him on. Flies swarmed indifferently around them and the four dead bodies. "Go ahead," Moondog said. "You can take your bull."

He tried lassoing the bull but it flicked off the lasso with its horns. He tried again and the bull lowered its head, eyeing him with disdain, and shrugged the rope off. Finally he twirled the rope around one of its hind legs and lashed it to the stubbing post. The bull tried to kick the rope off, lunged forward and split the post in half. Then it wheeled to face him, spraddling between him and the gate, daring him to take a step. It groaned and tossed its head, its sleek flanks glistening with sweat and swarming flies. It switched its tail and bellowed and pawed the dirt, then it raised its wide brow to the shrouded sky and roared out its demon chorus, just as the cattle traders said it would. Overcome with terror, he uncoiled his whip and lashed it over the bull with a crack like a rifle shot, screaming in an unholy fury: "Get back, get back you monster!"

When the bull heard his voice it sprang toward him in a frenzy and he brought the whip down on its glistening eyes. That was his last chance to fight back, his last chance to escape from the basin, his last chance to be a man. The bull snagged his red shirt on one of its barbed horns and tangled him up in it, twisted him around like a plaything, skewered him through the belly and dragged him through the corral fence. Then it tossed his broken body aside and charged across the plain with a strip of his shirt flapping on its horn like a matador's cape.

"We didn't even try to stop him," Moondog told Slater. "I told him, Go ahead, you can take your bull."

17

The yellow cur loped in ahead of the other dogs, grim and silent while the others bayed and howled, tails between their legs. It was the first sign that something was amiss in the balance of death between man and beast. The cur ran to the Captain on the porch and licked his hand while the others remained below, noses in the dirt, cringing in obeisance. "It's a sign," Jacinta said. "It's a sign that Luke is all right."

"Of course it is," Elena said.

There had been other signs—the drumbeat of the stampede, the smoke and shooting in the east, the sudden rain quenching the western fire—and to Jacinta they all meant that Luke was safe.

"I'll go out and look for him," the Captain said, slipping on his boots.

"No, don't go. He'll come back soon."

Then they saw the bull, the blooded Avileña Negra bull—there was nothing remotely like it in the basin—that Luke had gone to fetch. It wandered out of the sand wash and struck north across the range, trailing a red banner from one of its horns, a trophy of its combat with Luke.

"That's Luke's shirt," Elena said, choking on the tears she'd been holding back.

"Nonsense," Jacinta said.

A man they recognized as Murtaugh shambled toward them. As usual he wore a silver cross around his neck with Jesus hanging from it. He'd slipped away from Slater's camp on account of the debt he owed Slater, which he knew had to be paid in blood. He moved like a dead man walking and smelled like the filth that covered him. To the Captain's questions he responded like a spectator who'd played no role in the drama. He described the battle, the stampede, the fire and the catastrophe: the bawling cattle, the screaming horses, the maddened hoofs skidding down the rotten shale, the headlong pitch into the thundering silence of the distant riverbed. The cattle, a thousand, two thousand of them, groaning on the rocks.

The Captain's face bloodless, his voice faltering. "This was Vickery's doing?"

"Yes, sir, he led us out there."

"Did he survive?"

"I ain't seen him." Murtaugh's eyes tried to dodge the Captain's: right, left, down into the earth, away from the inevitable question.

"And Luke?"

"Your son is dead, sir. Gored by the bull."

"That's a lie," Jacinta cried out. "Why would you believe this man? Slater sent him up here to lie to you."

"I saw him where the bull tossed him, ma'am, folded almost in half. At Slater's camp."

She rounded on the messenger, bayed at him like a hound. "Luke is safe! Don't lie to me!"

"Jacinta—"

"Slater sent this man to lure you down there. Don't fall for his tricks! Have you no pride, letting him bait his trap with your own son?"

The Captain stepped in front of his wife and asked Murtaugh: "Is his body safe or has he been eaten by dogs?"

"He's on the ground, sir, drenched in his own blood, black with flies."

Elena, weeping, laid her arm across her mother's shoulders and tried to pull her aside, but she shook her off, flapping her arms, and twisted away screeching like some bird of evil omen. "What are you doing?"

The Captain had strapped on his holster and revolver and pulled a shotgun down from the gun rack. "I'm going to get the body," he said, without looking at either his wife or his daughter. "Murtaugh, you and Zeke bring the wagon out and yoke up the two mares. Put a blanket in the back to wind around him."

In the yard, as the Captain waited for the wagon, Jacinta gored him with her stiletto eyes. "You should be ashamed of yourself, going down there to beg for your son's body—as if he were dead."

"I'm not going to beg," he said, trying not to look at her. "I'll pay Slater to let me bring the boy home."

"Pay him? What a disgrace!" She circled him while the men hauled the wagon out of the barn and hitched the mares. "Listen to me: he's not dead. If they've captured him, make them release him."

"Let me go with you, Captain," Murtaugh said.

For the first time the Captain showed his fury. "Get away from this wagon," he shouted, raising his whip at Murtaugh. "You lost the battle, lost the herd, let them kill Luke. Stay here cowering with this woman where you belong."

Elena climbed on the wagon seat beside her father. "I'm going with you."

"No, stay here with your mother. She needs you here."

Jacinta tried to pull her down. "Don't go! They'll kill you."

"I'm going with him."

Jacinta seized the reins out of the Captain's hands and twirled them around her wrists, stopping the mares, pulling them back, whipping their eyes with the loose ends. They heaved and staggered, almost upsetting the wagon. The men jumped on Jacinta and dragged her away, screaming and scratching. Old Zeke tossed the reins back to the Captain and he lashed the wagon away.

His hands shook as he drove. "She's right," he told Elena, "you should get out of the wagon. They're going to kill us. They've killed everybody else."

She stopped sobbing when he said that. "They won't kill anybody while I'm there."

Slater's camp reeked of dead bodies and wounded and heartsick men. A dozen blear-eyed prisoners moiled in the corral, hatless, bound together with their hands behind them, Crazy Ike prodding them with a whip and a sharpened stake like cattle balking on the ramp into the slaughterhouse. Other men patrolled the corral with shotguns to remind the prisoners that their chastisement remained undecided. There was no forgiveness in their leaden eyes.

Slater himself lay propped up on a cot his men had dragged from the bunkhouse.

Moondog had removed the bullet from his shoulder but he remained weak from loss of blood. Wounded and weak is a dangerous condition for any leader—he's never safe with the tang of blood in the air around him. Mutiny is never more than a heartbeat away. The least irresolution or disobedience may trigger it. They all expected treachery, more treachery, from the Captain, and when they saw his wagon cresting the rise they reached for their guns and searched the landscape for his minions. That there seemed to be only two people on the wagon—the Captain and one other—only inflamed their suspicion of a sneak attack. "We ain't going to be sitting ducks this time," Moondog said, not as a hope or even an intention but as an order to the men and a rebuke to Slater, who'd been tricked into allowing the last ambush. "Who else they got in the back of that wagon?"

Rory was the first to realize that the other person in the wagon was Elena. "Hold off!" he called out. "That's Elena in the wagon."

Slater sat up and saw her. "No shooting!" he shouted, and to some of the men it seemed sickeningly like the last time, when Vickery had nearly guiled them to slaughter.

The wagon trundled closer and the Captain came into focus, his face tallow, as if he'd been bled and rendered. Elena sat beside him sobbing into a kerchief. No one could believe the Captain would hide behind a woman's tears, least of all his daughter's. Rory heard some of the men's guns click as they drew and cocked them. Without thinking, he stepped toward the wagon, hands up as if he was surrendering to the Captain—in fact only trying to keep from alarming him. The men sensed treachery. The ravens who'd lighted on the sheds stopped muttering and hunched up their wings. The Captain's dogs, who'd followed the prisoners to Slater's camp, ran out toward their master, then thought better of it. They stood and barked as if he was an intruder, and when the wagon kept coming they turned and skulked back to the corral.

"Rory!" Slater called out. "Get back here!"

Rory stopped but stood his ground between the armed men and the wagon, waited for it to pass. The Captain and Elena gave no sign of recognition, neither to him nor to the men in the corral, their own men, who watched them pass with baleful eyes. If they could have escaped from that corral they might have torn them to pieces.

The Captain refused to approach Slater unarmed, though Elena urged him to. "I do not come in supplication," he told her. "You stay in the wagon."

"I'm coming with you."

He climbed down and stumbled, queasy and light-headed. He felt his blood sinking—and it would drain all the way out of him, he thought, the earth was so thirsty for it—until Elena steadied him, clutched his elbow and helped him forward. Before Slater he bowed slightly, not with deference but the mere politeness of a gentlemen, a courtesy Slater had never merited before. Slater accepted this gesture without comment or reciprocation. Both of them boiled with anger and bitter regret but when they faced each other they played the parts fate had assigned them.

"This is a sad day," the Captain said.

"Yes, it is," Slater agreed.

"My herd is destroyed, my property burned, most of my men dead or captured."

"Who told you all that?"

"Murtaugh."

"He lived, did he?"

The Captain nodded.

"Well, he won't live for long." Slater pointed to his shoulder. "He put this bullet in me under a truce."

The Captain glanced at the bodies laid out on the ground, which were separated, for some fanciful reason, according to the outfits the men had belonged to. Some had been badly mutilated and were scarcely recognizable, while others looked no different than they had looked when they climbed out of bed that morning. "Will you bury the dead men?"

"Won't be no wolves feasting on them, if that's your worry. I'm clearing the wolves out of this basin once and for all."

"What about the men in the corral?"

"I ain't decided. Can I trust them?"

The Captain allowed himself a faint smile. "About as far as you can throw them."

"You don't care about them, then?"

"They owe me nothing," he said coldly. "I owe them nothing."

Slater stared back at him, thinking slowly, as he always did, about this man who stood before him, unrepentant, ignorant even, in the face of the carnage spread out before him. His own son heaped like a pile of offal a few feet away. His cattle swelling the river with blood. His daughter sobbing beside him as he paid her no mind.

"I come as a father," the Captain said. "My father was a proud man and he passed his pride on to me."

"Is that what you call it? Pride?"

Slater was astonished that he called it that. Your vanity killed them all, he wanted to say. All of them sacrificed to your vanity, and your fear. And if you had any, your shame. He felt the anger welling up inside him, bestial, uncertain of mastery.

"Do you have any sons?" the Captain asked.

"Rory's like a son to me."

The Captain's voice faltered. "Then... you must be proud of him."

Slater nodded.

"And you must have had a father."

"He lost two of his sons in the war."

"My father suffered the same fate."

They both lowered their eyes in a heartsick ritual of sorrow. Sorrow for that fate and for what it led each of them to. Sorrow for the shattered hopes which had brought them together.

"I came for my son's body," the Captain said. "I will pay you for it."

Slater's face darkened and his hand went to his gun. "Don't tempt me with your disrespect."

"I meant no disrespect."

"Some of these men want to shoot you, same as Vickery shot Crenshaw. Same as Murtaugh shot me. Same as you sicced that cur Vickery on all of us."

"I never told Vickery to do what he did. He disobeyed me."

"Some of these men don't think your son's body should be treated any better than the other men who died today, or even as good. Maybe we should throw it to the dogs."

"I beg of you—"

"I don't want no begging. I won't have no begging. Insult me once more and it'll be the last thing you ever do."

"Can I take him?"

Slater waited for his anger to die down. It would be so easy to throw him in the corral and let his own men tear him apart. So easy, short of that, to pistol whip him and make him thrash in the dirt, make him admit once and for all what kind of man he was. But there beside him stood Elena, sobbing even harder now, for her brother and now for her father and for herself in this basin where nobody wants to live and nobody can escape. He couldn't let her see her father beaten and humiliated in front of all these men.

"Take him."

The Captain hesitated, unsure whether he'd be shot if he took a step.

"Rory'll go with you," Slater said. "None of these men will touch Rory."

"I thank you."

"Some good men on both sides went down today. I don't want to see any more."

Rory helped the Captain lift Luke's mangled body into the wagon bed while Elena held the reins. The Captain wound the blanket around it so his wife wouldn't have to see him, though he might have spared the effort: half an hour later as they rumbled through the arching gateway she leaped into the wagon bed screaming and sobbing and tore the sheet off and threw it into the dust and threw herself down on top of his body weeping until the Captain pulled her off drenched in his blood. The men in the corral, the Captain's men, stood pressed against the rail, hands behind them, heads leering forward like a tangle of venomous lizards, their eyes small with hate. They hissed and spat at the Captain and he ignored them, loading the body, winding it in the blanket, climbing back up on the seat beside his daughter. "Do you need help finding the bull?" Rory asked him.

"I've got to bury my son," he said. "Then I'll go out on the range and hunt down the bull."

"If you need any help bringing it in—"

"I won't be bringing it in."

That night, after Luke was in the ground, the Captain sent Elena inside to mind her mother, sharpened his bowie knife and a cleaver on the grindstone in the barn and packed two loaded rifles and a shotgun and the cleaver and bowie knife on a mule. He took the yellow cur and shut the other dogs in the barn and rode out shirtless in the summer moonlight to hunt the blooded bull whose destruction, he knew, would make his ruin complete. With the cur he tracked it like a wild beast from the rise above Slater's camp to the timber gulch along the yellow bluffs where the cows and heifers grazed at that time of year. The bull must have sensed he was on its trail for he found it lying in wait for him in a cane brake, invisible in the still shadows but emanating the heat of its two thousand pounds in a mist of sweat and fetid breath that thickened the moonlight above it, and when the Captain spurred his mule closer (the mule balking as it also sensed the menace of the bull), the bull dug in its hoofs and burst from the thicket tilting its twisted horns toward mule and rider. The Captain was ready for it—as ready as any man could be face to face with that terrible creature which just that day had killed his son. He fired one rifle, then the other, into the bull's fierce eyes, and when it still raged forward, unstoppable, skewering its horns into the belly of the rearing mule, he dropped to the ground and fired up under the bull with both barrels of his 16-gauge shotgun and the bull's hideous face fell on top of him, bathing him in its steaming blood. He hacked his way out from under the dead animal with his bowie knife and sliced its throat and cut out its tongue and fed it to the ravening cur and then he went to work with the cleaver on its flanks and loins and rump, drawing out the coiled entrails and stringing them over the sand in the moonlight as if they held a hidden message, until the cur began to swallow them whole. Then he lighted a fire and burned the entrails and the monstrous slabs of fat he extracted from the bull's loins and the aroma of burning fat and flesh cloyed the air, delighting no one but the wolves that crept in around him, their eyes gleaming yellow in the night, and when he had buried the dead mule he heaped the bull's remains into a pulpit of bones and left it for the wolves to howl over.

Rory stepped back over to Slater's cot and propped him up on a grain sack. "That was a shame what happened to Luke," Slater said.

"Yes it was."

"A lot happened today that shouldn't have happened. Look at all these dead men. They're somebody's sons too."

"Elena said it was all Vickery's doing."

"I'm not sure as I believe that."

Slater glanced past Rory at two figures approaching, one on horseback, the other on foot. "Here's Buckminster. Who's he got with him?"

After the stampede over the cliff, Buckminster and Vickery had slipped away to settle their accounts privately. They'd made a deal neither intended to honor, and both of them knew it. When the tide of battle shifted and the Captain's herd started to run, Buckminster had leapt into the middle of it and drove it forward, double-crossing Vickery (Vickery would have done the same thing to him) because he knew that destroying the Captain's herd was the only way he could gain control of the basin. After that he would take on tomfool Slater who couldn't see what was in front of his face, and then the upstart Rory, and as for Elena, he'd have her one way or another, the gentle way or the rough way if it came to that. As between him and Vickery, he was the first to break the truce.

And now here he was, leading Vickery like a dog, gagged, hands tied behind his back, a noose coiled around his neck. When he lagged behind or stumbled, Buckminster yanked on the rope to keep him moving—bootless, hatless, lips curled, his burn scar blazing crimson with venom and outrage. Still he faced Slater with a certain haughty pride, as if he knew even then that before death tore him down he would play one last malefic card to seal Slater's doom, and the Captain's too, which, in the final reckoning, would make his a life well spent. Not by telling what he knew—there'd be no last-minute curses or revelations--but by concealing it. They'd have to learn the truth the hard way. And he could see that the end was near. The mob of prisoners in the corral, his loyal troops an hour before, pressed forward against the rail, cursing and spitting at him. If they could untie their hands they would have vaulted over the fence and torn him limb from limb, as if he was the one who should bear their sorrows.

"Tried to escape," Buckminster told Slater, shoving Vickery face down in the dirt.

"Where would he escape to?"

"He's been planning to kill you. Still is, far as I can tell."

"I'd say hang him from the nearest tree but that'd be about a hundred miles away."

Buckminster pointed to the cantilevered beam over the hayloft door, already fitted with a rope and pulley. "That ought to hold him long enough to die."

Slater nodded toward the mob in the corral. "I want them to earn their pardon, if there's going to be one. Let's give them a night to think about it."

They left Vickery gnawing the dirt while they savored their victory. Rory felt sick to his stomach. He hated Vickery but didn't want to watch him hang. "It's a whole new world, Rory," Slater said, "and it's ours."

To the northwest the fire had died under a gentle cleansing rain, having scoured the earth of every leaf and blade and bequeathed a new tranquility: a scarred badland not of rock and sand but of annealed earth purified of all life, the wolves dispersed, the ravens silenced, the mice and snakes and lizards fled or petrified in their holes. It was a deceptive peace, the peace of death, destined soon to give way to the entanglements of life and fate. But for now Slater was in the catbird seat. Occupier of the land, sole owner of the cattle, commander of men. The Captain was ruined, his herd destroyed, his prize bull marked for destruction at his own hand. There was only one thing he had left—and who would stand in Slater's way if he laid claim to that?

"I've a mind to marry that girl," he told Rory.

Part III

18.

West Texas, August 1865

Morning in a different country. Flatter, drier, nothing in sight but mirages. Blazing hot under a blinding sky, Mexico not long since. Wildfire wind whistling straight up from hell. Unless those clouds come closer, the dew on that prickly pear's all the water you're going to find.

Still early days in the cattle business, still wide open. Rounding up longhorns that've been running wild since the days of Cabeza de Vaca. They fight like crazy tipping their nine-foot horns at you before they're roped and trussed up and you spur your mount into the chaparral for the next one, scared of what you might find. Brand them and sell them to one of the bigger outfits that'll drive them up to Kansas. Only problem is you've followed them too far west and too far north—you're in Comanche country and those boys mean to scalp you. Painted warriors in breechclouts and leggings carrying ten-foot lances and bows and sometimes old army muskets. You'll never see them on the plains. They'll hide in the draws until after dark and before you know it you're surrounded.

That new man has a serious look, face dark and craggy, must think highly of himself to ride like that. Says he ain't afraid of the Comanches. If you believe that you probably ought to be more afraid of him than of them.

The new man—he called himself Bishop then—grew up on a small plantation south of Galveston Bay. His well-bred mother died young, leaving him with two older brothers who tried without much success to lord it over him. His hotheaded, hard-drinking father, well down the road to madness, had thrashed him more than once for his insufferable pride—baseless, he called it, though the boy knew better. They called him the Captain as a form of mockery but he took it into his heart as a badge of pride. The Confederate army never ranked him higher than first lieutenant but they put him in charge of a guerrilla platoon in Missouri where he perfected the art of command. In the early days he led one of the most vicious attacks of the war. It was brutal, sordid, demeaning—and dangerous. He knew he was not destined to die such an ignominious death. For the rest of the war he avoided violence, for which his men revered him.

He returned home to find his family landless and disgraced, his two brothers dead, his father insane, clinging to the ideals—he called them ideals—which had brought on war and slaughter and starvation. He had nothing to be proud of except his pride, which swelled as his world diminished. His father led him out on the plains on a mad mission to round up cattle driven away during the war. They quarreled—it was inevitable that they should quarrel, being so much alike. The old man, proud like his son, hated him for seeing through the sham that wrought his destruction, and abandoned him to wander alone on the yawning plains. That was Comanche country, where a white man's life was worth less than the clothes on his back. He joined a passing cattle outfit that rounded up wild longhorns and drove them to the old missions on both sides of the border, where the priests paid Spanish gold for beef on the hoof. There he studied the fine points of cattle—breeding, rearing, driving, trading— compliments of an old cowhand named Johnson, who was soon to lose half his nose to a Comanche blade.

"Them Comanches ain't your ordinary garden variety redskins, the kind you see back east," Johnson told him. "They don't plant corn or weave baskets or come to the trading post except to burn it down. They don't believe in anything we believe in, not good or evil nor anything in between, no Great Father in the sky, not even any right or wrong except what suits them on a particular occasion. Their only morals is revenge, which they practice with scrupulous devotion."

In those words Bishop heard the echo of his own heart, where he harbored a hidden likeness of the Comanches' beliefs. There's no good nor evil, he'd told his father, just what men do. For which his father, who knew nothing of good but much of evil, had turned him out into the desert wilderness. He admired the Comanches for their honesty and freedom, for the savage innocence that refused to worship false gods. But how could that anarchy hold its place against his pride? "They must believe in something," he said.

Johnson read the bafflement on his troubled face. "It ain't like they don't have their own code of honor, and a warrior's pride. They'll risk their life, even throw it away before they'll be dishonored in their own eyes. Is that believing in something? You tell me, when they're scalping you alive."

Slater first heard about him from Johnson years later, the night before he fished Rory out of the Rio Concho. Along with the wagon trains a dozen cattle outfits bivouacked along the river trying to keep their herds apart until they could swim them across. At night the men drifted from one camp to another to drink and smoke and scout for old friends. Slater had barely pulled himself back from his delirium of thirst and heat and wind in the mirage country and the bawling of the grieving cows that echoed inside him—he wasn't fit to console a man with half a nose. When Johnson plumped down beside him at the fire he began to turn away but when he saw the nose he made himself stay and pretend not to notice it. The least he could do for this mutilated but oddly cheerful man.

"I seen you looking at my nose," Johnson said, nodding—it was an old story. He leaned into the fire to light his cigar. "I bet you're wondering how I lost it."

"I reckon that's your business."

"Summer of '65, it was. Young fella named Bishop—thought highly of himself though nobody knew why—joined our outfit in San Antone. He learned what I could teach him about cattle and within six months he was running his own outfit. I signed up thinking maybe he still needed to learn a thing or two. Sure enough, ten days out we run across a band of Comanches. Heard them yipping and howling like coyotes in the night, worrying our horses, daring us to come after them. Well, Bishop was too proud not to take the bait, though I warned him. He admired the Comanches, he told me once, for not believing in anything. He rode out in the moonlight with four men, myself included, left the rest to guard the remuda and the herd. The Comanches cornered us in an arroyo, scalped three of the men alive while Bishop and I looked on."

"Why didn't they kill you and Bishop?"

"They spared Bishop just for sport, laughing at him, calling him *mujer* (one of them spoke a little Spanish), and let him go so he could tell his outfit what a coward he was. One of them backed him against a steep bank and whipped his face with a bullwhip, carved the shape of a fishhook just under his lower lip. Then he beat it out of there like a jackrabbit. Never once looked back at me and the three dead men."

Slater wanted to stand up and walk away before the old cowhand's tale stirred up the sunstroke terrors he'd barely survived a few days before. He raised his tin cup and took a sip of coffee. "I still don't get why they didn't kill you."

"I'm coming to that." Johnson leaned toward him, daring him to turn away. "You see, they left me alive as an eyewitness in case Bishop didn't own up to being a coward. Cut off my nose with a bowie knife so I'd have something to remember them by. I staggered back to the camp but the outfit was gone. Bishop had told them that me and the others was dead. They believed him or they wouldn't have left me to fend for myself on them sweltering plains."

Slater ventured a glance into Johnson's flickering eyes. "So that's how it happened." He doubted if this Bishop ever existed or that Johnson had ever seen a Comanche. Like as not he burned his nose off falling drunk into a fire or lost it in a bar room brawl. How sad that cowboys whiled away their lives with such tales.

"I made it back to San Antone two weeks later, about nine tenths dead," Johnson went on, flipping his cigar butt into the chaparral. "When my story got around, Bishop disappeared and was never seen again. I reckon he's still out there somewhere, and when I find him—the others in that outfit feel the same way—I'm going to finish what the Comanches started. He shouldn't be too hard to find. That scar under his lip marks him out like the brand of the devil."

It was the next day that Slater dove into the Concho to save the boy. He'd never been able to fill the hole left in his heart by his dying wife and child and a treacherous brother. He'd all but lost his mind in the scorching wilderness of dust around the poison lakes. He had little to say that any man would want to hear. All he had left was that mad leap, which might have been his last. The roiling river would decide.

19.

The Captain lived in a dark place. A place of anger and shame, despondency and impotence. When he trudged back from the yellow bluffs after he slaughtered the bull and offered its fat and flesh to the ravening wolves, he followed his yellow cur to the ranch, and when he opened the barn door the other dogs boiled around him and he whipped them mercilessly until they cringed into the darkness and disappeared. That was for Luke, the son he'd treated just as cruelly though deserving so much better. He could love Luke now only by hating himself. And hating other men he scarcely knew but for their tobacco'd teeth and stinking breath and leathern faces, who'd licked his hands like dogs when they worked for him but now spat when they heard his name. He was ashamed to have lost his kingdom, ashamed above all to have lost it to the likes of Slater, poor white trash that blew up out of nowhere like a thistle scratching the dirt. He had no plans, no hope, no future. Blythe and Gregson—agents of Matamoros, if Matamoros existed—would learn the fate of their bull as quick as a wildfire could spread to wherever they were. They'd file a judgment on all his property, the house and buildings, equipment, any remaining livestock, all to be sold at a distress sale within the month, if a marshal or his deputies dared set foot in the basin. Which they would, because the same wind would bring news of his humiliation. The days of his dominion were over. The dogs had never returned after he whipped them out of the barn.

Elena was the only person he talked to. Never while eating, never in front of his wife, who passed among them like a ghost. In the ranch office, which was his bedroom, he sat at his desk staring at payrolls of dead men and men who'd kill him if they ever saw him again. The only cowboy still on the payroll was Charlie Crow, who did odd jobs and helped Elena with the horses. She brought the meals in from the cookhouse, where Old Zeke lay drunk most of the time. Ever since she rode with him to fetch Luke's body and the next morning after he did his grisly work at the bluffs and they laid the body in a hole and she muttered some words she found in an old book—nobody from town came out, even Jacinta wouldn't leave the house—they'd stayed together most of the time, in the office or doing chores in the barn, silent, avoiding each other's eyes, yet closer than they'd ever been. They shared a common wound and it hurt when either of them pressed on it. Then one morning she walked into the office and found him weeping. He turned away and pretended to be clearing his nose.

"Were you crying for Luke or yourself?" she asked him.

"Myself, probably."

"You're just saying that."

"That's probably true too."

"It's harder to talk about Luke, isn't it?"

The silence they'd been smothering in started to close back around them. "He could never satisfy me," the Captain said, fighting it back, "no matter what he did. And now he got himself killed. I hope I'm satisfied."

It was hard listening to her father say that. Even in admitting he was wrong he couldn't let go of his pride.

"We're going to lose everything," he said. "They'll come after me for that bull and I don't have the money to pay them."

"They'll take the house?"

"They'll take everything that's left."

To that point Elena had cried only for Luke, and for her parents. Now she cried for herself. "What will we do?"

He touched her hand. "We'll survive. That's about as much as we ever did."

Jacinta could be heard calling out for Elena from her room.

"See to your mother."

She stood up to leave but her father held her back. "There's something else," he said. "I'm grateful for what your boy Rory did when we went down there to get Luke. Nobody else would look us in the eye."

"He's not my boy."

"Well, just the same."

She smiled for the first time in a week, surprised by the unaccustomed notes of sympathy and forgiveness in his voice. It seemed that he had been relieved of some burden he'd been carrying all his life.

"Are you grateful to Slater too?" she asked him.

"No," he said. "I plan on shooting him the first chance I get."

The Captain's fall freed his wife's dire spirit to rule the basin. In her black mourning weeds, wrapped high around her like a raven's wings, she prowled the ridges and gullies around the ranch, calling down curses on the land that spawned the race of men. From the porch she commanded the horizons and the four winds, conjuring her madhouse eyes and her terrible bone-white countenance to raise towering thunderheads, punishing rains, suffocating darkness. In her rage against the light she claimed the mother-right of endless sorrow and implacable revenge. Her fury found its voice in her weaving. The tapestry she'd been working on for as long as Elena could remember became a work of prophecy, a likeness of past, present and future that grew more horrific as the days brought new visions. It was all there: the pitiless landscape, the lowering sky, the butchering of livestock, the glutting of dogs on the corpses of men. Slater and his henchmen, the abominable bull, the Captain himself—all who had a hand in murdering Luke were woven into that fabric of doom.

At times she seemed possessed by a strange elation, floating over the dark vision that was never far from her mind. Her eyes would fix on some blank spot in the tapestry, as if she imagined that by concentrating hard enough she could weave a different world. "Luke will come back," she told Elena, "to claim this land and make it his own."

Elena took her hand and led her away from the loom. "Luke is dead, Mother."

"Then the whole world is dead. What does it matter?"

It was hot in the house, sweating August heat. A little better on the porch, if you stayed out of the sun. Elena sat her mother down on a bench and tried to talk to her. "We're going to have to move," she said. "Father has lost everything."

Jacinta's eyes glimmered with a mad certainty. "It's him that's lost," she said. "Look—everything's still right here. The house, the barn, the corrals—nothing's lost. It's all right here."

"Not the cattle, though," Elena said. "The cattle are gone."

"But he's still the cattle king. And I am still the queen."

Another time, one evening as the sun began to set, her fury overcame her and she stalked the range in her billowing black dress, her obsidian eyes as sharp as sacrificial knives, and cursed the fading light like a she-wolf mourning her young. "Men washed in the blood of the bull will feed their lives to the dogs," she howled in the wind. "I see the ropes of death knotted around their necks." Elena ran out to bring her home—she greeted her daughter as she would a stranger. "The land cries out for the son," she said. "The father will claw the dust with both hands."

Every day she searched for gods in her prayers and imprecations, finding none but slathering wolves, seething hosts of hornets, split-tongued snakes, her own fury boiling like scorpions out of the earth. At the shrine in her bedroom she bowed down to Santa Muerte, the end of all things.

Elena's own feelings had been smothered under the weight of her parents' suffering. Her dreams of a future were dead and buried, swallowed into the earth like everything else in that basin of lost souls. There was no future there and no escape. She seldom thought about Rory, and then only as a distant memory. At least (she told herself in a rare moment of reflection) her father had given up his project of marrying her off, having no property or status to preserve. In that she was mistaken. On those infertile plains where she was the only marriageable woman within a hundred miles, there were men who would calculate her future much more carefully than she did.

20.

The rain swirled in after the dying was done, at first a cleansing wash, then a tumult like the wailing of lost souls. Men who'd never looked into their hearts had found themselves on intimate terms with evil. They had learned what it meant to pitch in the dust, to breathe their last, to feed their lives to the earth. To see other men's lives gush out, tainting the earth. The evil saturated the basin, yet somehow it went unfulfilled.

"It'll take one more death to end this," Slater told Rory that first night after most of the men had bunked down. They murmured by lantern light as Rory cleaned and dressed Slater's wound, his own wound throbbing painfully. Unlike the Captain, Slater believed in evil, even while knowing it was a phantom, a shadow without substance in that country. But to pretend not to see it when it coiled around him would be to let himself be mocked by it. He would not be mocked by evil. Vickery had to die.

Buckminster and Moondog had confined Vickery bound and gagged in a meat locker in the barn, while his men slept on the floor, tied up and guarded by Crazy Ike and his crew. Two of Slater's men had caught Murtaugh scrounging for food in the garbage pit. They bound him and threw him in the meat locker with Vickery.

To Slater, Buckminster argued for killing Vickery without ceremony. "He'll run back and feed the Captain's dreams of conquest. We need to kill him."

Slater heard his foreman out, but there was something off-kilter in his arguments, something almost like guile, which Slater had never detected in him before. "I say give him a fair trial."

"He doesn't need a trial. He'll just lie his way out."

"I want the Captain's men to decide. I need to know if they're on my side."

"What about Murtaugh?"

You couldn't read Slater's thoughts, Rory knew that. Sometimes you'd wonder if he was even having any. So Rory was surprised to see a benign smile creep over his face, the smile of a merciful judge.

"I got a special place in my heart for Murtaugh," Slater said, "since he's the one who shot me. Put him on trial too."

At sunup they brought the Captain's men back out to the corral and stood Vickery and Murtaugh in front of them, tied back to back on the wagon, two mules harnessed in front. Vickery growled and grunted, a gag knotted tight across his foaming mouth, the cloth ragged, his lips dripping blood where he'd tried to bite it off. The men in the corral taunted him with raucous, stuttering imitations.

Rory stood between Slater and Buckminster, revolted equally by Vickery and the mob that mocked him. "I'm washing my hands of these two," Slater told the mob. "You can do whatever you want with them. You can set them free, as long as they clear out of the basin. And once you finish with them—no matter what you decide—you can keep on working here, if you swear your loyalty to me. If not, you'd better clear out fast."

Rory scanned the desperate, baffled men held at gunpoint in the corral, staring like cattle on their way to the slaughterhouse. He knew most of them but they were hardly recognizable after the fighting and a night tied up in the barn. They were Vickery's accomplices but Slater had made them his jury. Rory peered in their dull eyes and saw his own shame for everything that had happened and his own role in it, be it for praise or blame. Stampeding two thousand cattle to their deaths. Killing men he had nothing against except that they might kill him first. Exulting in his triumph, as if he enjoyed any of this. And now the men he hadn't killed stood ready to ransom themselves with treachery, turning on the man they'd followed into battle, mocking him, spitting on him, throwing dirt at him, scorning him for what they themselves had done. And was it any different on this side of the fence, standing next to Slater as he celebrated his victory? Suddenly Slater seemed capable of anything. He wanted Elena, seemed to think she'd be his just for the asking. Of course there was no chance that she'd marry him—Rory still wanted her and he was determined to have her. But neither of them had said any more about it. On those plains men kept their fancies to themselves and then one day they surprised each other and that was that. When the time came Rory would fight back and Slater would be the surprised one. How would he react? Disappointment, anger, jealous rage? It was a new world and it was his, as he'd said the night before. He was the boss now, the only boss, and in his wily, impenetrable way he even claimed the power of life and death over the men in front of him, the only uncertainty being how many of them he was about to sacrifice.

"This is just a lynch mob," Rory muttered.

"It ain't a lynch mob, it's a jury. Is there anybody who don't want to serve?"

Not a murmur of disagreement. "Buckminster will lay out the case against them. Vickery first."

Buckminster circled the wagon as Vickery watched from behind his gag with a mad dog's leer. Strutting, preening, he'd worn his black suit, as if he thought he really was a prosecutor. The men in that mob knew him for what he was, saw in him what Slater could not see. They hated him. "This man Vickery," he began, eyeing the snarling prisoner, "against the Captain's orders, set out to kill Slater and destroy his herd. He turned you loose against him like a pack of wolves. Too many men on both sides died—you know who they were, I don't need to name them. What Vickery did wasn't war, it was murder. He shot Crenshaw in cold blood, and he had Murtaugh shoot Slater under the cover of a truce."

Buckminster turned, took a step toward the crowd. "Don't take my word for it. Let me ask Murtaugh." He pivoted back to face Murtaugh. "Are all those charges true?"

"They are," Murtaugh said.

"Does any man dispute them?"

The mob erupted in anger, shouting indistinctly, hurling clumps of mud and manure at Buckminster and Murtaugh and Vickery. Buckminster brushed the debris off his suit and went on: "And you, Murtaugh. You shot Slater. What do you have to say for yourself?"

"I was following orders. We all were following orders."

A roar of approval. Murtaugh was right. They were all following orders.

"Take Vickery's gag off," one of the men shouted when the noise had died down. "He has a right to defend himself."

"He'll get his chance to talk," Buckminster said.

"String him up!" someone called out, and the cry echoed: String him up! String him up! No dissenting voices were heard, other than Vickery's grunts and snarls.

"That's your judgment then. Now what to do with Murtaugh?"

The tumult died at once. Those men had been asked to judge themselves, who'd all been following orders. Many had been soldiers and they knew the answer—an order was an order. They couldn't have done any different from what they did.

Slater stepped forward and took his time beginning to speak. A tremor of worry juddered through the crowd. "I'm going to step in here," he said. "As for Murtaugh, I'm the one he ambushed, so I'm the one with the right to judge him."

"You said that was up to us," one of the men objected.

"You said we were the jury."

Slater let them speak and then he went on: "He tried to kill me and I've got a painful wound to prove it. I can hang him just as high as Vickery and he deserves it."

"You said you washed your hands of him."

"My hands are clean," Slater said. "Cleaner than any of yours. But enough good men have died and I won't add to their number. As an act of mercy I'm going to pardon Murtaugh—"

The men clapped and cheered as if they were the ones being pardoned. If they had their way, they wouldn't have let him finish his sentence. He waited for quiet.

"On one condition." He let that linger in the air like the echo of a distant gunshot. They needed time to grasp the gravity and contingency of the situation. It could still go either way.

"That he carries out your judgment against Vickery."

21

Moondog and Crazy Ike mourned Polecat by lighting a fire and burning his belongings. A blanket, a pair of socks and a denim shirt, a tin canteen, a deck of racy playing cards, a crumpled letter in a woman's hand, and surprisingly, a well-thumbed Bible, which was spared from the flames, along with $8.75 in specie, shared among the mourners. Smoke and fumes rose heavily and sagged in the clouded sky, leaving a foul smell in remembrance of the deceased. No tears were shed, but Moondog—solemn in his fleece chaps, his buffalo robe and his bear-claw necklace—offered a meditation on Polecat's lifelong bad luck and the lessons that could be learned from it. "Luck is a fickle friend," he said, "while fate is as constant as the stars, for all men the same. A few days ago Polecat lived and breathed, same as you and me. Now he's dead and buried and gone to heaven. That's where he'll stay for all eternity, no matter what kind of luck he ever had."

"Heaven?" some of the men muttered. Polecat was the last man you'd expect to see in heaven.

"Cowboy heaven," Moondog said. "It ain't real, any more than any other heaven. But you all knew that. That's one thing we got over them farmers and shopkeepers and church ladies. We know this damn basin is the last place we'll ever be."

None of the other dead were honored with private obsequies. Their belongings were hauled out of the bunkhouse and parceled out, so much as anyone wanted, the rest burned. A pious delegation of ravens flapped in for the ceremony, croaked their condolences, and vanished into the haze.

Rory drifted away from the fire, stung by the smoke. He'd been surly, uncommunicative, his shoulder more painful than ever. That was to be expected with a bullet wound, Buckminster had told him—his version of sympathy. It would take a month to heal. He tried to keep his mind on his work instead of trying to hack through the tangle of lies Buckminster had gathered around Elena. Elena's view of Rory was a reflection of the way he saw her: a clouded image of lost hope, an imagined promise broken, the pity of a longing that died before it bloomed. Both of them too shy, too proud, too hurt to reach through that entanglement to touch the truth.

The heat of August had withered the grass and maddened the cattle to destruction. Soon the late summer rains would resume, soaking into the land, then on the burned-out northwestern ridge the saturated soil under the burn scar would slough off and slide down the slopes as mud. Those attuned to such portents—ravens, scorpions, rattlesnakes—saw disaster written on the land. They fled, except for the ravens, who batten on death. Men became entangled in webs of cunning, revenge, doom, even love.

First came the chastisements. Vickery was hanged by his own men, led by Murtaugh, who slipped the noose around his neck. and was then, true to Slater's word, set loose on the plains with a day's rations and the clothes on his back. At the last minute Buckminster removed the gag so Vickery could talk. Did he speak the truth, exposing his own and Buckminster's perfidy? No, he understood that nothing could save him. He cursed the Captain and Slater and Murtaugh and every man in that mob, spitting and clicking as he ranted, but he kept secret the web of deceit that he and Buckminster had spun around them. In that web and its silence he envisioned his revenge and their undoing. At the last minute, before the hood went on, he favored Buckminster with a sly, sinister smile, unfathomable to the other men. He spiraled down to death with that smile on his scarred, hooded face.

Thus Slater never learned that Buckminster had betrayed him. But what Buckminster had done to the Captain's herd sickened him—infuriated him, when it visited his sleep—and he considered letting the men string him up as they had Vickery. And they would have done it without hesitation. They felt a deep, gnawing shame at what they'd done and held Buckminster responsible for it. They saw him as a tempter who'd found a blind spot in Slater's perceptions and wormed his way in to corrupt him and the outfit. Those were their cattle he'd destroyed, the cattle they'd saved from wolves, branded and castrated, whipped into obedience. Some of them sobbed and tore their hair when they heard how those cattle had perished. "Why did you do such a thing?" Slater demanded.

"It's what Vickery planned to do to you," Buckminster said, taken aback at his reaction. He always saw himself as blameless.

"You're no better than Vickery then."

"It had to be done, to break the Captain's power. Now all this belongs to you." Buckminster swept his hand in a grand arc across the landscape, as if the empty plains held all the kingdoms of the earth.

It sickened Slater to think of those cattle as sport for the wolves. He sent out a crew to hunt down and kill all the wolves they could find in the basin, along with the Captain's dogs, which still ran wild. Buckminster tried to convince him that destroying the herd had been a necessary evil. The Captain's outfit would never have capitulated if their herd was still intact. For his part Buckminster resented Slater's upbraiding him in front of the men. But he found consolation in watching Rory writhe like a hogtied calf every time Slater mentioned Elena's name. Rory's interest in the girl had escaped Slater completely. He talked freely of marrying her and set the men to building him a two-story log house like the Captain's where he could set up housekeeping with his bride. He even sought Rory's advice, without catching a glimmer of his resentment. He was as blind to

Rory's feelings for Elena as he was to the snares of Buckminster's cunning.

Buckminster bided his time, gave Slater a chance to cool down. Then one morning he shaved and washed and put on a clean shirt and went to Slater with what seemed a sudden inspiration. "I'm sorry you're so mad about the cattle," he told Slater. "To tell the truth, I thought you'd want it done that way."

"I don't know how you could've thought that."

"Well, I'm sorry."

The moment was awkward. When men on those plains got crossways with each other, they snarled and spat, they laughed, sometimes they shot each other. But they didn't apologize. Slater felt like he'd been ambushed.

"Let me make it up to you," Buckminster said, smiling back at him. "Let me go over and talk to the Captain about his daughter—on your behalf. I know you want to marry her."

At times like that Slater dismissed the anger and misgivings he'd felt toward Buckminster, who'd always been loyal to him. He needed Buckminster's diplomacy, his gifts of speech and charm and sincerity, and he felt grateful for his willingness to approach the Captain, who for all he knew might be waiting for him with a shotgun cradled in his lap.

The Captain had been living in the darkness of his own private hell, curled around himself like a snake in a cold cellar. Then slowly he began to uncoil and make his way back to daylight. He shed his shame and despondency and wove a new skin around his anger, lithe and lustrous with the promise of revenge. Nightmares followed him out of the darkness: Luke with a skeleton face clinging madly to the horns of a raging bull. Jacinta trampled by horses, himself cast down in a ravine, eaten by dogs.

Forewarned of Buckminster's visit by Old Zeke, he waited on the porch with his shotgun. It was another sweltering day, misty in the morning before a blistering, windless noon. The yellow cur, indifferent to the heat, curled at his feet with a murderous eye. It sensed Buckminster's approach long before he came in sight, growling, lashing its tail, and then, when the foreman's horse trudged out of the sand wash, leaping up to snarl and bay like a hound of hell. That dog sees through Buckminster the same way I do, the Captain thought with satisfaction. A man as false as the hope for salvation.

Buckminster had worn his black suit, a vest, a dress hat. He rode slowly through the arching gateway, hitched his tall black mare and climbed the steps to the porch. The Captain hefted his shotgun and considered swatting him out of the air like a fly. This was the man who'd driven his herd to destruction. He hated him more than he hated Slater. Slater at least was not a snake.

"Good morning, Captain," Buckminster said, removing his hat. "I wanted to express my condolences about your son. Luke was a fine young man."

The Captain checked his rage. "Luke was a damn fool. What do you want?"

"I just wanted to say those things and ask how you and your family are getting along."

He winced at the nicety of the words. "You've destroyed me and taken everything I owned. That's how we're getting along."

"I apologize for that, sir. To be honest, I was only following Slater's orders."

A snake and a worm at the same time, he thought. "Don't call me sir, unless you want me to have you horsewhipped."

"I'm sorry."

"And stop apologizing or I'll whip you myself."

Buckminster took his time answering, sidestepping the threats. "With all respect," he said, "you do have something left. Or someone, I ought to say: your daughter. She's of marrying age."

The Captain studied his clean-shaven face, his empty blue eyes. "Surely you can't be thinking she'd marry the likes of you."

"No, surely not. I'm here on Slater's behalf."

The Captain feigned outraged surprise. "The day my daughter marries that swamp trash is the day hell spews its devils on the earth."

"Slater's a rich man now. He's got the basin to himself."

"He's a thief, is what he is. What happened to Vickery?"

"Vickery's dead," Buckminster said. "Hanged."

"He's a murderer too then."

"He could help you get back on your feet.   Eventually—"

The Captain cut him off. "Get out of here, Buckminster. My daughter's not for sale."

Of course she's for sale, Buckminster mused as he rode back to camp. She was for sale before and she's still for sale, even more urgently. It's just that now there won't be any takers. Those men of property and substance you dangled her in front of two months ago won't give her a second look now, will they, Captain? You know that—you're desperate to recoup your losses and she's the only way you can do it.

But when he arrived back at camp Buckminster didn't tell Slater exactly what had passed between him and the Captain. In fact his version of events, as with most things he said, bore little resemblance to the truth.

It was late afternoon and the sky had lost its luster to wispy clouds drifting in high from the north. All outward signs of the war had been erased, the dead buried in sand under a makeshift cross that wouldn't last through the winter. Most of the men were out on the range, still rounding up Slater's scattered herd, which in a few weeks would be driven down from the high country for the winter. Buckminster noticed Slater grooming his horse in the corral but didn't approach him until Rory rode in.

"The Captain'll let you have her," he told Slater when Rory had joined them in the corral. "It's just a matter of what price you're willing to pay."

Slater wheeled on him with flaring eyes. "It ain't a purchase. I hope you didn't present it that way."

"Not at all. That was how the Captain put it."

Rory felt himself curling up inside. "Surely Elena won't let herself be bought and sold."

"I ain't aiming to buy her," Slater said.

"Don't kill the messenger!" Buckminster laughed, backing away as if in fear. "I'm just telling you what he said."

"Was Elena there?"

"Sure she was there. The Captain said she had to agree, and she did."

"She said she wanted to marry me?"

Buckminster caught himself before he laughed again. "Well, to be honest, it wasn't exactly a question of wanting to. She's willing to—let's put it that way."

Slater had worked himself up into a sweat. "But that's not what it has to be," he insisted. "This is marriage I'm proposing. She has to want to get married."

"All I can do is tell you the truth," Buckminster said. "Maybe you ought to go over there and talk to her yourself."

Rory watched Buckminster carefully. "Maybe there's some other man she's sweet on."

"No, there isn't." Buckminster said. "I asked her that and she denied it. And I asked her another thing." He glanced around until he caught Rory's eye. "There's a story going around—I don't know where I heard it, probably at the saloon—that she's been with a man. Had a fling with some cowboy, pretty serious, to tell you the truth."

"You heard that?" Slater asked.

"Not that I believe it, at least the way I heard it. You know how men exaggerate when it comes to that sort of thing. So I wouldn't give it any weight. But I knew you'd want to know, so I asked her about it."

"You asked her? What'd she say?"

"Whatever it amounted to—and like I say, I don't believe half of what I heard—she says it's all over and done with."

Slater turned to Rory. "You heard about this?"

"No, I ain't," Rory said, glaring at Buckminster. "I sure ain't."

"You don't know who the man was?" Slater pressed Buckminster. "Ferguson, maybe? I saw her out on the range talking to Ferguson once."

"No, this man's still alive. She said she wouldn't marry him, though. She don't want to marry a pauper."

"Well, good," Slater said, calmer now. "I still got a fighting chance."

"But she is, some might say, damaged goods. I hope that doesn't spoil her for you."

Slater allowed himself a faint smile. "I been a cattle man all my life," he said. "I know what I got a right to expect."

22.

All life in the basin was unsettled by the fate of the Captain's herd. The glutted wolves fled north ahead of the hunters dispatched to kill them. The ravens grew bold, the hornets menacing, the rattlesnakes spiteful and shrill. The remaining cattle—Slater's cattle—groaned mournfully from dawn to dark; the horses trotted in circles, ornery and skittish. The men kept their heads down, ashamed of both triumph and defeat. There was work to be done and they gladly rode out to do it. They were sick of war, sick of death, in a few cases sick of life. Some wanted nothing more to do with the accursed business of raising cattle for slaughter, a sacrifice, so it seemed, that offered no protection from the caprice of evil gods.

In those ill-omened days, if you could have looked down from the sky arching over that parched range into the legend unfolding there—into the heart of that legend, the human drama which had chosen that basin as its stage—you would have seen four men and two women (Slater, the Captain, Rory, Buckminster, Elena and Jacinta) yoked together like a six-mule team dragging a heavy load of sorrow and anger and ambition and love and hate, all toward the same destination, the only possible destination, though none of them standing alone would have chosen it. When they reached that destination they would curse their fates, each of them, though it wasn't fate that brought them there, it was their own decisions. Yet those decisions were so unquestionable, so necessary and compelled by events as they saw them, that even as they were made they seemed but a submission to fate.

Rory's heart churned with painful and unfamiliar passions. It hadn't occurred to him to marry Elena until Slater announced his own intention to do it. Then suddenly he felt thwarted, betrayed, jealous. Annoyed—no, angry—that Slater never suspected he might have a rival with at least as good a claim. And seething mad that Buckminster, who surely did suspect it, would insult him to his face, and Elena too, with his insinuation that she'd been despoiled by him but would never marry him. When he saw Buckminster on the range he raced up to him like a Comanche hungry for a scalp and pulled back on his reins about twenty feet short of a collision. "I don't like them nasty rumors you're spreading about Elena," he said. "There's no truth to them."

Buckminster tried to look friendly, though his lips were a ghastly white. "That's what I figured—I said that, didn't I?—but I thought Slater needed to know."

"They're lies and I don't want to hear them again. Anyway, Elena's spoken for."

He favored Rory with a wry smile. "Well, if you're the one doing the speaking, she ain't been listening. The fact is, she's made up her mind against you."

"You're crazy if you think she'd marry Slater."

"She said she would. And I reckon it'd be a good move, from a business standpoint. Merge the two kingdoms, so to speak, so they're not always trying to destroy each other."

The business standpoint—who owns what, how many cattle they run, how the profits get divided. That was something Rory hadn't even thought about. He was in water over his head. "This is all supposed to be mine someday," he said.

"Not all of it," Buckminster disagreed. "Slater told me if I stuck around, there'd be something here for me—"

"And he told me he was just stringing you along to keep you working here."

"No, that ain't right. He said—"

"You know what he said to me?" Rory thought fast—with a man like Buckminster you've got to strike like a rattler—and said the last thing he would want to hear. "Buckminster's just a hired hand and that's all he'll ever be. I never made him no promises. That's what he said."

The foreman answered with a deadly stare. "I don't believe that."

"Anyway that marriage ain't going to happen. You think a pretty young girl like Elena's going to marry an old swayback like Slater just because her father tells her to?"

The pretense of friendliness had flickered and died. "That's your idea but it ain't any of hers," Buckminster said, his voice level and cold. "She wants to marry him. Sees it as a way to improve herself. That's what she said."

"You better pray that she changes her mind," Rory said before he spurred his horse and trotted away, "because if she don't, the most you'll ever get out of Slater is a month's wages and a place in the grub line."

Buckminster rode back to the bunkhouse cursing and spitting, ready to pick up a rock and smash Rory's head with it, Slater's too if Rory could be believed. He was the kind of liar who holds other men to the strict letter of truth and is outraged when they deviate from it. Slater had promised him a piece of his outfit, said it was already written down. Was that just a lie, a ruse by that unsubtle man? Was Slater mocking him, laughing at his good faith in believing him? Just the possibility of that vexed him, bedeviled him as if it represented something sinister, inhuman, like the mocking smile Vickery had aimed at him as the hood slipped over his head—had Vickery been laughing at Slater and the Captain for what he knew Buckminster would do to them, or at Buckminster for what they would do to him? Vickery was another liar who'd failed to deliver on his promises. If he'd kept his word—if Murtaugh's shot had hit home, and Rory'd taken the next one—Buckminster wouldn't have to play this complicated game to set Slater and Rory against each other, spoiling the girl for both of them by repeating rumors he never heard. They'd both be dead and he'd have her for himself.

Slater stood sorting out some ropes and hanging them on hooks in the barn. He nodded to Buckminster but kept his eyes on his work. The foreman stood waiting for him to finish.

"Something you need?"

"Something I'd like to talk about if you've got time."

Slater's eyes challenged him. "Shoot."

"A lot's happened, and you know I've been a loyal and hardworking foreman."

"Appreciate it."

"It makes me wonder, what we talked about that time after the drive up north. About you giving me a piece of the action."

"What of it?"

"Is that deal still good? I mean—"

"You doubting me? I told you it was."

"I was just wondering. So much has changed."

"Well that ain't changed."

Slater turned back to his work and Buckminster slouched away to get some hay for his horse. He asked himself if he trusted Slater. He had no reason not to, except what Rory had said, which he knew was a lie. But when Slater turned his back on him, something changed, just enough to lure him down a dangerous road. If a liar can't believe the people he's lying to, he'll believe anything.

Buckminster's visit, repellent as it was, kindled the Captain's cunning hope of salvaging something from the wreckage of his life. He still had Elena, his last trump if he played it right: through her, he imagined, he could recover everything he had lost to Slater. He mulled the question and discussed it with Jacinta, who hated Slater more than the devil. All the more reason to lure him in, he told her. He kept to his dark place, laying plans for Buckminster's next visit.

Jacinta forgot her madness in the deep absorption of weaving, playing on her loom like an infernal harpist as she threaded the shuttle among its mute strings. Draped in mourning, hands as gnarled as her imagination, she called Elena into the room and wove her future like a spider casting its web around a fly. "Do you remember when Vickery saw you with Slater's boy Rory," she asked her, "and I told you to stay away from him?"

"I remember."

"Have you seen him again?"

"I have," Elena said, "the night they took the bull." No reason to lie now, with nothing at stake. "Luke shot him and I bandaged him up."

"Luke shot him?"

She met her mother's astonished eyes with wary composure. "Yes, and the next morning, before the fight, I pulled the bullet out of Rory's shoulder so he wouldn't die of infection."

"Who knows about this?"

"Slater's foreman, Buckminster. He was spying on us."

"By now he will have told other men. They'll draw their own conclusions."

"We were just talking. That's all we ever did. You can ask Rory, he'll tell you the truth."

"Don't you realize the truth doesn't matter? Why do you suppose I married your father? He rode out of the desert with a few rawboned longhorns and paid court to me like a queen. If he'd heard the rumors about me he would have ridden on—though there was nothing to them, no more than the ones about you. They damaged me in the eyes of the few men who were worthy of me. My father took what he could get for me and sent me north."

Elena turned and fled to her room. The disaster had left her so devastated that she'd thought the whole world had changed, and now she realized that most of what she thought she escaped from hadn't changed at all. Men and women, fathers and mothers, pride and greed and shame—none of that had gone away, it had just been twisted into a different shape. She was still a pawn among kings and queens and that would never change. She felt the future twining around her as never before.

Buckminster again found the Captain on his porch with the big yellow cur curled at his feet. His shotgun lay on the table beside him. He seemed in better spirits than before, though still not of this world but of some darker chaos outside its creation. The hot spell had broken leaving a confusion of wind and wispy clouds behind. A few unsaddled horses browsed from a manger in the corral. Charlie Crow watched Buckminster with a wary eye from the open barn door. Buckminster hated Crow for the intimacy he imagined between him and Elena. There were no other men left on the ranch except Old Zeke, who spent his days in the cookhouse and slept in the barn, too blind to be anywhere else.

"Good morning, Captain."

"I knew you'd be back," the Captain said. "This pup's been expecting you." The dog growled and showed Buckminster one of its baleful eyes. "What tomfoolery have you got in store for me today? It better not be trying to buy my daughter."

Buckminster stood on the stairs, a few steps down, at eye level with the Captain. "Slater isn't of a mind to buy her. He just wants your leave to court her, same as any man courts a woman."

"That's very gentlemanly," the Captain said, "for swamp trash. What does that mean to him, courting?"

"It means the regular kind. Sweet talk and all. Let her choose for herself."

The Captain nodded as if he agreed, but then he asked, "Why would he need my permission to do that? I don't rule over her."

"Well, in case you did."

"I ought to warn you—she's sweet on Rory."

Buckminster expected that. "That's just the thing, Captain," he said. "I told you about them false rumors going around about her and some man. Well, I don't know who that man was, but I know what Rory says about her and I wouldn't repeat it, not to you or to her or anybody else."

"Does he admit he was the man?"

"He won't say, but he does say he'd never marry her. Just a roll in the hay, I guess is what it was for him."

Cunning, the Captain thought. This man is cunning, or seems so, which means he's not. Unless showing you his cunning is part of the ruse. "Does Slater know anything about this?"

"Not yet, but like as not he will before long. I don't know if he'll want to marry her when he finds out."

"Finds out what?"

"About them rumors."

"Come on up and sit down." The Captain reached down to stroke the dog's neck, then stood up to go inside. "Elena needs to hear this."

"No, sir, I wouldn't want to be telling her this."

"You'll tell her or I'll set this dog on you. It's less than you deserve for telling me."

He stepped inside and in a few minutes brought Elena out and sat her down on a bench across from Buckminster. "You know Buckminster, don't you?" The foreman tipped his hat and ventured a nod. "He has something he wants to tell you."

She eyed Buckminster with undisguised contempt. He twiddled his hat on his lap, eyes goggling, in a fair imitation of embarrassment that fooled no one. "Well, it's like this," he stammered, "based on what I heard anyway—but I want you to know, miss, I don't believe a word of it—that you've been with a man, in a way that a young girl shouldn't be. The fellas at the saloon laugh and make jokes about it, Rory most of all—I wouldn't repeat the things he says—he lets on he knows all about you, though he won't say it was him, and far as he's concerned there ain't no question of making an honest woman of you—"

Elena cut him off. "What are you trying to say?"

He stopped twiddling and smoothed his hat with his thumbs. His words had piled up and stopped.

"What he's saying," the Captain explained, "is that your Rory doesn't want any more to do with you. He thinks you're a whore. Does that about sum it up, Buckminster?"

"I wouldn't exactly put it that way, Captain."

"That's the way you put it to me."

Elena lowered her eyes, then covered them for fear of showing any part of her pain to this man who chilled her heart like none she'd ever known. Her breath quickened and even that left her exposed, as if she'd cried out. The numbness she'd felt since the day Luke died could not protect her. Even in that numbness she'd kept a place for Rory, a special place like an ember in a cold fire. Now she knew she would never feel that warmth again.

With a show of respect her father waited until she'd regained her composure. Buckminster kept his head down as if expecting to be whipped. Without looking at either of them she stood up, walked inside, and shut the door behind her.

"You say Slater don't know about any of this," the Captain said. "What is he, deaf or a fool?"

"He don't mix with other men."

The Captain studied Buckminster with detachment, the way you might study a toad or a curious insect. He saw through his falseness, yet the man remained a mystery. What was there about him that wasn't false? "You're an honest man, Buckminster"—they exchanged glances and with them an acknowledgement that what he'd just said was a lie—"and I'll be honest with you." Another lie, worthy of the first one.

"I'm glad we understand each other," Buckminster said.

The Captain nodded without smiling. "If Elena consents to marry Slater, there will be financial requirements."

"Of course," Buckminster said. "You got a figure in mind?"

"She's not for sale. I thought we agreed on that."

"Begging your pardon. I didn't mean it that way. But then what—"

"Just set and listen. My only concern is for Elena's happiness. Like any loving daughter she wants her parents to be secure. We don't know where we'll be living a month from now. The owner of the bull that killed my son filed a judgment that covers everything I have and then some. In a few days some marshal or deputy'll be out here to take this house, the barn, the horses and everything else."

"That's a shame, Captain. I wish there was something—"

"Unless somebody buys that judgment and hands it over to me. That would be Slater if he wants to marry Elena. And before the wedding he'll execute an irrevocable deed of trust putting everything he owns in her name in the event that anything happens to him."

Buckminster seemed, for once—and possibly for real—befuddled. "I'll be honest with you, Captain"—groping for words, the usual hollow words—"That's something I hadn't counted on, Slater disposing of all his property like that. I've been with him since he came out here. He promised me if I stayed loyal to him, I'd get half of the outfit some day. And I've stayed loyal, right up until this very minute. But the idea of giving everything to Elena—I just don't know."

"Isn't that what usually happens in a marriage?"

"I reckon so, if there ain't a prior claim against it."

The Captain smirked at his legalistic paltering. "Just so there's no misunderstanding: Elena won't be marrying him unless she gets an irrevocable deed of trust on all his property. You go back and tell him that."

Buckminster swallowed hard, fighting the realization that all his fawning and cunning had resulted only in his own impoverishment. "Slater won't like it."

"It's you that don't like it. It cuts you out. But it's not as bad as it sounds. It cuts Rory out too. And that leaves Elena in sole possession of the outfit and you as the only man capable of managing it if Slater was out of the way."

"What do you mean out of the way?"

"Anything can happen out on the range—you know that. A man can get struck by lightning, bit by a rattlesnake, crushed by his horse."

"That's true, but I still don't see—"

"Any of those things could happen to Slater the day after Elena marries him. And then what would she do? She couldn't manage the outfit by herself, she'd need a husband, and if you play your cards right that just might be you. If I was a betting man I'd give odds that it would be."

"I don't know, Captain. You're asking me to put everything on the line for the far-fetched possibility that Slater might be eliminated by some unlikely misfortune. I'm not a betting man, but if I was, I wouldn't put a nickel down on that hand."

"A man like you," the Captain said, "I'm sure you can think of something."

23

Bear Creek, Missouri, 1870

They called the Slaters backwoods but the whole town knew they were smart. The old man set his pastures along the river, the barns uphill. Built up the herd and trained his sons to it, driving the stock out of the woods to St. Louis and coming back with cartloads of guns, powder, molasses, calico for the local trade. Then with the war came the raids, the banishments, the burned-out farms, the orphans and ravished wives. Bushwhackers, Jayhawkers, militias, armies: murder was their trade, blood their legal tender. Whose side are you on? It don't matter, they're all just as bad.

The old man never came back. Killed, captured or deserted, nobody ever knew. His wife dead of a fever, two sons killed, daughters carried away by Jayhawkers. Only two sons left and they were as close as brothers could be. Jake the younger, bright and cheerful, liked to talk more than he liked to work. Aiming to be a politician, people said, maybe president someday. Afterwards everybody said Slater how could you trust that fella, you're a shrewd judge of character. People joked, tried to warn him, but when it came to farming and cattle feeding Jake never let him down, never shorted him on the cash from a sale, never made a promise he didn't keep. It was in just that one thing—women, women and men, and the tricks they play on you—that Slater had a blind spot, he was like a little child. In everything else he was the one you trusted, listened to, followed, quiet and patient as he was. Knew cattle, knew horses, and more important, knew men—and he took pride in that knowledge, pride enough to brush off the warnings about Jake. He knew how to lead men without lording it over them, how to command loyalty and obedience without demanding it. You needed that to run a cattle outfit after the war, when the Texans started driving their herds in and the Missouri stock all caught the Texas fever and died, and you had to shoot the longhorns on sight and some of the Texans too to keep them away from your herd. Slater kept the cattle safe from the fever, the men safe from the Texans, the farm safe from the tax-collector. He didn't mix with other men, or drink, or play cards. His thoughts were dense and seldom heard.

Then he met and married Cynthia, a marvel who brought love and warmth into his life. Blue-eyed, golden-haired, barefoot much of the time, she laughed at the discomforts he and his brother were accustomed to, the smoky fires, the leaky roof, the tumbledown porch, and saw to it they got fixed. She planted a garden of poppies and asters and sunflowers and filled the house with flowers. She coaxed Slater out of himself and away from his work and showed him the joys of living in the world. And after a year she told him she was going to have a baby. Nothing changed at first, they went on the same way as before, but toward the end she seemed to lose her bloom, her eyes blanched, her skin turned blue, her fine teeth fell out. She prayed to God and only got worse. Slater had never prayed, never trusted God. The only person he'd ever trusted, apart from his brother, was Cynthia.

He never lost that trust until the day she died, giving birth to a son. Her death about broke his heart and what was he to do with that poor sickly child? He swaddled and nursed it as best he could, with a little help from some church ladies, but mostly they turned away, couldn't look him in the eye because they knew the truth, everybody knew the truth except him. The child belonged to Jake, a charmer they'd always called him, a ladies' man. And finally Jake, seeing how broken-hearted he was, tried to comfort him (or so he claimed) by hinting at the truth, but it took much more than just hinting before he saw the light. Jake had to rub it in his face and mock him for a fool before he got the message and even then he couldn't believe it, or understand why his brother, if it was true, would reveal his crime when he could have kept it hidden, until he understood that seeing the first glimmer of the truth in his eyes and laughing at him as it glowed brighter was as enjoyable for Jake as it must have been to bed his wife. He had an evil streak or more than a streak and Slater could see it now, to take advantage of his blindness on this one subject, to betray him and at last to taunt him with his evil. Slater picked up a rake and chased after him. Out of the barn and across a soggy field until he caught up with him, swinging wildly, landing the tines in his leg, then in his back, until he limped away cursing in indignation. Even his curses had the ring of mockery as he ran away. And everyone who saw Slater then, furious, beside himself, inconsolable, laughed at him behind his back. How could it be that this patient, quiet man had so much fury inside him? How could any man have been so naive? And when the child died, in the ordinary course of things, his fury turned cold and froze him to his bones. He buried the child and climbed on his horse and rode south and into Texas until he found a cattle drive headed west. They drove two thousand longhorns into the mirage country, a land of poison lakes and prehistoric skeletons and boiling quicksand where every morning the cowboys clubbed the newborn calves to death in front of their mothers and somewhere amid the heat and wind and agonizing thirst of that country the mirages became real and he began to see things that weren't there. He knew that sooner or later in that immense cauldron of evil he'd see his brother again and be taken in by him once more. And when his fever broke he escaped from the mirages and his own madness, and it was a few days later, camped with the outfit along the Rio Concho, that he plucked Rory off the bottom of the river and made him his son.

Many years later, after Slater came to the basin, he recognized the Captain as the man he'd heard about from the old cowhand

Johnson along the Concho. The man with the fishhook whipscar under his lip who admired the Comanches, so he thought, for not believing in anything. They'd lured him out, scalped his men and spared him just for sport, laughed at him, so he could run back to his outfit in disgrace, leaving Johnson behind to be killed and mutilated. But the Indians spared Johnson as an eyewitness to his cowardice and betrayal, sliced off his nose and let him go, and the Captain—that's what he called himself now, the Captain—pressed farther west, picked up a wife in Santa Fe and led his new outfit north into the wilderness. He was not an evil man, Slater divined, but a man who knew evil, and had found it in his own heart, and rather than to hide it or expunge it he would taunt himself with it, and any other man who could see it there.

24.

Nothing had changed in that vast tideless sea for ten thousand years. The sun was the same—fierce in summer, distant in winter, fickle in spring and fall. The clouds that cast their shadows on its emptiness puffed themselves up, darkened, sometimes raged, then drifted away without a trace. The wind never stopped. The land stood vacant, hollow, scarred with ancient waterways and dunes. Torrents of rain vanished into the dust, snow blew away in the wind. Salt and sulfur boiled out of the earth. Short bunch grass, stunted juniper, sagebrush, cactus—those were all that grew there. Except on the clearest of days you couldn't see across it. Staggered ridges to the east. To the south the crested abyss, to the north the badland. To the west, beyond the cliffs, canyons counting their years in dinosaur bones. Extinct beasts had roamed there, leaving their successors— elk, antelope, bear—to be feasted on by wolves, ravens, buzzards, always the same. And the invaders of recent times: wild horses and their doomed hunters, crook-horned cattle and the men who drove them to slaughter. Renegades and outlaws and would-be kings.

Elena rode her sorrel mare out to the mustangs in her mourning dress and bonnet, black from head to toe, bereft of her brother and her own hopes. The September rains had risen in the sky along with banks of fog and braying crescents of geese. The mustangs huddled close together in the first thickening of their winter coats. Susannah trotted out to greet her, then wheeled and raced away. Elena climbed down, hitched her anxious mare to a juniper and strolled fifty yards in a zigzag path cooing to the mustang, which kept her distance, then curveted closer in a game of playful disobedience. But it was a serious game. Susannah was acting out her freedom and demanding that it be recognized. She had not been subjugated like Elena's mare and she wanted Elena to acknowledge that. They played this game whenever Elena went out to see her, and it always ended the same way: Elena astride the mustang's back, clutching her thick mane, the two of them racing in a wide arc across the range. In exchange for a few loving words and a handful of oats, Susannah loaned Elena a little bit of her freedom.

Jacinta said she'd shoot Slater if he set foot on their property.

"If you shoot him," the Captain told her, "it won't be our property for long. We'll be sleeping under the wagon—if they leave us the wagon—and eating what we can scrape out of the dust. Is that what you want?"

"You'd sacrifice your daughter?"

"Didn't you hear what I said about the deed of trust? She'd only be marrying him to get back what's ours. And once that's done..."

They sat before the fire in what Jacinta called the parlor. The house was dark at midday, all curtains drawn against the drizzling sky. Jacinta had taken to wringing her hands, biting her bloodless lips. Her eyes flickered like spyglasses on some distant watchtower.

"Buckminster'll take care of him. He has a high opinion of himself. He thinks he'll be marrying Elena next."

"Buckminster?" She coughed, nearly spat. "You can't trust him to get rid of Slater. That man is a snake."

The Captain hesitated.

Jacinta dug her nails into the back of his hand. "I want to hear you swear that you'll kill Slater. Hunt him down and kill him like a dog. Hang him the way he hung Vickery."

"I'm telling you—"

"That's what you have to do. Swear that you'll do it or I'll do it myself."

Elena rode down from the cliffs at sunset to fix supper for her parents. The two of them still grieving so, that neither would eat (so she believed) unless she cooked their food and put it in front of them. They depended on her for everything now, almost like children. The wind was cold and damp but the house was warm inside, though nearly dark.

Her father squatted in front of the fireplace, adding a log to the blaze. Her mother, wrapped in mourning, raven hair pulled straight back, perched on the sofa wringing her hands.

When the Captain finished his fire-stoking he sat down beside her. Elena's spirits had been raised by the mustangs; they sank like a stone when she faced her mother and father. "We need to talk to you," the Captain said.

"About your future," Jacinta added. Her eyes a pair of black mirrors flickering in the firelight.

"Our family's about been destroyed," the Captain went on. "In a few days the Spaniard's agents will take this house and what's left of our livestock, the wagons and the saddles and tack and everything else we own. We'll be thrown out on the plains with nothing but the clothes on our backs."

An unnerving image: all her clothes on her back as she staggered under the vast, hollow sky. "Where will we go?"

"There's no place to go. I doubt if we'll get out of the basin alive."

"We only want what's best for you," Jacinta murmured.

"You're a grown up woman and you have to act like one."

A memory made Elena shudder: The Captain telling Luke he was a man and had to act like one as he sent him out to be killed. Now he was doing the same thing to her.

"There's one man in the basin who could support you," her father said, "give you a decent life and keep us from losing everything we have left."

"And who would that be?"

"Mr. Slater."

"Mister is it now?"

"Speaking with all due respect."

Slater rode out to the Captain's ranch in a faded black suit that made him look like an out-of-work undertaker. Charlie Crow watched from the open barn door but did not return his nod. Elena had confided in him about her father's plan to marry her off to Slater. He wanted to tell her not to do it, there were other men, better men, but when he opened his mouth he couldn't find the words. She never suspected that he might be in love with her.

The big yellow cur met Slater in the yard, snarling and baring its teeth, and followed him up the stairs to the front porch. He removed his hat and smoothed his shirt front and wiped the sweat and grime off his face before he tapped on the door, rehearsing the condolences he would offer the Captain and his wife. They did not appear, then or later. Elena came to the door and opened it without inviting him inside. He stumbled back, hat in hand, bowing slightly as she stepped forward and the dog slinked past him to kiss her fingers.

She was also dressed in black, still mourning her brother. She bent over and whispered something gentle to the dog, whose ears lay flat as he curled around her legs. Slater felt like he should have been selling sewing machines or farm implements.

She shook his hand, which embarrassed him. "My condolences for your loss," he said.

"Which one?"

He blinked in confusion. "All of them. Your brother. Luke."

"Thanks for letting us take his body," she said. "Did you hang Vickery?"

He nodded, fumbling his hat.

"Can't say as I need much consolation for that."

He nodded again, ventured a smile. "He wasn't included."

Her amber eyes steady, neither amused nor disapproving. "You're here because you want to marry me," she said.

Her directness unnerved him. "Well, yes." Trying to sound humble without seeming hesitant. "If you'll have me."

That was the wrong thing to say. "You've decided before you even met me?" Her voice skeptical, almost mocking.

"I've always liked you. Seen you out on the range plenty of times."

"That's not much to go on."

"I can see what I'm getting." Another faux pas.

She started to turn away, then met his eyes. "It's not like buying a horse."

"No," he said, wary of elaboration. "I can see that."

At last a small smile. "A horse you get to ride first."

He grinned and his eyes darted away. He would have had better luck talking to a horse, he thought. They would have understood each other, him and the horse, even before he rode it. With this girl it was like trying to talk a foreign language. Which is what he was doing, because women are from a different country than men. A country he'd visited briefly as a young man but never really understood, and which he'd fled after his wife died and he learned what she'd done. And now here he was twenty years later, knocking at the gate to get back in and still not knowing the language or the customs or even where it was on the map.

"We need to get better acquainted, is what I meant," she said with a slightly bigger smile.

"Sure we do," he said. "I never thought we didn't."

And so for an hour, sitting across from each other, they stammered and rattled on about nothing, which is generally how men and women get acquainted and how they stay acquainted even through a long marriage, until at last their words were spent and they stared at each other in silence.

"It's settled, then," Slater said.

"What's settled?"

"That we're getting married."

"Nothing's settled," she said. "I need a couple days to decide."

25.

It took her three days. Methodically, she weighed the choices laid out for her. Poverty, homelessness, unending hardship, or a comfortable existence as Slater's wife. Marriage is a woman's lot, her mother told her. To be used as men use women and brought to childbearing, with its travail and smell of death.

"I won't be a pawn," she told her mother.

Jacinta smiled. "A pawn can be a queen if the game goes on long enough."

But still a pawn to the hand that moves it, she wanted to say. And what moves that hand? The answer seemed obvious. The pain of her rejection and shaming by Rory had made her believe in fate. There was no arguing with what was meant to be.

When Slater called his men together and told them that Elena had agreed to marry him, they greeted the news with cheers and bawdy jokes. Nobody noticed Rory slinking into the barn where he threw down stacks of hay bales and pounded feed sacks with his fist and hurled saddles on the floor. He jumped on his horse and spurred it to gallop five miles out to a run-down cabin near the vermillion cliffs where he could sit alone smoking and wishing he'd never been born. That night in the saloon he drank eight shots of whiskey and socked a cowboy who made a joke about Elena. A dozen men whaled on him until Moondog and Crazy Ike pulled them off and dragged him home where he stayed in his bunk for two days.

Slater looked in on him, made sure he was still alive, but could get no response. He walked out and found Buckminster smoking by the bunkhouse. "What's got into Rory, I wonder?" he asked him.

"Well, boss—if I can speak confidentially—it's the marriage."
Buckminster glanced around and lowered his voice to keep anybody
from overhearing. "Not that he objects to you marrying Elena. It's
just that he counted on inheriting something. Some land or cattle or
a piece of the outfit. But now if you're going to have a wife and
family he's wondering if there'll be anything left for him."

"Sure there will. I never said there wouldn't."

"That's what I thought. That's what I told him. But I'm sure I
told you—the Captain says you have to leave everything to Elena."

Slater's eyes narrowed. "That's what the Captain says."

"He wants it all in writing before the wedding. A deed of trust—
"

"I know what you told me. There's ways around that."

"Well, I'm glad to hear that, for Rory's sake." Buckminster kept
his voice soft, his tone ingratiating. "And if you don't mind me
saying so, for mine too."

Slater cocked his head. "Yours?"

"Sure. You said there'd be something here for me, if I stuck
around."

"That wasn't no promise."

Buckminster tossed his cigar down and stared into the dirt as
those four words—"That wasn't no promise"—echoed in his stony
heart. He knew that until the day his heart stopped, stifling that echo,
he would not forget this betrayal. He would have the justice that was
his due. "No, I guess it wasn't," he said.

"Just an idea. Not that I won't do it. You just got to wait and see
what happens after all this gets squared away."

Slater waited until Rory was back in the saddle doing a day's
work before he approached him. The boy was still embarrassed
about the licking he took in the saloon, still keeping shy of the other
men, even when they went out of their way to be friendly. Anybody

would feel that way, Slater told himself, though it irked him that Rory treated him the same as the others. He'd hoped the boy would share his happiness about Elena and the future he looked forward to with her, that for once he'd show a little awareness that Slater was a man with a life of his own instead of always being the parent, the teacher, the boss. But that was probably too much to ask of a young man who still hadn't had a chance to find his own path. Slater was grateful to Buckminster for confiding Rory's worries about his inheritance. And there was something else that needed to be straightened out. The two of them had been like father and son for over twelve years, with no wife or mother to get between them. Naturally the boy would worry that the new wife might be an intrusion. So it was important, Slater decided, to reassure Rory that he wouldn't be excluded from his new life with Elena.

He caught up with Rory watering his horse at the trough by the corral. "Can I have a word?" he asked him.

A sullen grunt, not meeting Slater's eyes. "Sure."

"There's something I just wanted to make clear. When I get married, I'll have a will and naturally, if I died, my wife would get everything. But I'll carve your part out ahead of time."

Rory kept his eyes on the trough, as if the horse might stop drinking unless he watched.

"Just thought you'd want to know."

"Much obliged."

Slater felt a twitch of anger, tried to swallow it. Was Rory laughing at him? No, it must have been the other thing: the boy was jealous, afraid Elena would come between them. "You're young," Slater said. "You got plenty of time before you need to worry about such things."

That got Rory's attention. "What things?"

"Inheriting and the like. In the meantime you ought to get to know Elena. She's a fine gal, I'm sure you'll like her. The new house is almost ready to move into and you'll always be welcome there. In fact I was hoping you could help us out with setting up housekeeping."

Rory stared back at Slater in wonderment at his blindness, his goodness, his childish folly.

"The Captain's wife—Elena's mother—she don't like the sight of me, says she'll shoot me if I ever show my face over there. So I'm wondering if you'd drive over in the wagon and bring Elena over here. I want to show her the place, show her where she's going to live, give her a chance to start feeling at home here."

"You want me to go pick her up?"

Another twitch of anger, this time at the boy's mocking tone. "Is that too much to ask?"

"I couldn't do that," Rory said.

"She won't bite. You're going to have to get to know her sooner or later."

Fall whirled in like a whip, flinging the dust of a long hot summer into the sky. The sudden cold stung with its touch. If there'd been anything green in that basin it would have shriveled and died, except for the scrub pines, so gnarled by drought they paid no mind to the seasons. The men worked long hours getting the ranch ready for winter. Culling the herd, branding the calves born since the spring roundup, hauling in what little hay had survived the fire. Sledding timber down from the mountains to hew it into planks and firewood. Painting tar on the floor beams of the barn and the corral posts before the ice settled in to split them apart. Amidst all this activity Slater set a crew to finishing and furnishing the new house so his bride could move in right after the wedding. He was proud of the house and anxious for her to see it. And he was anxious about something else (which was why he could not be dissuaded from sending Rory to fetch her): it was important that she and Rory like each other.

When Rory arrived at the Captain's with Slater's wagon, he was met by Charlie Crow, who stood guard at the arching gateway, sullen-faced, brandishing a shotgun. He wondered if that show of force was directed by Elena or her father, and if it was aimed at him or Slater. He flicked the mules forward and stopped in front of the house to wait for Elena. "Morning, ma'am," he said without looking at her. "I'm here to take you to Slater's."

"I thank you." She climbed up and sat beside him, gathering her skirt around her ankles to keep it from touching him. "I could've ridden over there myself but my father wouldn't let me."

He turned the wagon around and drove toward Slater's without acknowledging her, taking the long way around rather than to whip the mules through the sand wash. It was a cold, gray morning, acting like rain. The junipers quaked as the wind lisped down from the bluffs.

"It sounds like the wind is whispering, doesn't it?" she said.

Rory took his time answering, as if she'd asked a hard question. "I never thought that, one way or the other."

"My father didn't like it when Luke and I used to whisper. He said whispering is lying."

"I guess the wind is lying then."

He stared at the sky, the bluffs, the speckled plain, the mountains in the distance. The backs of the mules, the flies around their muzzles, their tails whisking beneath him. Everything he'd seen a thousand times before instead of looking at Elena or talking to her. He hoped she'd say something but whatever it was, he wouldn't believe it.

"How is your shoulder healing up?" she asked after a long while.

"Fine." It still hurt something fierce but he wasn't about to tell her that. "Appreciate what you done."

"I'm sorry Luke shot you. I tried to stop him."

"I guess I had it coming." Too humble. Pathetic. "Taking the bull and all."

It sounded so simple. Borrowing a bull, a bullet in the shoulder. As if all the rest never happened. All those men never killed, the herd still alive. Luke never gored to death.

"I'm sorry about Luke," he said.

"The bull killed him. It was his own fault."

"No, it was ours. We shouldn't have took that bull. Then he wouldn't have come to fetch it. I'm sorry."

She cried when he said that and he pretended not to notice. When they came in sight of Slater's camp, she said, "You'll have to get used to having me around."

He drove in silently and pulled the wagon up in front of Slater's cabin. Slater heard the reins jangling and came out to greet them. Rory had never seen him so excited.

Slater did everything he could to make Elena and Rory like each other. That almost seemed more important than whether Elena liked him. He praised Rory for his riding and roping and his hard work as if she'd never heard of him before, and he told Rory all the good things he'd heard about her. They listened grudgingly, nodded but had nothing to say, more distant in his presence than they'd been in the wagon. They both felt embarrassed and a little guilty that they'd ever been friends. Obviously Slater didn't know that, and for some reason—they couldn't have said what it was—they felt the need to hide it from him.

Slater took them in the new log house and showed them how he planned to outfit the various rooms. The bedrooms were along a gallery on the second floor, overlooking the main rooms on the ground floor. "This'll be our room," he told Elena. "The biggest bedroom, naturally. And Rory that one'll be yours."

Elena turned her head, avoiding Slater's eyes. Rory backed away, his face burning. "I'll be sleeping out in the bunkhouse," he said. "You can save that room for the baby."

Slater looked up, sensing the awkwardness between them. "I'm sorry if I'm acting like a fool. I just want you to like each other."

"We're okay, aren't we, Elena?"

She nodded. "Sure we are."

Rory forced a smile and headed down the stairs. "Let me know when you're ready to drive back."

The ride home was worse than the one that brought her there. Slater's efforts to make them like each other had only brought out their mutual hostility. Each of them, if you asked them, would have told you they'd been scorned, lied about, laughed at by the other, so there was more than a little anger bottled up inside them. And now they'd have the added vexation of belonging to the same family. Slater had warned her that Rory would be jealous—not of her, but of him. She took a much darker view. She knew he'd do his best to make all three of them miserable.

They barely spoke for most of the trip. Then, as the wagon rattled close to the ranch, she tried to break the ice. "I can see that living there is going to be awkward."

"Don't worry, I won't be living in that house. I told you that."

"Just because I'm marrying your father, that doesn't mean everything has to change between you and him."

"He ain't my father."

"Foster father, then."

"That's over and done with. I don't need no fostering anymore."

"Just the same, I don't want you to think I'm horning in. We don't have to be rivals. We owe it to him to get along."

Rory allowed himself a sardonic smile. "I guess we've got to stop hating each other all over again."

"I've never hated you. Do you hate me?"

"No, ma'am."

Wedding preparations proceeded on both ends of the sand wash. The ceremony would take place at the Captain's, the newlyweds retiring afterwards to Slater's new house. Moondog volunteered to officiate, being the only man of god (he never said which god) within a hundred miles, to which the Captain agreed, overruling his wife who insisted that they send for a priest. Jacinta had never withdrawn her threat to shoot her future son-in-law if he set foot on their property; Slater and several of his men, including Moondog, planned to come fully armed in case she tried to carry it out. Slater bought the judgment levied on the Captain's property and promised to surrender it, along with the deed of trust, when the bride said 'I do.' Elena busied herself with sewing her dress and assembling her trousseau, though she thought about Rory more than about Slater. Every word of their conversations in the wagon echoed through her mind like some bittersweet melody she'd heard long ago and couldn't forget. Rory thought about her too, though the tune he heard was more bitter than sweet.

Five days before the wedding Slater invited Elena back to oversee some finishing touches on the house and he asked Rory to pick her up again. Rory balked and Buckminster offered to make the trip, but Slater insisted that Rory be the one to go. It was another chance for the two of them to make friends. Buckminster couldn't help but smile at his folly. He rode out after Rory, far enough behind to keep out of sight, mulling his next move.

Fetching Elena had already become a routine, it seemed. Presenting himself to the sullen guardian at the gate, more sullen each time, reining in the mules and turning the wagon around, repeating the exercise once she'd climbed on board. Barely polite greetings. Inauspicious grunts. No inkling that anything important was about to happen. They rode silently almost as far as Slater's camp, harnesses creaking in the wind. Rory as distant as the clouds, Elena brooding, choosing her words.

"I know we're supposed to like each other," she said. "So I just want you to know, if that's going to happen, there's things that'll have to change. First of all, I won't stand for any more of your insults."

"Insults?"

"I know what you've been saying about me at the saloon."

"And what would that be?"

"For one thing, that would be your boast—your false boast—that you've taken me to bed."

"You ever seen my bed? It's a pine bunk about a foot wide. You wouldn't even fit on it."

"Is that one of your jokes? I've heard you tell some pretty good ones."

The mules stepped up their pace, startled by the angry voices. "I did hear that you've been with a man," Rory said. "But it sure as hell wasn't me. I think I'd remember that. But you were probably thinking of me when you said you wouldn't marry a pauper."

"I said no such thing."

"No, you're going to marry Slater because that's your way to get back what you've lost. For that you'd sell yourself—or did your father collect the money?"

The mules had begun to trot, pitching the wagon from side to side in the ruts. Rory strained to rein them in while Elena waited for a chance to jump off. The insults just kept coming and she'd had enough of them. "Stop it! Stop the wagon!" she yelled, and when the wagon stopped she climbed down.

"What's the matter with you?"

"You're calling me a whore, just like Buckminster said."

For a breathless moment they stared at each other as a sudden silence trembled between them. In the junipers the wind was whispering again, words you couldn't quite make out. What was it she'd said the last time? Whispering is lying. You couldn't even trust the wind.

"Who did you hear all this from?" he asked her. "Buckminster?"

"Mostly from my father."

"Who heard it from Buckminster?"

Her lips pinched together. Not ready to admit the plain truth. "Some of it."

He reached down to help her up. "Climb back on. It's too dusty to walk in that black dress."

She pulled herself up and brushed the dust off her dress. "Just because Buckminster said it, that doesn't mean it's not true."

"No, but I'll tell you a funny thing. Everything I heard about you, I heard from Buckminster too."

They rode quietly, both trying to grasp the enormity of what had just happened. "I'm still engaged to marry Mr. Slater," she said as the wagon rolled into Slater's camp.

Rory leaned around to face her, incredulous, as if she was a wonder of the world. "You're going to marry a man you call Mister?"

"Does he have a Christian name?"

"If he does I never heard it. Never heard of him being a Christian neither."

Slater rushed out to greet them before their feet touched the ground. They met him awkwardly, eyes averted, words straggling. For the rest of the day they walked in the sudden grace of recognition. Play-acting unfriendliness now as Slater tried to bring them together. Careful not to look at each other lest their eyes meet. Ashamed, because in their hearts—as some might have said who knew their Bible—they were already committing adultery.

Rory left Elena with Slater and went looking for Buckminster. In the barn he found a bullwhip coiled on a peg, took it down and lashed it a few times at a wooden post. When he stepped outside hefting the whip he saw Buckminster rubbing down his saddle on the other side of the corral, whistling as he worked. He moved toward him, near blind with anger and hatred. It would have been easy enough to carve up his smooth-shaven face, strip the flesh off his lying lips, reel him in like runaway calf, but he checked himself. To do that would ruin him in Slater's eyes, finish his days in the outfit. Best to bide his time, talk nice, get Elena alone. There would be plenty of time to whip Buckminster.

All day Elena's spirits were spinning, hanging on Slater's every word. She was warmer toward him than ever before, to his unsuspecting delight. The greater his delight, the deeper her treachery; the deeper her treachery, the brighter her smile. By the time she was ready to leave, they were both giddy with anticipation, knowing that their fondest hopes would soon be fulfilled. Though in each case that meant something different, as she knew, and he did not.

She called to Rory to bring the wagon around, and when he'd done so she kissed Slater's cheek, climbed on board and waved goodbye, all smiles. Rory yelled at the mules—"Git up! Git up!"— and the wagon plodded forward. Before it had gone half a mile, just around a curve behind a sand hill, he stopped the wagon and he and Elena fell into each other's arms, lost in a kiss that seemed to last far into the night.

26.

Less than a week until the wedding date. The weather had turned cold and damp, massive cloud banks towering in from the northwest like a herd of mythical beasts, dark, brooding, bellowing as they unleashed broadsides of rain that ran off invisible mountains and bluffs into the clefts and crevices of the earth. The men fed the cattle what little hay they had, waiting for the rain to end before they could drive them down from the high country for the winter. Even at midday you couldn't see farther than half a mile. If a man rode into the mist, that was the last you'd see of him until the end of the day.

Rory remembered that broken-down cabin out by the vermillion cliffs, where sometimes, when the herd grazed nearby, the cowboys spent the night. In this weather nobody would go out there. Elena met him there every day, riding out on the pretext of taking care of the mustangs. There was a straw pallet and that was where they spent most of their time.

Neither had any experience with sex except what they'd observed of the cattle, which proved to be laughably inapplicable. Fortunately nature took them under her wing and taught them everything they needed to know.

"I've had my eye on you since the day we got here," Rory told her. They lay twined together in the melancholy mood that follows love.

"It's been the same for me," she said.

"I knew there were other girls in the world, but I had to have you. Slater wanted to leave the basin and I made up all sorts of reasons not to, shamed him into staying even when your father threatened him." He raised himself on one elbow and looked down into her eyes. "This is something you need to know about me. By making him stay here, I'm responsible for all the bad things that've happened, all the hatred and bloodshed, because I wouldn't give up on you."

"Hush." She reached up to block his lips with her finger. "You can't live your life worrying about how you might have changed somebody else's."

"It's true, though. If Slater had left the basin, you wouldn't even know me."

"In that case, I'd be very unhappy."

And Luke would still be alive, Rory thought—though he didn't say it—and she wouldn't be marrying Slater. There were so many things they couldn't talk about. The suffering, the deaths, the destruction and disgrace—they couldn't be erased by a few words of love. And the future couldn't be avoided either: it was a book which had already been written. By its lights they were traitors, sleeping with the enemy.

"Does Slater know?" Elena asked him as they dressed to go their separate ways. She would leave first, Rory fifteen minutes later. Their horses stood hidden in a thicket along the ridge.

"No, I'm sure he don't," Rory said. "I try to avoid him but he seeks me out. Always some question about you and the house. Do I think Elena'd like this, or that, or the other thing."

"He doesn't suspect anything?"

"He don't know anything about men and women."

"What do you think he'll do when he finds out?"

Elena had seen enough of men, enough of their pride and their anger, their violence, their heartlessness, to guess the answer to her question. She wished she hadn't asked it, and she was glad when Rory didn't answer. She pulled her boots on and kissed him goodbye.

Before she left she asked him, "Wasn't he married once before?"

"He was. Whatever happened, he never talks about it."

Buckminster waited nearby, invisible in a cane brake around a spring along the bluff. In the gathering dusk he watched Elena unhitch her sorrel mare and trot away, followed by Rory ten minutes later. He considered his position and the options open to him. An artless insinuation was all it would take to end this affair, his word being trusted on all sides. Tragic it would be, yet just, and he fancied himself an instrument of justice. But he had his personal interest to consider. The blandishments of the Captain, the faithlessness of Slater, the pleasure of seeing Rory banished from the basin—all these he took into account. But there were voices within him stronger than ambition or spite, breathless voices that spoke to him in the night in dark, urgent tones. One way or another, he would have that girl.

The men in Slater's outfit had no use for the days of the week, any more than the cattle did. They knew there were seven of them, but save for a few Bible thumpers they paid no mind to which one today or tomorrow happened to be. The same work had to be done no matter what day it was. Slater's wedding changed all that. It would take place on a Sunday, which meant that Friday and Saturday would be spent getting ready for it, in addition to the perennial chores of caring for the livestock. Saturday night earmarked for a celebration at the saloon, with a barbecue to follow on Sunday afternoon. Thursday and Friday to be spent putting the finishing touches on the new house and butchering the beef for the barbecue.

Slater oversaw all this activity with newfound enthusiasm and sociability. The prospect of marriage had released him from the stoic reticence which was all anyone had ever known of him. Suddenly he was voluble, eager, even a little argumentative. The men seemed apprehensive, on edge.

Thursday night Rory stood silent, red-faced, in the grub line, fearful of some joke the men might toss his way. Surely the fact that he was sleeping with Slater's bride was written all over him. He avoided Slater altogether, reflecting not guilt or fear but his secret superiority over the man who was destined to be the loser in their rivalry, of which Slater seemed still innocent of all knowledge. Sometimes, for fear of challenging this innocence, he dreamed of running away.

Slipping outside for a smoke, Rory stood leaning against the top rail of the corral. It was a clear, chilly night but rumoring change. A full moon had just risen over the lacy white of the plain. He sensed danger but before he could step away Slater was at his side, biting off the end of a cheroot. Cheerful, talkative, baring his thoughts with unaccustomed openness. "For once I feel I've got something to look forward to," he said, lighting his cigar. "What do you think, Rory? Is Elena everything I hoped she'd be?"

"Sure." Rory bit his lip, his face warm. Why would Slater think he could answer that? Did he know more than he let on?

"That's what I was hoping you'd say. I want you to like her."

"I like her fine."

Slater blew a smoke ring and watched it drift into the moonlight. "Who'd have thought I'd marry the Captain's daughter?"

Rory forced a laugh. "It's some kind of miracle."

"Even miracles happen for a reason," Slater said. "You see, the Captain and me, we have something in common. He's got a secret and I know what it is."

"A secret?"

"It's something that happened in his early days, after the war. Some cowboys got scalped by the Comanches because of him, and I heard about it. He saw me staring at that whip scar under his lip. That's how we got off on the wrong foot."

Rory rolled a cigarette and lighted it. "What I don't get," he said, "is why he didn't kill you like he said he would. He's had other men killed. Why didn't he send Vickery to kill you?"

"He was too proud."

"Too proud to kill you?"

"The Captain's got a madness of pride—vanity, my mother would've called it—and it's what drives him, the way we drive the cattle. He can't shake free of it, any more than the cattle can find the next pastureland without us goading them."

Slater blew another smoke ring and the two of them watched it spiral into the night. "Oh, he might have done it for business reasons," Slater said. "He could have told Vickery to shoot me just like you said. But he was too proud to have another man fight a personal battle for him. He'd have to do that himself."

"But he didn't."

"No, he couldn't do that either. He don't like to think of himself as a murderer. And in a funny way I think he wanted me alive. You could almost say he needed me."

That was a strange idea, Rory thought. "Needed you?"

"Think back to that first day we met down in front of his stock pen. You and I came drifting into the basin like a couple of Russian thistles, white trash, he called us, driving a wasted herd that wasn't worth browsing on the same shriveled grass as his. And he could tell right away, from the way I looked at that scar, that I knew his secret. He'd been living with that secret for twenty years, dreading the moment when a man would show up who knew it, not just the secret itself but the shame it stood for. And I was that man."

"Then it wasn't revenge for the insult?" Rory asked.

"That was the story he put out, but it never was that. It was because I knew his secret, and his shame."

Rory dropped his cigarette and ground it underfoot, still puzzled. He'd never thought the insult, if there was an insult, could account for the depth of the Captain's hostility.

"All those years," Slater went on, "he'd been haunted by a devil whose face he never saw, who never spoke, never stood in his way, and then suddenly it rose up in front of him and called out his name. He didn't know how much I knew or if I'd been sent here by the law or some kin of the men he let die, or whether it was just happenstance that sent me here. But as time went by and I didn't mention his secret, I must have seemed like an improvement over what he'd been dreading all those years. I was real at least, not some frenzy of the imagination. I guess you could say I was the devil he knew. The two of us sharing that secret made us like brothers under the skin. He was proud of the life he'd built to make up for what he'd done on the Comanche plains. He needed somebody to know about it, maybe to offer some kind of grace or forgiveness, and that somebody was me. I was the one man who understood him."

That was it, then, Rory thought. That was where his argument came out. That somehow he and the Captain were brothers, or partners, or maybe even closer than that, enemies, for so long they couldn't tell each other apart. Maybe that was Slater's plan all along, to replace the Captain and marry Elena. The devil you know.

"Probably this is all hogwash," Slater chuckled. "I don't know. I'm just jawing in the moonlight. But the thing is, Rory, you've got to realize the Captain ain't an evil man. He thought he was going to be a great man and instead he found evil in himself out on those plains in Texas, and he's been living with it ever since."

"We've all got evil in us, I guess," Rory said.

"There was plenty of evil on those Comanche plains. I've seen it myself, and not just there. Back home, too. That's why I left."

The words drifted out like one of Slater's smoke rings and hung in the air waiting for their mystery to be dispelled.

"Something to do with your wife?" Rory asked.

"My wife, and my brother too. A man I trusted. Loved, even."

He waited, not asking or expecting anything. Whatever would come must come by itself. The air seemed almost too heavy to be moved by words.

"She had a child that wasn't mine."

Not responding too quickly. Give it time. "What did you do?"

Slater coughed out a dry, mirthless laugh. "I didn't kill them, if that's what you're thinking. But sometimes I wish I did. At least the Captain was man enough to see the evil in his own heart and pay the price. I was in the middle of it and didn't even see it. Let it mock me behind my back."

He took a last puff and flicked his cigar sputtering over the corral. "I won't make that mistake again."

The men grew more and more uneasy, like cattle moiling at the approach of a storm. In a marriage brokered between the Captain and Buckminster they sensed disaster: their instinct was to protect Slater and the outfit. Two of them—Moondog and Jameson—went to Slater and begged him to postpone the wedding until spring. He wouldn't hear of it. He was peeved, condescending, offended that they questioned him. Did they think he didn't know what he was doing? That (as they came close to saying) he'd been naive to trust Buckminster, after relying on him all these years? Once he challenged them with his pride they could only back away. They knew he didn't know men the way he thought he did. In their devotion they'd let him believe that, like a boy who, after secretly taking to evil ways, lets his father fancy how well he knows his child. But they couldn't say that, even if they'd thought of saying it. And they couldn't mention the rumors about Rory and Elena. That was the last chance to call off the wedding.

Jacinta had grown increasingly distracted and fantastic, driven both to deny Luke's death and to swear to avenge it. She sat for hours at her loom, muttering in a language of her own, weaving oracular visions in the colors of her tapestry. It was as if she had left this world and journeyed to another, from which she returned only to issue inscrutable pronouncements. She was mad but her madness had an audacity that consumed the sanity of everyone around her.

In her presence Elena felt like a little girl again. She tried to find in her mother's desperation some sympathy for her own. "I don't know if I can go through with this," she said. "I can't marry a man I don't love."

"You won't be the first woman who's had to do that."

"He's twice my age. He's got gray hair, bad teeth."

"It must be done."

"I can't." She began to sob. "I can't."

Taking her hand, Jacinta led her into the bedroom and sat down with her at the loom, expounding the woven figures as if reading her future from a deck of cards. Near the top of that endless tapestry she had woven a labyrinth of colors and geometric shapes in a folkloric Mexican style which at first glance seemed mere decoration, but which, as Elena squinted through her tears, resolved into the picture of a man reaching out across a speckled landscape of sagebrush and cactus and crook-horned cattle, a serpent twined around his ankles, and above it all, her arms embracing the man and the landscape and all its hellborn creatures, the unmistakable image of Nuestra Señora de la Santa Muerte, holy death, smiling her baleful skeleton smile. Whether this vision was truly depicted in the tapestry, or whether Elena's perception of it resulted from her mother's hypnotic crooning or her own fevered imagination, she would never know, but at that moment it was as vivid and real as the beating of her own heart. "Is this Slater?" she asked her mother, pointing to the figure of the man.

Jacinta nodded. "You are to be Slater's wife, used as men use women, until parted by death."

"Yes," Elena said. "That is the marriage vow."

"And that death will come—you see, it is shown right here—and everything that is his, what was once ours, will be yours, and ours again."

"Ours? You mean our family's."

"Yes, ours. And this will happen soon."

"Soon? But how?"

Jacinta pointed to the serpent coiled around the man's ankles. "That is his faithful servant, who will kill him with a single bite."

"Slater will die from a snakebite?"

"So many misfortunes can meet a man out on that range! A snakebite, an unruly horse. A blow to the head. So many misfortunes."

"And that servant?"

"He has a mind to marry you after the misfortune. But he won't, I can promise you that. He will suffer his own misfortune not long after the first one. I will see to that."

She reassured Elena with a sinister smile. "Then you can marry your cowboy."

Elena came away from Jacinta shaking and short of breath. She climbed into bed and pulled the covers over her head. It took her a long sleepless night to decipher her mother's mad auguries. Slater would be killed after the wedding, as soon as he had signed his property over to Elena. The angel of death would take the form of Buckminster, the snake trusted by Slater as his faithful servant, who imagined (with what encouragement she could only guess) that Elena would then be his. But again Santa Muerte would intervene, in the form of Jacinta herself.

In the cold morning light the burden of the plot became clear. To marry Slater (that grizzled but kindly man, who had done everything in his power to please her) would be to sign his death warrant, and Buckminster's as well. Having recovered her father's property, she would be allowed to marry Rory. But what joy could she find in a marriage predicated on two cold-blooded murders?

Her heart ached as if she had eaten of the tree of evil. But she resolved to keep her misery to herself. She would not tempt Rory with such knowledge. She had made her decision.

27

Friday night—the last night they would spend together, the wedding being Sunday—Rory and Elena met outside the broken cabin. The wind whispered around them, lying, as they knew, about freedom and forgiveness and happiness, but they chose to believe it—and why not, this one last time? For half an hour they sat entwined in the moonlight, amusing themselves with banter and playful kisses, as lovers do, before submitting to the yoke of passion. As that began to weigh on them, their breath quickening, their kisses longer and hungrier, they spurned the moonlight's cold calculation and the wind's whispering lies and fled inside the cabin to lock themselves in love's dark embrace. There as before they found a joy seasoned with guilt and fatality, as if doom had cast its toils around them the first time their bodies met. They lay together in silence, feeling each other's warmth like the first touch of life, listening as their mingled breathing lost its urgency. Rory grazed his fingertips over the skin of her face, her shoulders, her breasts, and followed, just as lightly, with his lips, as if to touch deeper were to tempt temptation before its time, to rekindle proud desire and threaten the hard-sought peace. She paid him back in kind, her fingers lighter, her kisses deeper, until history repeated itself, harder and more fiercely, as if a serious debt had to be paid before their passion could end. And when it did end they lay silent against each other again and they heard their hearts beat against the rising wind—keening now instead of whispering—as it sang out that love and death will always cling together.

On Sunday morning Slater's party rode into the Captain's compound in a wary cavalcade, Buckminster in the lead, eyes alert, Moondog behind him, resplendent in a buffalo robe, suede vest and leggings, a Colt .45 tucked into his belt. Only then came the anxious, clean-shaven bridegroom, unarmed, astride his best horse, the gelded buckskin, in his undertaker suit and deerskin boots and a beaver hat he'd bought from some traveling Comancheros. A pair of cowhands slouched behind him, cradling shotguns across their saddles, followed by Crazy Ike, his mad eyes rolling suspiciously, his horse meandering as if it were drunk. The rest of the outfit—including many who weeks before had served the Captain—followed at a respectful distance. It did not resemble a wedding party so much as a Masonic funeral procession or the remnants of a lost regiment straggling home from a war. The wind nicked them with its claws and darted away. Their saddles creaked like the bones of old men who would never see another sunrise.

Earth and sky were uniformly grim and gray. Looming dark clouds, dour battlements rimming the distance. Those clouds, still quiet, would soon rear up and flood the faded land. The Captain's party, what could be seen of it, seemed equally gray and slow and noiseless. If that was an omen of what would come—that something would come, something startling and devastating—it was lost on Slater. He had ridden from his ranch pondering another omen of hurt and loss: Rory gone missing in the night, after the celebration at the saloon. In his saddle bag Slater had brought the papers to be signed before the wedding—the deed of trust and his last will and testament—and he'd meant to discuss them with Rory, to explain about the land and cattle he'd carved out for him, but now, with the boy gone, he couldn't help but think with a sinking heart that Rory, in his hot-blooded jealousy, might have run away. He should have talked to him sooner.

Some of the men had drifted back into the Captain's service, to what end remained unclear. He had few cattle, though he hoped to rebuild his herd after Slater discharged the judgment. Two of those men, Warner and McCool, stood beside the Captain in an L-shaped formation flanking out from the porch like an open bear trap. The Captain clutched a shotgun across his chest. Warner and McCool, on either side of him, watched with hair-trigger eyes. All motion ceased as Moondog and Crazy Ike resisted the temptation to reach for their side arms. Buckminster, the unfaithful servant of two masters, felt his throat tighten with desperation. Random sounds fled into the wind: horses chuffing, stirrups rattling, reins jangling. The Captain's yellow cur skulked at his feet.

Slater held his hands steady on the reins and looked the Captain dead in the eye. "I thought this was going to be a wedding," he said.

The dog raised its snout long enough to bay at Slater's blood-drained face. The Captain clouted it down and it slinked behind him.

"There can't be a wedding without a bride," the Captain said, raising his shotgun.

Slater's sinking heart quickened its descent. "Where's the bride then?"

"She run off in the night."

Slater stared down the barrel of the Captain's shotgun, where any sudden movement would have taken him, snuffing the unbearable realization that spiraled in his mind. But there were others, innocent if that word could be applied to such men as Buckminster, Moondog, Crazy Ike—they did no wrong or had aught to gain from what he'd lost or hoped for. He could not take them with him down the barrel of that gun.

The Captain's eyes were intense and unforgiving. "Where is your foster son?"

"He run off in the night."

There were more, much, that could have been said. Questions that could have been asked, though unlikely to have been answered. Accusations of insult and trickery and deceit on all sides, threats of retribution and violence. Slater felt sick, the way he'd felt when he saw the calves clubbed to death on that trail in Texas. The way he felt when his brother had claimed his baby. Of some wrongs there is no righting or oblivion.

But now the spring must be uncoiled, if it is destined to be uncoiled. To turn your back on a man who hates you, a man who blames you for destroying him and killing his son—and who is pointing a shotgun at your eyes. To trust a dozen armed men not to panic, to suppress instincts of fight and courage and action bred over a lifetime—instincts that make them worthy of being called men—for the sake of breathing another hour. To swallow your pride to avoid a fight that would be your last. To flaunt the disgrace of being shot in the back.

And so the procession must reverse course. The horses must be turned, the men must keep their hands steady on the reins, their faces blank, their trembling lips mute. They move the horses along gently, unhurriedly—the crack of a whip could end their world. A deep sigh marks the outer limit of their fear and they escape with a single thought: there will be another day. Buckminster casts a last baleful glance at the Captain that pleads for mercy.

As the Captain watches Slater ride away, he confesses to himself that he feels a certain sympathy for him. Not on account of his daughter—Slater hardly knew the girl and he's better off without her. But he knows what it means to lose a son. He would have shot any man before he wished that on him.

The outfit rode slowly back toward camp. When they were halfway there, Slater stopped the procession and gave the men their orders.

"Moondog, you and Crazy Ike ride out and bring Elena back. I ain't going to let her go this easy."

"What about Rory?" Crazy Ike asked.

"Tie a rope around him and drag him in. Like Buckminster done with Vickery."

Part IV

28.

You, Rory? You done this to me?

Is there anything in this world I can trust after you done this to me? Not my own eyes, my own heart—yes, I got a heart, I thought you knew that. You left it scattered and swirling like a dust devil, howling after you, your past and future paid for with my shame. What's left of truth after you tangled me in your lies and hung me up on a post for the mules and the ravens to laugh at? Ain't nobody important, you tell them, just old Slater. You can laugh at him all you want. He's a empty snakeskin, a dried-out gourd rattling with dead seeds. But he was a man once, a man respected and obeyed, who didn't care to be loved by anybody but you. Who pulled you out of a raging river, raised you like his own son, gave you all he could give. Who never wanted a wife or a child, after the ones he'd had, so you, no kin at all, could be his child and there'd be no other. Who kept that vow until he got it in his head to marry that girl he should have known would never marry the likes of him. And the Captain, he humored me, mocked me, let on like I was his equal, his brother even, because I knew his secret, let me believe that if I could forgive his evil ways I could take on some of his arrogance for myself. He made a dupe of me, didn't he? Didn't I even say he wasn't a bad man? Then he held out his daughter, dangled her in front of me like a prize calf. Just the thought of that turned my head, left me soft, unguarded, open to pain. Why didn't you just tell me you wanted her for yourself and leave me to my loneliness? I would have given her to you, given you my whole kingdom, more land than you could ride in a day, asked for nothing in return, as long as you wouldn't have turned against me, lied to me, betrayed me. You took all I gave you and that wasn't enough. Did you have to take my pride? Did you have to take that?

Now I'll tell you something you must know in your traitor's heart. With Moondog and Crazy Ike on your trail, your life ain't worth a damn. I wouldn't give you three days.

29

The elopement had proceeded according to plan. Elena laid out her dress and her flowers and finished her wedding preparations with her mother and went to bed. At midnight she sneaked out to the barn and changed into some of Luke's old clothes and made her way along the familiar route to the clay butte, where she met Rory. He'd gone to the saloon with the rest of the outfit to celebrate Slater's marriage, pretended to get drunk, and told the others he was going home. Instead he rode out on his palomino, having packed his rifle, his revolver and a saddlebag full of hardtack and beef jerky. The plan was to catch a few hours' sleep in the cabin, then follow the cattle trail up through the badland to the first railroad town and catch the mail train west.

They were awake and on the trail at first light. Over and around them on all sides loomed towering reefs of cloud that dwarfed the mountains rimming the basin: dark, churning clouds that trembled with distant thunder. As they rode north the first waves of rain scudded in on the wind. Ahead of them lay the badland, darker than the clouds, a vast rockscape of lost hopes and fantastic, wind-carved statuary. To their left, scarcely visible in the mist, stood the towering ridges that blocked any escape to the west. Elena sighted the mustangs and climbed down from the palomino, waving to them. Rory trotted away, leaving her alone on a sandy rise. Susannah pranced toward her while the rest of the herd circled at a distance.

Elena whispered to her, rubbed her neck, let her nibble some grain from her hand. Then she twisted her fingers in her mane and pulled herself up, leaned forward, kneed her ribs and raced toward Rory. His horse, pricked by the mustang's wildness, slung itself from side to side, stamped and reared. When Rory pulled back on the reins it staggered and skidded on the wet clay and toppled screaming into a rock-strewn gully.

The horse went down hard, squealing in desperation as it tried to right itself on a broken foreleg, each time flinging itself harder into the rocks. Rory could see the ragged edge of a bone sticking out below the knee. His own ankle had twisted on the rocks as he followed the horse in its fall. Rolling out of the saddle, he fell down when he tried to stand up. He pulled out his revolver to shoot the horse but stopped short of pulling the trigger. A shot would be heard for miles around. He drew his bowie knife from his belt and with one swift motion cut the horse's throat. Blood spurted three feet in the air and rained back on him in the wind. After the first gush it flooded the sand under the horse's head and the earth drank it in.

Elena, on the mustang, witnessed this act of mercy—which to the mustangs was cold-blooded murder—from the rim of the gully. Her mount reared up and tried to throw her—she clutched its mane for dear life. The herd raced in a circle around them snorting and wheezing as if in some ritual of sacrifice. When Rory climbed out of the gully they turned on him, rushed at him rearing and kicking. He waved them off with his revolver, which only seemed to madden them further.

Elena released her grip and slid off Susannah, who joined the attack. The others ignored her, intent on trampling Rory.

"I'm going to shoot them," Rory yelled.

"No! Don't shoot them!"

He raised the gun and fired over their heads.

The mustangs stopped and stared, angry, incredulous, feral.

He fired again, and like a flock of startled blackbirds they turned as one and raced away.

Slater had sent Moondog and Crazy Ike to search for Elena and Rory in a cloud of disbelief almost as dark and violent as the thunderheads rampaging in the sky. Was he so bad that she'd leave her whole life behind and ride out in a storm to get away from him? He never hurt her, always treated her with respect, fitted up the house just the way she wanted it. Angry as he was—and hurt, though he didn't call it that—he'd welcome her back, and he felt sure she would come. He knew she didn't love him, probably never would, but he'd never expected that. And even on his side it wasn't exactly a fairy tale romance, which nobody expected in that rough country. But they were well enough matched to come together, start a family. Rory stealing off with her had been a blow to his pride, a kind of pride he didn't know he had. He'd held her up as a prize which now he desperately wanted to recover. When he looked into his heart he saw things he didn't want to see. Himself as a proud man, corrupted by his pride, like the man he'd defeated and now, it seemed, he'd become, blinded to what actually mattered to him. So he looked the other way, anywhere but into his own heart.

Buckminster saw into it effortlessly, and unlike Slater he found pleasure and self-justification in what he saw: a sorry fool getting what he deserved and on his way to getting more. "She'll come back," he told Slater. "She's probably regretting it already."

"You think so?"

"Rory must have tricked her. I can't believe she really wanted to leave you."

"I appreciate that, Buckminster. You've always been somebody I could trust."

"Thanks, boss. I've got to say—no, I won't." He turned and went back to combing his black mare. They stood in the barn, apart from the other men.

Slater grabbed his arm. "What? Don't hold back on me."

"It's just that"—Buckminster lowered his voice—"Moondog and Crazy Ike, they're good hands, but frankly they're sort of unpredictable."

"Unpredictable?"

"That's all I'm going to say. You know I never gossip about the men."

"Gossip? What're you holding back?"

Buckminster cast his eyes about aimlessly, not wanting the others to think he wanted to keep them from overhearing. "Well, I've heard some of the things they've said about Elena, things I wouldn't repeat. Things they'd like to do to her if they got her alone. You know how men talk."

"Why didn't you tell me about that?"

"I didn't think it meant anything. I still don't."

"It means something. It means they're going to catch up with her and do those things."

"OK, if you believe that, you want to ride out there and stop them?"

"I can't do that. How would that make me look? Chasing after her after she run out on me? That's why I sent Moondog and Crazy Ike up to the badland to bring her back. Now you're telling me I can't trust them either. You go, Buckminster, you go out there and keep those two dogs away from her. You bring her back. Tonight, if you can find her."

"What about Rory?"

"It don't matter a lick to me what you do with Rory. I don't want to see him again."

All day after Buckminster left, Slater wished he hadn't said that. In fact he worried about Rory, hoped the men would spare him so he would come back. I should've seen this coming, he told himself, the way the boy was acting. Moping around, disappearing half the night. He was out running after that gal. Why couldn't he just tell me he wanted her for himself? Instead he tricked me, lied to me, spirited her away and made me look like a fool. It angered him to think about it, but Rory was more important to him than his anger. He felt hollow without him.

Buckminster rode out in the drenching rain, about an hour behind Moondog and Crazy Ike. As if to show the seriousness of his mission, he rode his tall ebony mare, the one he valued so highly, caparisoned in deerhide to fend off the rain. On that horse in his black duster and high black hat he towered like a knight thirsting for blood. He and Slater had agreed that the most likely route of escape was up the cattle trail and through the badland to the railroad towns. He set off in that direction, but as soon as he was out of sight he turned south toward the Captain's ranch, where he had unfinished business. The morning's events had stymied his plans, for which he blamed his own naive faith in his own calculations. He'd seen Elena and Rory together at the cabin but he never thought they'd elope. He'd counted on Elena marrying Slater so she could inherit his property before he was eliminated. Some people just couldn't be trusted. Would the Captain still make her marry him if he brought her back? No, he couldn't trust him either. He wasn't a fool like Slater.

He tethered his horse in front of the big log house and climbed the steps to the porch, rain cascading down in front of him. The house was dark inside, shades drawn, scarcely a candle or a lamp lighted. He tapped on the door and the Captain invited him in. Still dressed in his best suit, coat buttoned to the neck, as he was that morning, his wife upright on a ladder-back chair in her black mourning dress, both staring with an air of weary expectation.

Buckminster fumbled his hat and bowed humbly. "Shame about what happened, Captain," he said. "I never saw it coming."

"Nobody did," the Captain shrugged. "What's Slater going to do?"

"Well, that's why I stopped by. He sent Moondog and Crazy Ike up to the badland after them."

"He can bring her back if he wants to but she'll never marry him."

"It's not that he wants them to bring her back, or Rory either."

"What do you mean?"

"He sent those boys out there to kill them. I never seen him so mad."

The Captain's face paled. He stumbled back and sat beside his wife.

"I'm going out to warn them," Buckminster said. "I hope I can get there before the murderers do their work."

"I'll kill those two," the Captain said in a low grinding voice. "Slater too."

"Captain"—Buckminster tried to hold him back—"Those boys, I've been their foreman for years. I think I can talk sense into them."

The Captain stood up and unbuttoned his suit coat. He eased it off and hung it on a hook behind the door, taking down a rough leather coat which he eased over his massive frame. "You bring Elena back here, you understand?" he told Buckminster. "Not to Slater. He's not going to marry her."

"I'm still hoping she might marry me."

The Captain laughed in his face. Was this a joke? Or was Buckminster an even bigger fool than he thought he was? Buckminster turned aside, his face flushed, and the Captain knew he'd been serious. That was the first time he'd ever seen Buckminster lose control. "Kill those two animals and bring her back here and you just might have a chance," he said, anxious to keep him in the game. "Where is Slater?"

"Still at his ranch"—Buckminster's voice a little weak—"the last I knew."

The Captain walked to a cupboard and took out his gun belt, strapping it on. "I'm going over there to kill him. Then I'll join you up there on the trail."

Jacinta was on her feet, wrapping a shawl around her shoulders. "I'm going with you."

"Nonsense."

"Luke's over there. He went to get the bull."

The Captain found his hat and headed for the door, stopping to face his wife one last time. "Luke is dead. Will you get that through your head?"

She followed him onto the porch. "I'm going with you. I need to see Luke."

He pushed her back inside—"Get in the house!"—and shut the door behind her. Then cursing the rain he trudged to the barn to saddle his fastest horse. Charlie Crow appeared in the stall and helped him lead the horse outside. "Where are you going, Captain?"

"I'm going to Slater's camp to kill him. The boy too if I catch up with him."

Crow stood shuddering in the rain, sick at heart. Slater would die, Rory would die, and Elena would curse the day she was brought to that malignant landscape. And what was he in this calamity? A minor, unrecorded casualty. A maverick calf, branded with the sadness of having lost what he never had.

Buckminster, his black duster cowled around his shoulders, thought about shooting Crow and leaving him to thrash in the mud. Leaving him alive to judge him and tell the truth about him had been a mistake, which could still be remedied. But that reckoning could wait for another day. He waited on the porch for the Captain to ride out. Then he mounted his ebony mare and headed north into the darkening afternoon.

The Captain rode away leaving Jacinta alone, more alone than she'd ever been in that house. Luke gone, Elena gone, the Captain gone. The men, who'd been given the day off for the wedding, drinking down at the saloon. Nobody to watch her, obey her or defy her. She picked up a ceramic oil lamp presented by a favorite aunt upon her own marriage and hurled it against the wall. She ran into the kitchen and smashed china, glassware, crockery, howling all the while, yipping like the coyotes she'd heard on the range, barking and baying like dogs. In her room she yanked the tapestry out of the loom, the tapestry she'd been working on as long as she could remember, bringing its prophecies to a sudden consummation. She knelt before the shrine and prayed to the saint whose hour had come, conjuring her presence and her power as she muttered her name. Nuestra Señora de la Santa Muerte.

She opened the Captain's gun cabinet, selected a shotgun and loaded it. If anything had happened to Luke, she would kill Slater herself. Outside she felt the pounding rain lash her face as she stumbled through ankle-deep mud to the barn, where she waved off Charlie Crow, harnessed the mares and hitched them to the wagon. She carried the shotgun cradled under one arm, a whip in her free hand. The mares shied when they saw the whip, shied more when she barked at them, even more when she howled. They remembered her whipping them when the Captain took the wagon to fetch Luke. She pulled the reins to lead them out and they balked, tossed their heads, refused to move forward. They were stupid, stubborn; they needed to be taught a lesson. Screaming, she whipped them on the back, the withers, the neck, finally on the eyes, the ears, the mouth. Still they defied her, lurched backwards, from side to side, every way but forward, and she whipped them again, harder this time, barking uncontrollably, until they lowered their heads to the floor and moaned, tried to lie down but she yanked up on the bits, their mouths bled, and at last they pulled the wagon out of the barn to the arching gate. Crow ran out to stop her but too late. She stepped in front of the mares to open the gate and they reared up and brought their hooves down on top of her, kicked her unconscious, trampled her into the mud, until all that could be seen of her were the torn skirts of her mourning dress. And then they pulled the wagon over her and through the gate to their favorite grazing spot along the road.

30

Moondog and Crazy Ike followed the muddy trail north, black clouds looming around them as far they could see. There was no sky, no horizon: the basin had no boundaries, it might have stretched forever in all directions. "This rain's going to slow them down some," Moondog said.

"Slow us down too."

Moondog stopped to examine a muddy slough churned and trampled by unshod hooves. "Looks like that whole herd of mustangs come this way."

"That gal runs with the mustangs."

"So she does. Here's one that's shod." He pointed to a track leading away toward the badland. "That'd be Rory's palomino."

Two hours later they found it, bled out in a muddy gully. "It must've broke its leg and Rory cut its throat. Looks like they took off that way on foot. Got your lasso handy?"

They shared a dispirited laugh. Neither of them was happy to be there. Trying to hold back the forces of nature, is what it seemed. They could have told Slater he'd lose his bet putting money on that girl. Now they had to do his work for him, fighting the odds to set things right.

Crazy Ike laughed the kind of laugh that earned him his nickname. "Capturing Rory's a waste of time," he said. "And dangerous too."

"That's what we're here for."

"Slater's fixing to hang him anyway, same as he did Vickery. You heard him."

Moondog stopped his horse so they could have a proper conversation. When Crazy Ike halted beside him, he pulled his revolver from his belt and cocked back the hammer, just to raise the stakes. He wanted to emphasize that what they were doing was serious business.

"You're going to die someday, Ike," he said. "Does that mean I ought to shoot you right now? Of course it don't. Old Man Death'll get us all but you got to let him take his own sweet time. You try to rush him along he'll come back to bite you."

"I've rushed him along for a lot of men," Crazy Ike said, "and so have you, Moondog. What about Barlow up there with the Tatum gang? And the blacksmith John Riley—didn't we send him to hell a little earlier than he counted on?"

"Those were fights, not executions."

"Giving a doomed man a leg up is all it is. It's a blessing, like him cutting that horse's throat."

Buckminster rode out a couple of hours after Moondog and Crazy Ike. The world seemed to be dissolving in mist, melting into mud, mad rushes of water running in circles. The maelstrom drew him in, spun its invisible net around him, dizzying his mind. But he felt confident that he was on the right course. Give Moondog and Crazy Ike enough rope and they'd do his work for him. They'd find Rory and Elena, kill Rory or at least tie him up, bring Elena back. And he'd meet them half way, nothing suspicious. When they turned their backs he'd shoot them, take Elena north, put her on a train to San Francisco. If anybody came looking for them he'd kill them too. Elena would love him as other women had done—if not, he'd take his fill of her and leave her in some crevice in the badland. What had pushed him to such extremes? First Slater's betrayal, reneging on his promise of land, then the Captain's laughing at him, mocking the idea that he could marry Elena. The Captain had been playing him all along, which he hadn't thought possible. Like every cunning man, he fancied that his own guile was insurance against others' deceit.

Two others would join the fatal cavalcade that slogged its way across the range. Slater was shaken by Buckminster's revelation that Moondog and Crazy Ike meant to kill Rory, heartsick that in his fury he had suggested it. Why did they just accept what he'd said? Why didn't they talk him out of it? All those years of quiet authority—what he'd always seen as his strength—had been his undoing. They never questioned him, never disobeyed him, even now when he talked like a crazy man. They'd always been jealous of Rory, because Slater loved him like a son. Had they secretly wished for his fall? Was this their revenge—to carry out Slater's orders to the letter? He was on the verge of tears for the first time since the baby he'd thought was his son had died, shuddering from deep inside as he'd done when he watched those calves clubbed to death in front of their mothers, before he pulled Rory out of the Rio Concho and breathed new life into him and into himself. Why couldn't those men have seen that? How could they not know him better than to believe he wanted Rory dead? He had to stop them before it was too late. He would ride out and bring Rory back, him and the girl, save them both from the killers he'd sent after them, forgive them both and set them free to live their lives without him. If he could get there in time.

Finally the Captain, who arrived at Slater's camp after he'd left, joined the cavalcade. He had vowed to kill Slater and his henchmen, Moondog and Crazy Ike, before they could reach Elena; Buckminster, too, in spite of his protestations of noble intention—the man was a snake who couldn't be trusted closer than a whip's length. And what about Rory? He was from Slater's outfit and as such was marked for death. Elena could be forgiven but not allowed to run wild.

The Captain had armed himself with a shotgun, a rifle and two revolvers. He'd taken his fastest horse, the white Arabian, and

brought his yellow cur to scout the way. He had no time to waste.
There was much work to be done.

Even after a lifetime in that basin, Elena had never felt so
desolate as when the mustangs turned and ran away. Their horror at
Rory's killing his horse and her complicity with him was a judgment
that marked them both as enemies. They had left the human world
behind when they fled to this wilderness. They were in nature now,
and the mustangs saw them as invaders, subject to nature's law, the
law of kill or be killed. From now on everything would be different.
In her desolation Elena longed to be back with her family, even with
Luke though he was dead. She felt like crying but there was no place
for tears in this brutal world. Instead she searched in Rory's
saddlebag until she found a scrap of cloth she could use to bind up
his ankle. When she was done he could stand up on it.

"Walking's going to be a little slow for a while," he told her.
"We've got to keep moving, though. Whoever's coming after us
must have heard those shots."

"Maybe they took it for thunder."

"Ain't a man on this range who'd make that mistake."

The thunder, moving closer, had brought lightning and pelting
rain. Cold water lapped over their ankles and into the gullies to slake
the thirst of the earth. The walking was slow. They took turns
carrying the saddlebag, which held their food, dry matches,
ammunition. Rory held his rifle close and kept his revolver in his
belt.

"They're going to find that dead horse," he said after a while. "If
we stay on this cattle trail they'll be on our tail before we know it."

"Where else could we go?"

Abandoning the cattle trail, they wended their way between
roaring gullies and washes toward the dark masses of mountains and

clouds that loomed in the west. They gave up trying to talk through
the relentless din. After two hours they came to a range of high bluffs
cut by a steep gorge that carried a muddy torrent down from the
high country behind the bluffs. When Rory saw that mud and the
burn scar on the bluffs he knew they'd come the right way. This was
the landscape devastated by the wildfires of six weeks before. Not a
tree standing, not a shrub or even a weed, the earth itself baked and
blackened like a clay pot, whole slabs of its crust sloughing down the
bluffs and cliff sides into the draws and melting back into clay. The
gorge seemed to be flowing with molten earth.

"Maybe if we get up to the top of these bluffs we'll be able to
find a way over the ridge," Rory shouted into the wind.

"Why can't we just keep going north?"

"We'd be in the badland before long. No shelter there."

They followed a broken path into the gorge, a relic of
prospecting days, and made their way up along the raging creek. As
they climbed the rain became mixed with hail, frozen pebbles
stinging their faces like hornets. The gorge narrowed, its walls on
either side hollowed by hanging ledges carved out by some ancient
cataclysm. Elena wanted to shelter where a tributary cut in from the
south, but Rory insisted on climbing farther up along the north side
of the creek, knee-deep in water and mud, holding his rifle and the
saddlebag over his head. They tied themselves together so that if one
slipped they would share the same fate, whatever that might be.
When the light began to fail, they stopped under an arching overhang
where the rain couldn't reach them. Rory tossed the saddlebag on
the rocks and untied the rope that bound them together. "This is
where we'll spend the night."

The overhang sheltered a wide ledge and the back of it opened
into the cliff side like a cave, a black hole about the size of a man. As
they approached the cave they heard growling and snarling. They

leaped back in fear of a bear, but the snarling gave way to a devils' chorus of howling and barking and a dozen frenzied dogs burst out and ran toward them, then backed away. They were the Captain's dogs, gone feral, with just enough ancestral memory to recognize Rory as a man waving a gun at them and shouting threats. The growling rose as they slunk past him and stood in a half circle around the overhang, teeth bared, tongues drooping, eyes empty of all fidelity to man—all that remained was loathing, dread of punishment, gnawing hunger.

Rory brandished his revolver and ran at them, chased them from the ledge into the downpour. They ran about fifty feet, then skulked farther up the gorge, looking backwards. Later when they returned to the overhang he tossed them a little of the meat he'd brought in his saddlebag. They snarled and fought among themselves for the food, turning their hatred toward each other, and allowing themselves, for the sake of another chance at that meat, to again be subjugated by man. Rory knew, as they did, that the truce was never more than temporary. He built a fire near the mouth of the cave and the dogs crept back to spend the night out of the rain. He tossed them more meat and watched them fight. The fire and smoke kept them away from the cave. After he and Elena had eaten, they crawled into the cave and found a place where they could stand up and lie down. The stench was nauseating—of dogs, rats, bats, and of something else. A little farther in they found it: what was left of a human corpse, bones scattered and gnawed on by the dogs. Rory recognized the little chain around the man's neck that had a figure dangling from it. Jesus on the cross. It was Murtaugh.

Two hours behind their quarry, Moondog and Crazy Ike rode into the canyon as far as their horses would go, then hobbled them on a gentle slope where a tributary entered from the south.

"Hard to see what they'll find to browse on in that mud," Crazy Ike said.

"It's the best we can do, ain't it? We'll have to go the rest of the way up on foot."

"You sure they're up there?"

Moondog could track a toad in a tornado. "I'm sure."

The two men built a fire under an overhang and squatted down to eat. Wet hard tack, wet beef jerky, cold beans. When supper was done they made a bed on some wet moss and went to sleep.

Buckminster had trailed Moondog and Crazy Ike unseen into the canyon. When he spotted their fire blazing under the overhang, he rode back down half a mile, tied up his horse, and huddled under his deerhide slicker debating whether to go back up and kill them. Easy enough to do while they slept, and it would save him time and trouble tomorrow. But wasn't it better to let them tangle with Rory first? Maybe they'd kill him, or he'd kill them—no matter how it turned out, he'd have one less thing to worry about. Their horses, though, were a different matter—he'd seen them on the slope, rooting in the mud for something to eat. If they captured Elena and killed or captured Rory, they'd need those horses to get home, something Buckminster wasn't about to let happen. So before going to sleep he'd sneak back up the canyon and slit the horses' throats. If those boys noticed it in the morning, they'd blame it on Rory. One more reason to kill him.

Slater followed the same trail into the canyon but stopped sooner, before he found Buckminster. He built a fire in a sheltered spot and settled down for the night. The Captain was close on his heels, guided by his yellow cur, which began to pace and growl as they neared Slater's camp. The Captain retreated to an overhang farther down where he could spend the night. The next morning he would kill them all—Slater, Buckminster, Moondog, Crazy Ike, Rory—to save Elena from the designs of men. He should never have let Slater take over the basin. He should have listened to Jacinta and stayed true to his vow. When his bloody work was done they could start all over again, he and Jacinta and Elena, build back what they'd lost, take back their kingdom. Salvage what was left of their pride.

His reverie was broken by a horseman slogging up the trail, his horse wheezing and gasping as he whipped it through the mud, hot breath pluming above it like a ghost. "Captain? Is that you?"

It was Charlie Crow. Ashen, wild-eyed, lips trembling as if mumbling a prayer.

"What are you doing here, Crow?"

He climbed down from the horse and edged toward the Captain. "It's your lady, Captain."

The Captain stepped back. "What are you talking about?"

"Your wife. She's dead. Trampled by the mares on her way over to shoot Slater."

The Captain remained still, rain dripping down his face like tears. He tossed a glance at Crow and pointed back the way he came. "Get out of here."

The earth and the sky and the relentless rain had revealed their hidden purpose. The land melting, rendering, purging itself of everything he'd ever done or been, then washing away. There would be no starting over. The kingdom and all his pride were lost forever. Jacinta gone to join her patron saint, Santa Muerte. All he had left was his daughter and the yellow cur.

He lay down with the cur beside him. Waking out of a whirling dream the next morning, he thrashed and cried out in terror. The yellow cur was gone.

They made a bed of juniper boughs and pine cones the rats had stashed in the cave, as far away from Murtaugh's bones as they could crawl. Too exhausted to go on, too cold and wet not to cling together, they had no choice but to steal a few hours' sleep. There were men coming after them, ruthless men skilled in tracking and hunting who would have no trouble finding them even in that transfigured landscape.

"They're going to try to kill us," Rory told Elena as they lay beside each other. "Or me at least. They probably want to take you back." Or something worse, he thought.

"I won't go back."

"Don't worry, they won't get us." He had to say that even if neither believed it.

She squeezed his hand. "I know you won't let them."

Such touching faith, and they both knew it was a lie. Until that day he'd thought he knew what it was going to be like, being a man. Strength, courage, confidence. Not what he felt now. "I'll make sure they don't."

How wrong he had been. He knew so little about himself or the world—a couple of cow towns, a railroad town, a few roughhewn men running from life, like Slater, or already defeated by it—and about women, nothing. Was there anything he could say to her that wouldn't be a lie?

"Rory," she said, "I won't go back because you're the only man I could love. I know that as well as I know anything."

He pulled her closer and laid his head on her breast, grateful not to have to show her his weakness, though she must have felt it. "I don't know that I deserve it."

"It's not about deserving," she said. "You can't earn somebody's love. It's more like faith."

He pulled himself up and peered into the flickering mirror of her eyes. "Why should you have faith in me?"

"I can't explain it," she smiled. "But you proved me right by having the courage to carry me away."

"That was your idea."

"I know that. It was my decision and I made it. But you actually carried it out."

He kissed her and they laid their heads together on the saddlebag. As Elena drifted off to sleep she found a new peace in Rory's embrace, far from the suffering and strife of that day and the one to come. She felt as light as a butterfly and as free, knowing that her life, however short it might be, could be a new one, and all her own.

The fire had died to embers by the time they woke up. In the dim light they gagged on the rotting corpse and the smoldering fire and the stench of rats and mud-soaked dogs. The dogs confronted them as they crawled out of the cave, growling and snapping for handouts. Outside the hellish roar continued, the rain still thundering down, the creek foaming, the earth spewing mud as if it were melting. Serpents wound out of clefts in the earth, lizards too, rats, toads, an army of ants—all fled to shelter under the overhang. Each breed kept its distance from the others, as if under a truce. The dogs, unsure of their status, cringed near the cave entrance, but when Rory and Elena stepped forward they fanned out snarling to block their path. The snakes—most of them rattlers—closed in behind them, coiled, raising their heads, whirring to strike if the couple tried to cross the ledge. The rats bared their teeth at the prospect of gnawing human flesh. Rory wondered if this was how Murtaugh had met his end.

It's not just those men who want to kill us, he thought. It's the land and the sky and every living creature in this basin. He ducked back into the cave and lighted two juniper boughs on the smoldering embers. Then he and Elena ventured forward waving the flaming sticks in front of them. The dogs cowered back, the snakes feinted an attack and retreated, the rats squinted at them through narrow vicious eyes. They held them at bay with the flames, locking eyes with the rattlesnakes long enough to cross the ledge into the river of mud and the driving rain.

31.

In the half light of dawn they struggled uphill, roped together, pulling themselves up the muddy slope by the roots and remains of burned-out junipers and pines. When one of them slipped both would go down, flat on their stomachs, clawing the ground. Getting back on their feet was an ordeal, but they couldn't let themselves slide farther. The low places were filling with mud.

The gorge narrowed around them as they climbed farther up, as if drawing them into the womb of the earth. Elena carried Rory's revolver in the saddlebag while he struggled to keep his rifle out of the mud. They heard men shouting below them in harsh muffled voices. Those were the men who would kill her or try to take her back. To Slater? To her father? It didn't matter—she wasn't going. If they killed Rory, she would slide down and drown in the mud before she'd let them take her. To think that yesterday was to have been her wedding day.

A rifle shot rang out below, then a volley of gunfire. The muffled shouting rose and died away.

When they reached a flat ledge Rory untied the rope and sent Elena ahead to shelter in a crevice while he huddled behind a boulder overlooking the path. At its upper end the gorge was a maze of blind alleys, small box canyons piled on each other against a sheer rock face a hundred feet high. Waterfalls cascaded down from the top but there was no path up or around that wall. The only way you could get out of there was to go back down. If Rory or Elena had had a clear line of sight through the hazy twisted gorge, they might have seen their pursuers filing up after them: Moondog and Crazy Ike, followed by Buckminster, then Slater and the Captain—yesterday's cavalcade battered into a slogging death march. Each on his own mission: Moondog to rescue Elena and bring Rory back, Crazy Ike eager to shoot Rory if he resisted. Buckminster to shoot the three of them and take Elena for himself. Slater—who still believed Buckminster's lies—to protect Rory and Elena from Moondog and Crazy Ike. And the Captain, aware of all these nuances, to kill all the men for the sake of his daughter.

Moondog could be seen trudging up about fifty feet below, rifle in hand, trying to keep his footing on the slippery path. Rory raised his rifle and fixed him in its sight. He could have shot him but couldn't bring himself to do it. Moondog had always been kind to him, protected him, trained him in the lore of the range. But that didn't mean he could trust him. He'd seen the man in the rage of battle. He had the soul of a wolf.

Behind him he heard a boulder slough down the cliff. At the bottom it was sucked down in the mud and disappeared. Looking up he found himself staring down the barrel of Moondog's rifle through the sight on his own. He'd lost his advantage in an instant's inattention.

"Rory," Moondog said, peering up at him along the top of his rifle, "I guess you know why we're here. I ain't happy about it. I've always liked you."

"That won't keep you from killing me though, will it?"

"We ain't here to kill anybody. It's to bring the girl back. Bring you back too, alive if you'll let us."

"Like Vickery?"

"The men wouldn't let that happen to you."

The men, he'd said. Not Slater. Slater had said he didn't care what they did with Rory. And Crazy Ike—that's why Moondog had left him fifty feet down the trail—didn't want to risk trying to capture him.

"Don't make me shoot you, Moondog," Rory said.

"I'd just as soon nobody got shot. Throw down your gun and so will I."

Rory had to admire Moondog's courage, standing exposed while he huddled behind a rock. He wondered if a single shot would kill him or if like a bear he could tear you apart with a pound of lead in him. "Back off!" he yelled. "You ain't taking me alive."

Moondog stood his ground. "You have my word I won't shoot you, though I can't speak for Crazy Ike. He's about fifty feet behind me. I made him wait down there while I talked to you but he won't wait long. If you surrender to me he won't touch you. But listen to me, Rory. He don't care about you the way I do. If there's any shooting he'll be up here like a mountain lion and you'll be cursing him in hell along with O'Rourke and that black devil John Riley. He won't stop until he's split you down the middle."

Rory's heart was pounding. "I'll take my chances on how I get to hell."

Moondog seemed strangely calm. He lowered his rifle and took a step forward. "I know you won't shoot me."

"I've killed men before," Rory said.

"I heard about what you did in that Vickery fight. You about threw up when you shot that man. Couldn't talk for the rest of the day."

"There was more than one." His voice faltering.

Moondog smiled and came a step closer. "Good for you."

"I'm warning you. Don't take another step."

Rory never knew how that conversation would have ended if it had been allowed to run its course. Would he have shot Moondog? He never knew because Crazy Ike came up the path swinging a shotgun like a war club, howling and shrieking for Moondog to get out of his way. He really was crazy, crazy enough to think he could charge through bullets and bludgeon Rory to death with the barrel of a shotgun.

There was an explosion, two explosions. Crazy Ike fell face
down in the mud, the back of his head spewing blood and brains.
Moondog toppled backwards over him and slid halfway down the
slope. Rory stared at them in sickened disbelief, dropping his rifle as
if to prove to himself that he hadn't shot them. Elena stood beside
him clutching the revolver in both hands, her cheeks burning. The
bitter reek of gunsmoke drifted around them.

Before either could speak Buckminster appeared before them.
He strode up the path and kicked at Crazy Ike to see if he was still
alive. Then he turned to Elena and gently took the gun from her
hands.

"The blushing bride," he smiled. "Looks like she has a couple
of murders on her hands."

"Self-defense isn't murder," she said.

"These boys weren't here to kill you. They were sent to bring
you home."

Why did she let him take the revolver? Now she and Rory were
both unarmed and Buckminster had the gun. She wasn't going to let
him touch her.

"Don't worry," Buckminster said. "I'm not here to take you
home."

Rory had always loathed Buckminster. His square, clean-shaven
face. The icy clarity of those crystal-blue eyes. "You're going to let
us go?"

Buckminster's smile curled into a sneer. "You think I'm going
to let you live?"

He grabbed Rory by the hair and shoved the gun against his neck
while he weighed his next move. Farther down the gorge, dogs
yipped and howled in some unholy celebration.

The Captain had risen from his terrifying dream with a sense of
aloneness he hadn't felt since he married Jacinta. Elena was up in

that canyon, marked for murder. Could he still save her? He had a deathly fear of what he might find in that canyon. I should have known it would end like this, he thought. Out in some desolate canyon, alone, death boiling up around me like the blood of cattle driven to slaughter.

Slater would be his first quarry. He left his white Arabian hobbled on a patch of burnt grass and stalked up the sodden trail toward Slater's camp with his rifle cocked and loaded. The fire was still smoking but Slater had already climbed higher into the gorge. The Captain hurried behind him, hoping for a shot before he caught up with the others. At last he caught a glimpse of Slater's waterlogged hat, his slicker puffing out in the wind, the rain running down his back. A clear shot but the Captain didn't take it. He wanted Slater to know who'd brought him down to death.

"Slater!" he called out, and Slater whirled around, stumbling in the mud. He cursed the Captain and lurched sideways toward a ledge as the Captain fired and put a bullet in his thigh. He waved his revolver, firing wildly, and ducked behind a fallen tree. His leg was useless, pulsing blood. But from his redoubt he could check the Captain's movement in both directions, firing into his path if he tried to retreat, driving him back if he came forward.

The shooting stopped when the Captain found shelter behind a rock no bigger than a bale of hay. They were both trapped, but Slater's weakening pulse set a limit on his endurance. Before he lost all his strength he would crawl out from behind that fallen tree and open fire. He and the Captain knew their fates were raveled together and so would be their deaths.

"I should have killed you when I had the chance," the Captain said.

"Why didn't you?"

"I'm not a murderer."

"No," Slater said. "You're a coward. That's what you found out in that arroyo in Texas and that's what you've been running from ever since."

"I could have had you killed."

"Sure, by one of your henchmen. Has there ever been a time since you left Texas when you didn't have a gang of cutthroats around you, or that hellfire wife of yours, or that yellow cur? You wanted to make sure you'd never be tested again."

"Stick your head out and I'll kill you now."

"That was your secret and I knew it the first time I laid eyes on you."

"You've taken everything I had," the Captain said. "My son, my cattle, my wife—"

"Your wife?"

"She was trampled on her way over to kill you."

"I'll save my condolences then."

"My daughter's all I've got left and the only thing I care about is saving her from the men you sent up here to kill her."

Slater shuddered with the dread of a recognition that hovered in the mist, just beyond his grasp. Hadn't he sent Moondog and Crazy Ike out there to bring Elena back? What was this about killing her?

"Don't try to deceive me," the Captain said. "Buckminster told me why you sent those two men up here."

"No, no. I never said that. Is that what Buckminster told you?"

Now the Captain faltered, incredulous, his thoughts spinning wildly. Suddenly he understood: it wasn't Slater who'd deceived him, it was Buckminster. How had he let himself be duped by Buckminster? He'd known him for a liar and a traitor all along. "Buckminster told you that?"

He breathed heavily, trying to center himself. "I had it all wrong," he said after a long moment, cursing himself for his stupidity. "It's Buckminster we ought to be worried about. He's going to kill all of them—Rory and Moondog and Crazy Ike—and take Elena for himself."

Slater's slow, intricate mind circled around the Captain's meaning, tested it against what he knew and believed. "I trusted him," he said.

"You trusted him to negotiate your marriage too. Do you have any idea what kind of man he is? He was planning to kill you as soon as you married Elena."

"Why would he do that?"

"So he could be the next one to marry her."

Slater's knees went slack as the full weight of his folly fell on him. No relief in that collapse, no sudden illumination, only the agony of betrayal, and in that agony the inchoate realization that he, a hardened man of the plains, had been naive, blind, proud of knowledge he didn't have, and that had been his undoing. He pulled himself back up and aimed his gun over the rock the Captain hid behind. The blood seeped from his leg, reddened his boot. "You were in on it."

"I wasn't going to let him marry her, if that's what you mean."

"It was a way to get your outfit back. That deed of trust..."

"Of course it was. You think I was going to let you waltz off with everything I owned?"

They had to stop there or come out and kill each other. Their rivalry, feud, death pact—whatever it was—couldn't bind them any longer.

The Captain made the first move. He swallowed his fear and it went down hard. Scorched him all the way to his toes like a fire-breathing serpent, almost turned him around. But he kept it down, held his ground against it. He edged out from behind the rock, tossed his rifle down, and stood defenseless on the path. Slater could have shot him.

He seemed smaller, his pride dissolved in the mist. "Listen to me, Slater," he said. "You've whittled me away till there's nothing left and I don't care. All I want now is to save my daughter."

Slater held him in his gunsight, his mind drifting, forefinger trembling on the trigger. He was back in Texas, at the bottom of one of those poison lakes, peering out of a mirage. Pride sank its fangs into me when it was done with him, he thought, but I never wanted it. I ain't that man. The only man I ever wanted to be was the one that pulled Rory out of the Rio Concho and gave him his life back.

"It'll take both of us to stop him," the Captain said. "You shoot me and you're killing Rory."

Slater weighed those words, hesitated, made up his mind. All he wanted was to save Rory, and for Rory to have Elena. Nothing else mattered.

Two shots rang out above them and a dozen echoes scattered through the gorge.

"He's gone and killed them," Slater moaned, collapsing on his wounded leg. His gun dropped in the mud.

"Somebody shot somebody," the Captain said. "We don't know who." He scrambled up to the ledge and knelt beside Slater, tore off his shirt and wrapped it tight around the bleeding leg. "We've got to keep going. You think you can walk?"

"I reckon so." Slater hoisted himself on the Captain's arm. "Let me tell you something. If I get out of here alive, the basin's all yours. I'm done with it."

The Captain's face was gray, his eyes blank. "Don't kid yourself, Slater," he said. "Neither of us is getting out of here alive."

Slater nodded. "All right then. If that's the way it has to be."

"If those men don't kill us, we'll have to kill each other. You know that."

He picked up Slater's gun, wiped the mud off and handed it to him. "Better hang on to this."

Buckminster wanted to give Elena a thrill of fear, a preview of what would come next. And he wanted Rory to feel it too, so the last thing he saw before the bullet tore into his brain would be a vision of her defilement and degradation and his last thoughts would be of his powerlessness to defend her and the cowardice that kept him from trying.

"Like I say," Buckminster told Elena, "I ain't going to take you home. At least not right away. First you're going to give me what I want. I know you've been whoring it with Rory in that cabin so don't act like it's something you ain't done before."

She took a step back, desperate for an escape. But at the top of that gorge, where in a hundred small cataracts the creek sprang out of the sheer rock face, there was no place to hide.

He pressed the gun against Rory's neck, just below the ear, his grip clenching his hair. "Don't even think about going anywhere or I'll blow his brains all over your pretty little face."

Rory trembled, breathing hard. "You son of a bitch."

"Watch your mouth, boy, or I'll speed your demise. Now, Elena, let me tell you the rules. You can come easy or you can come hard. Either way suits me. In fact I enjoy a gal with a little spunk in her. But if you fight too hard you might end up getting hurt. There's some things I won't put up with from a woman."

"I've always hated you," Elena said.

"I expect you ain't done hating me yet."

The Captain led Slater, staggering, up the path, a rope looped around their waists to keep them from slipping apart. He wondered if he really needed Slater to stop Buckminster. Slater dragged his leg and cried out with every step but he held his head up and his revolver ready to fire. Anyway it was too late. They were already roped together.

They passed the overhang and a rabble of dogs swirled around them yipping and switching their tails. The dogs jumped up on the Captain to lick his hands, strained for his face. The yellow cur lorded over them. At a sign from the Captain he growled and they cringed away, tails between their legs.

The Captain praised the cur in a low croon and rubbed his neck. "Go on up there and find Elena. Get on, now!"

The dogs charged up the path in full cry but with an unreal slowness, their paws heavy with mud. When they reached the top they found a man they didn't know holding a gun on another man they didn't know, two corpses sprawled on the path, while Elena stood off to one side. Baffled, they hung back, whined and showed their teeth. Only the cur seemed to recognize Buckminster and not with affection.

"Stay back!" Elena yelled, fearing they would startle Buckminster into shooting Rory.

"Smart girl!" Buckminster said. "If I didn't have both hands full I'd shoot them sons of bitches." He swung Rory around and pushed him down on his knees as a bulwark against the dogs. "Get back! D'you hear? Get back!"

The shouting and violence excited the dogs. They stood baying, darted in and out. The yellow cur held Buckminster in the vise of his blank agate eyes.

The first thing the Captain saw was Moondog and Crazy Ike where death had overtaken them, face down in the mud. Above them Rory kneeling in front of Buckminster with the gun to his head, Elena frozen with terror, the dogs snarling around them in unearthly harmony. Buckminster so preoccupied with the dogs that he didn't notice the new arrivals stealing up from below.

The Captain moved cautiously. It was just possible that Buckminster had done exactly what he'd been sent there to do. Capture Rory, send Elena back.

He untied the rope, pointed Slater toward a vertical crevice along the cliff and whispered in his ear, "Sneak over there and see if you can line up a clear shot, but don't let him see you and don't shoot until I tell you to."

He counted to ten, then raised his rifle and called out: "Buckminster!"

Buckminster smiled back at him. "Captain! Just the man I was hoping to see. Call off your dogs."

"Don't listen to him!" Elena called out. "He's going to shoot all of us."

He forced a laugh. "Pay no attention, Captain. She's overexcited because I've got her boyfriend right where you wanted him. Now do you want him dead or alive?"

"Father! Stop him!"

"Call off your dogs, Captain."

The Captain whistled and the dogs backed up a few feet. "I see that you already took care of Moondog and Crazy Ike."

"Your daughter done that."

She burst into tears and he knew it was true. It shocked him to see his daughter become a killer as nothing else had shocked him in that season of terrors, more than Luke's death or Jacinta's or the death lying in wait for him a few heartbeats away.

"See that," Buckminster said. "She don't deny it." He whipped Rory on the cheek with his gun. "She did it to save this sorry son of a bitch."

The Captain understood: she'd killed for Rory. He couldn't risk killing Rory to save her.

"Put the gun down and we'll talk about it."

"I've done all the talking I'm fixing to do. Take your dogs and go home."

The Captain glanced toward Slater, his face blank. "Let them both go. I beg of you."

"Begging. That's what I like to hear. You've been humbled all the way down to human, Captain. Never thought I'd live to see it."

"I've got no pride left, nothing. Please, let them go."

Slater leaned against the wall of the crevice where there was no wind or rushing water to mask the din of sorrow. The pain filled his leg and his head and all the space around him. He could hear himself inhaling and exhaling, and it seemed that he could hear the Captain and Buckminster breathing in the same rhythm, and he knew, as he'd once only imagined, that this was the sound of men breathing for the last time. He staggered out, steadying himself with one hand against the cliff face, his revolver in the other, and he heard the breathing still, even in the wind. He raised the gun and aimed it unsteadily. "Buckminster! You heard the Captain. Let them go."

Buckminster, startled by the voice, darted his eyes toward Slater, remembered the Captain, tried to look both ways.

When he dropped his guard the Captain whistled and the dogs leaped on Buckminster like a swarming hive. He spun around and started shooting wildly to fend them off, the dogs snarling and roaring as Rory squirmed out of his grasp and went down in the shooting and writhed on the ground. Slater fired and missed and Buckminster took him down with a single shot. The Captain rushed forward but death outraced him as Buckminster put a bullet through his heart and his life flew away on the wind.

Buckminster tottered in momentary triumph. Then the yellow cur leaped up and sank its teeth into his throat, knocking him toward the slick muddy slope. The rest of the dogs piled on and in their fury drove him down toward the coil of molten clay that writhed through the gorge. He snarled curses, fought tooth and claw, bound in the slowness of the mud. And when the dogs were done with him the churning stream pulled him in, smothered his last breath and swallowed him back into the earth.

Elena was the sole witness to this reckoning. She crouched over Rory, who'd been shot in the foot, and over her father and Slater, who were both dead. She had nothing but dullness in her heart. The rain had tapered and the wind had died. In the saddlebag she had packed her first aid supplies. She stretched Rory out on his back, stuck a strap between his teeth and dug the bullet out of his foot with the needle-nosed pliers. It hurt but he was beyond caring. After she'd sewn and bandaged it up she covered him with his slicker and told him to rest. She would come back in an hour.

"They all must have left their horses down below," she said. "I'm going to bring a couple of them up so we can get you out of here and get my father and Slater home for a decent burial."

The dogs had disappeared but she could hear them baying and yipping in the distance. She followed the path down and found Moondog's and Crazy Ike's horses where Buckminster had left them, bloated now, whining with flies, their eyes pecked away by ravens. A little farther down Slater's horse stood tethered to a scrub pine. She left it there and looked for the Captain's, finding it guarded by Charlie Crow, who'd brought the report of Jacinta's death. He felt obliged to repeat it to Elena. "I have some bad news, miss."

She doubted there could be any bad news she didn't know.

"It's your mother," Crow said. "She's dead."

"Dead?"

"Trampled by the mares."

Finally she broke down in tears. It was the last thing that could have happened. She had nothing left except Rory.

"I'm sorry."

She turned away without another glance at Crow, who stood with his head bowed, hiding his shame at realizing how little she cared about him. She bridled the Captain's horse and led it back up the gorge. Near the top the Captain's dogs swept down, slavering, excited. A few of them had bones in their dripping mouths. After what they'd done to Buckminster, Elena felt a tremor of fear, for herself and for Rory. She'd left him lying on the ground. But no, they sniffed and circled the horse, whining pitifully—they were searching for their master, inconsolable at not finding him there. Elena spoke to them and that seemed to calm them—they recognized her voice, wagged their tails. They trotted after her and the horse, still sniffing and searching.

At the top, to her relief, she found Rory sleeping peacefully. All that was left of the Captain was a few scattered bones. The dogs ran in circles, desperate to find him.

Epilogue

She dropped her father's bones and Slater's remains down a crevice and piled rocks and scree on top of them. Rory couldn't walk or carry anything but he could ride the horse. She led him down to where she'd seen Slater's horse and they struck north across the badland, turning their backs on the basin. They'd spent their lives immured in that high desert, come of age there, watched men and women fall prey to the demons of pride and fear and their own brutal instincts, adding new pages to the bloody chronicle of history. How much of that could they leave behind? They could lay no claim to innocence: they had killed and would never be the same. And they'd seen suffering that would never leave them: Luke gored through, the Captain torn apart, Buckminster sucked into the mud. If you had asked them, they could not have told you what they expected to find outside the basin. They wanted something better but they had no idea what it would look like or even whether it existed. It was the love of life that drove them, and love for each other. The past seemed a legend they'd once heard, not real but not imagined either, a tale to tell their children.

Stories are still told by those who remember them, a dwindling number. They say they found some land up north and settled down, had their share of joys and sorrows—of some, more than their share—and found their destiny in another legend that played out on the divide, where the contraries meet and separate. All we know for sure is that they never came back to the basin. That country bore the stamp of doom even before they fled—some say because of the Captain's fall. For years the northern plains had been overgrazed, degraded by delusions of invincible destiny. That summer the reckoning came due. First the heat and the drought and the fires, then in autumn the rain and the floods and the mud. The snakes burrowed deeper, the mustangs fled south, the wolves swept back down from the north. The blizzards started in November and would not end until spring. Snow twelve feet deep, drifting to thirty feet in places, winds howling down to fifty below, sealing the earth under a pitiless sheet of ice. Buried, blinded, the cattle marched to their doom in the draws and drifts from New Mexico to Montana and the Dakotas, their hooves breaking through the ice floor, teeth scraping the frozen ground for a nibble of grass that wasn't there. They bellowed out their last breaths, tens of thousands of them, with nobody left to listen, the frostbitten heartsick cowboys having fled to the towns to drown themselves in drink. The Big Die-Up they called it, when the plains became a vast boneyard sifting back into dust. In the spring carcasses piled ten deep in the gullies, bloated, reeking, whispering with the hum of maggots at work, the wolves fattened to lethargy. The men struggled back to the range, not knowing if there'd be work or not—for most there was not. They saw it as a duty, like going to a funeral. They'd spent their lives driving cattle to be slaughtered, but when they found those pitiful beasts starved and crippled and bawling in the snow drifts, the few that were still alive, they cried like babies, they comforted them with soothing words, they asked forgiveness if they'd ever mistreated them, and then they shot them so the wolves couldn't eat them alive. That's when you knew there was some good in those men, even the worst of them, who wouldn't have cried at their own mothers' funerals.

Charlie Crow never cried for the cattle but there were times when he wanted to cry for himself. He'd lived his whole life among cattlemen and that big empty hollow in his heart was the same one all those men had, whether they knew it or not. It wasn't the cattle, it was the other half of the human race, the half, until he knew Elena, that he'd never loved or hated or even paid much attention to. Now she was gone, along with everything else he'd ever loved. To the east stretched a vast empire of empty space, where in a like expanse of time other worlds would rise and fall. He saddled his horse and rode toward it, like a man striking out across the ocean in search of a new land.

Most of the cowhands, when they talked about times past, remained loyal to Slater. Yes, he'd succumbed to weakness, and he was driven by inner demons that nobody knew or wanted to know, but he'd never cared to lord it over the land or the men who belonged there. With the Captain they shared a secret bond that made them reluctant to talk about him. Those who'd ridden with him in the early days, witnessed his rise and fall, knew both his greatness and his shame. Some said his death and what the dogs did to him was a kind of purgation, the natural order rising up against its violation. And some, in later years, when the memory of his character and deeds had blurred into legend, maintained that he was a great man who'd paid a terrible price for crimes that were not solely his own: for invading that country and destroying the buffalo and its native hunters, for subjugating and debasing the land for the sake of beefsteaks to be served to gentlemen in Chicago and New York.

Echoes are long in this part of the world, with the flats so wide, the ridges so far between. A startled cry, a shouted warning, a wail of despair can take a long time to come back around. Long enough for the wind to gnaw it to bits and howl it out like a wolf on his pulpit of bones.

The End

About the Author

Bruce Hartman is the author of eleven previous novels, including *The Philosophical Detective* and its popular sequels, *The Philosophical Detective Returns* and *The Philosophical Detective's Last Case. Legend of Lost Basin* is his first western, the first book in a projected trilogy. He is married with three grown sons and divides his time between Pennsylvania and Colorado.